WET

WET

WET

By Starzpen

WET

Copyright © 2019 by Radiah Johnson

Published by Pen 2 Pen
Est. 2012

Printed in the U.S.A.

This is a book of fiction. Names, locales, places, events, and people contained herein are purely from the author's memory, and/or from public record. This story is not intended to defame, intimidate, or ridicule any persons, living or dead.

Starzpen

WET

This book is dedicated to Brooklyn...

Starzpen

WET

WET

Juicy's Revenge

Starzpen

WET

Cynthia and Quez had been together ten years when she hopped out of a cab in midtown Manhattan to take her man lunch. Stepping across snow piles, she looked up and saw Quez exiting his office building. She went to call for him, however, some chick came out behind him, laughing and grabbing on him like they were besties. Before Cyn could react, they hopped into a car that was waiting out front.

What the hell? Cyn thought. Her FBI senses kicked in. Cyn hopped back into the cab, handed the driver some cash, and told him to follow the black Lincoln Town Car until it stopped. They drove for about thirty minutes and pulled up at the Ritz. The driver opened the woman's door, then he opened Quez's door. Arm in arm, they walked into the hotel. Cyn didn't need to see anymore.

Now, I understood keeping it classy and not coming unglued in a situation like this; however, nobody would have gotten wet in that moment! There would have been absolutely no fucking at all. Hell, I'd probably catch a charge myself. Listen, I knew three things for sure. First, I knew that the kind of hurt she was enduring was tremendously damaging. So, I knew Cyn had to be all messed up inside. Second, I knew that you should never jump ship that quickly; no reaction, no flipping the fuck out! Hmmph, unless you knew there was a life boat nearby. Finally, I knew that the only way to get over a man fucking over you was to slide up under another one.

In the midst of it all, Cyn was woman enough to accept the fact that she played a major part in his infidelity. Wrong as it was, they took vows and as soon as they hit a

Starzpen

rough spot, Quez sold out to the passed around pussy posse. Cyn never went outside her marriage. She did the total opposite. She dealt with boring nights of no conversation. She lived through his erectile dysfunction. His dick couldn't stay hard for five minutes.

Cyn dealt with curbing her wild side and ultimately forfeiting her individuality to please another - bad move. If roles were reversed and he caught her going into a hotel room with another man in broad daylight, he'd flip. Men couldn't take that. They couldn't take a third of what they dished out. Their hurt usually manifested in chaos and ended in destruction. I found that men used infidelity, cheating, and the ability to juggle multiple women as a defense mechanism for their own inadequacies. Insecurity 101.

The male species was quite greedy as well. I wondered if Quez could feel what she felt or saw her heart break literally, would he think twice about his actions. I wondered if knowledge of that pain would discourage him from hurting her again. Cyn was devastated. She took the food she had for Quez and sat in central park for hours, picking over the cold fries and her brain, wondering what she did wrong. Fear of being alone consumed her. She never shed one tear or even tried to call him and rant, though. What good would that do?

Cyn didn't appear angry. She seemed to be plotting. She wore just a blank stare and you could tell her mind was wandering. Somehow, I knew Cyn had other plans for his lying ass. Surprisingly, Cyn never mentioned what she saw or showed her husband the pictures she had hired a P.I to take a few days after the hotel sighting. Cynthia semi forgave

WET

the infidelity, but not fully, because she had him on the couch. Let's be realistic, he was a man. So, she took credit for her 40% of the blame, which was what she decided was fair. Now ladies, you know that a man was supposed to wake up with his dick in ya' mouth every morning. It wouldn't take long, trust me. Just slurp on it while he wiggled out of his dream. It'll be over in four minutes, tops.

Anyway, she knew it was her responsibility to ensure that his sipping spoon stayed at attention on a regular. She couldn't even blame the side piece for her trick ass behavior. It was all on her. Cyn knew she wasn't doing all she could to keep him home. She took the L and owned up to all her shortcomings. Nevertheless, I had other plans to push her past the trauma. She was really sick of his ass, anyway. So, I decided to show her how to use his infidelity as her way out.

By the way, I'm Juicy, well I used to be until these two started acting up. Seems to be a damn drought in here lately. Didn't she realize hydration was the key to life? Didn't she understand I was literally like marine life and that I'd die without moisture? I was not about to let her starve me just because this dummy was acting a fool. I still needed daily grooming!

This bump in the road was a major blow to Cyn's ego. She couldn't believe her spell had been reversed. Cyn would cringe at the thought of her sipping spoon resting on other lips. She thought of all the times she faked a nut. *Fuck this*, she thought. She wanted revenge.

WET

Cyn's mind would mirror flashbacks of his love with her. She reminisced on his heartbeat as it always seemed perfectly in sync with hers. She often thought of how dope it was, how amazing love was with him. She had vivid sweaty flashbacks of how dope sex was with Quez and *her* before they began to drift. All of that died at the confirmation of him with another woman. I had to do something. This shit was affecting Cyn's dope girl swag. When she looked in the mirror, she wondered if she was still a "bad bitch". He had her trying to figure out what was wrong with her. Cyn needed a makeover or some shit.

"Girl, get the fuck up and LIVE honey. If Quez dies tomorrow, you will still be a queen! These peasant thoughts are so unattractive." I whispered to her mind, hoping she would feel me. "Shoes. Shoes. Shoes." I inserted into her thoughts. They always made things better. She was addicted to them and I was elated when she decided to go shopping. She tried on a pair of black 4-inch red bottoms and strutted toward the full-length mirror. She could already feel the trouble that my need for hydration was about to cause. She was feeling herself and wondered if anyone else was feeling her.

Ironically, she spotted an old sipping spoon, no rust, no blemishes just mmmm… fione! I myself began to crave moisture and a little poking. Cyn was still in denial, fighting it a bit. She and I had been all too familiar with this block of chocolate. We hadn't seen or felt him in a little over ten years but, he looked better now. It was like the Garden of Eden and that damned apple all over again.

11

Starzpen

Across the long row of designer shoes, Mac and Cyn finally locked eyes. He recognized her immediately. Mac smiled excitedly, like he was having flashbacks of the fuck session they had in the girls' locker room their junior year in college. Mac walked over, leaned in, and hugged Cyn. He lightly kissed her cheek as he let go. "Well, well, well. Mac the snack." She laughed and hugged him again. "It's good to see you, Cynthia. You look amazing." Mac said. "Thank you! You look great yourself." Cyn replied. I could feel them both screaming silently with their bodies. They were saying, "please say you still wanna fuck me."

After reminiscing about college and current events, they decided to go have a drink. On the way to the parking deck, Cyn noticed I... she... I mean, we were doing Kegels repeatedly. Cyn was beginning to sweat a sweet, sticky, juicy sweat. She fantasized about her nipples between Mac's teeth. She giggled as she could literally feel the tingle in her naval. Hell, I knew an orgasm was inevitable, even if she had to work it out herself.

Mac knew the moment he saw Cyn, she still had it and he wanted it. I had also cosigned this episode and decided for Cyn that she wanted it too. Cyn's heart was racing a mile-a-minute in anticipation of a gut-wrenching orgasm. Mac helped to put some of her bags in the car. Cyn was aroused by his sweet dark chocolate scent. Seeing Mac again was calming, like standing on rocks in a creek as the river flowed over your feet; like a ballerina reciting a dope Jazz routine. Startling Cyn out of her fantasy, the trunk of the car shut and Mac gently slammed Cyn's head onto it as it closed. Shocked and somewhat startled, she slightly resisted, but I was completely in sync with Mac's rhythm. I needed to assist her in this ego boost. I had to convince her to take the win! News to me, Cyn had decided off the rip she was going to sip from his fountain right there in the parking garage. However, I could still feel her uncertainty. She was still pondering over that boring ass marriage. Nevertheless, she thought for sure a revenge cheat would make her hurt heal and I urged her to act on it.

Suddenly, Mac forcefully but pleasantly put one hand around Cyn's neck and the other pressed down in the small of her back. She trembled with pleasure, wanting more. Mac slid Cyn's cute black lace thongs a little to the left, as she noticed the outline of her fingerprints in the dew on the hood of the car.

Mac found his way inside, gripping her ass cheeks while hammering Cyn's body into the car, clit smacking up against the cool firmness. Complete silence masked the open area and the adrenaline was as good as the dick. "Hell yeah! Cyn, don't stop, bitch. I deserve this shit." I chanted. Suddenly, she began to go harder. She felt the extra pulsing in me. Her flower bud was hardening, and I was begging for relief.

"Pleaseeeeee, don't let him stop."
As Mac spit all his humongous chocolate swag from behind, Cyn could feel Mac's tongue gliding across her skin while simultaneously hydrating her juice box in full throttle. I was soaking wet, Cyn was feeling like a cheating hoe, and Mac was drowning. Hormones raging, we were all in now.

Cyn dropped down to her knees and begged him to let her sip from his spoon for a while. Mac didn't protest. He dropped back against the car as she slid between him and the bumper of the car in an attempt to conceal the ultimate public display of affection. Revenge at his best!

Cyn allowed me to continue pulsating at an all-time high. By this point, she was all in, headfirst. She examined Mac's dick curiously, awaiting its connection to her throat. It was a pretty, round, thick, spongy, slightly pinkish head. It had sweet dark smooth fudge-like skin covering its foundation. The veins popped out like the root of a tall strong tree.

Cyn closed her eyes and shrugged her shoulders. She let out a giggle in semi shame and embarrassment. She put both of Mac's balls in her mouth, while tracing the bulging veins in his dick with her forefinger. Mac was losing his mind. His knees were buckling. He was moaning profusely, while holding himself up against the car.

"Cyn, what the fuck are you doing to me?" He whispered, grabbing her head on both sides, joining in the flow. "Shit. Yes, Mami. This is your dick. Yes. Yes. Slob it up, Cynthia. You look like a goddess down there."

Cyn, now quite clear on her position, decided she wanted to be in complete control, she slid Mac's Goodbar out of her mouth, guiding it with her hands. Cyn then slithered her way to the other side of the car and opened the door. Mac followed. Now holding his chocolate bar in his hands, she pushed Mac into the seat and slid me and all my juicy, sticky loving all over Mac's hot strong stiffened fist of honor. Cyn hopped on top of Mac and tickled his naval with her flower bud. He gripped her booty with both hands as I spewed and clenched more honey from the hive.

They got me all slippery. I screamed in ecstasy. "Thank you, girl! I'm so glad you decided to see it my way." Mac lightly dropped his head between her two melon-like pretty ass titties, bouncing in front of him. Sweating, screaming, fucking like rabbits. They were going at it hard... wild... crazily intense. Realizing the apparent movement of the entire car, they laughed and enjoyed the moment of intimacy in the midst of their sweet and nasty, yet raunchy and disrespectful fuck.

She had better not stop. That's all I knew. Cyn arched her back just a little and the flower bud hardened and pulsated faster. It extended in preparation of a bloom. They both began to sing a song of defeat, thinking it was all about to end, neither could hold on much longer.

Their time was up. Fingers on the trigger, Mac kissed her like she was the only woman on the planet, increasing the explosions' intensity. They consciously decided to release their souls at the exact same time. Mac couldn't move as she continued their ride, resembling a seesaw with a faint breeze streaming across their bodies. It was like a cannon hitting the ocean after falling from the sky. Cyn rested her hand on Mac's shoulder in full go mode, her body blazing. She wasn't fully satisfied yet. But the juicy surprise was when Mac slid her body onto the dashboard and began to taste the honey.

Cyn gripped the hood of the car with both hands. Mac braced each cavity with class. I liked how Cyn and sticky meeeee were getting the best of both worlds. I was enjoying this. I was down for hitting the mark as many times as Cyn could take. I wanted to see Mac's face when we crossed the finish line.

The intensity was increasing tremendously, feeding Mac every drop of me. Silently screaming, Cyn exhaled the most amazing nut. Her eyes rolled back as she looked up and peered out of the foggy window with her handprints smeared into the dew. She saw her husband standing there, watching. Now me... Juicy, I was still extremely in a state of pleasure, frantically trying to compose myself; although, it was too late.

Cyn convinced herself that the damage was done. She wondered how he'd react. Would he break windows and snatch her out? Would he come for Mac?

Cyn was on cloud nine and her juice box was overflowing. She was secretly satisfied as well. Somewhere in the back of her mind, she was glad he was standing there. She was glad that he felt what she felt. Somewhere in the back of her mind, Cyn became Juicy; mind, body, and spiritually.

Mission accomplished, she thought, sarcastically boasting, celebrating what she perceived to be a WIN. Although, the revenge was somewhat the sweetest thing Cyn ever knew, reality was the end game.

Now, she was left with the questions. What did she gain? What did she prove? She finally realized the harsh truth. When you decide on a revenge cheat, a get back at him scheme, that make him feel what I felt mentality, that my queen was a losing battle and it was a fight that we women would never win.

She got him, yes. Let's face it, though. No man wanted another man's hands on his woman. Ninety-nine percent of men can't take it. All of that stemmed from you having him on the couch to begin with; the seduction of a sofa, which sent him into the arms of another woman. You decided to be just like that other woman and pass yourself around trying to fill up your juice box, trying to see if you still had it, trying to see if you were still a badass.

Ladies, submission is not for suckers. A man will not leave home if he has every reason to stay. With some mishaps, for the most part, a happy man stays home. Are we willing to work hard enough to make that happen? Are we willing to be consistent enough to keep him happy? Make no mistake, he must do the same for you. In all reality, he is the head of the household. He is the king. We teach. We love and nurture. Debatable, yes, but we bow down willingly to a deserving king; provided, he stays that way. It will come naturally. Then, and only then my Queens, you will reap an awesome reward. He'll have an undeniable respect for you. He will exhibit a breath-taking passion and he will love you for a lifetime.

Take it from me, my box has had a few straws and one thing for certain and two things for sure, a man will never look at you the same once he knows that other straws have slid into his box.

WET

Sincerely,

Juicy

P.S. Cyn, next time, let's make it worth our while and shoot for 60 seconds.

WET

Sin-Claire

19

Starzpen

WET

She came from a long line of strong black queens. Queens who washed massa's feet; queens who ripped cotton until their fingers bled and witnessed the lynching and beatings of their Kings. They were bred from royal stock that rose from oppression. An amazing strength with an amazing instinct to survive was permanently stained in their souls. It was the kind of bloodline that stood for everything and would die before falling for anything.

Claire, she too was from that long line of strength and she was well rounded, well raised. She was God-fearing and could quote bible scriptures as if it were the alphabet. She also had a beautiful voice, the kind that didn't need a microphone. She sang from her spirit. She sang from the sorrow she saw in others. She sang of a lonely heart. Clair was seemingly afraid of being noticed. She didn't think she deserved great things. Her self-esteem was... hell, non-existent.

Contrary to popular belief, she did have somewhat of a love life; a little boo. His name was Peter. *Peter?* What black man was named Peter? He was the organist, the usher, the youth director, and some other shit at her family's church. She wasn't too excited about him; however, she seemed to just tolerate him. He was probably a good handyman or something because he obviously wasn't fucking her properly. It came across as if she didn't even like him; maybe she dated him just to please the church hens.

Claire often expressed her desire to practice the *no-sex before-marriage* thing. I shrugged. If that floated her boat. However, that's definitely not for me. I needed to see if it was enough sugar in that Kool-Aid before I served it to Nay Nay and dem'. I had to taste the cookie and all its crumbs, prove to me you were worth a lifetime.

WET

Claire was well educated. She was gainfully employed and quite content with her life at this point. Or was she? Claire began sleeping a lot, not going out much. Her cleaning skills seemed to dwindle a bit as well. She began having thoughts of suicide and was sinking into a state of depression. Loneliness and loveless lives withered and died like a plant without water. You had to water your flowers every damn day and do that thing that makes you move, that thing that pumps your blood. Do you! Fuck the rest! At least, that was my philosophy.

Claire was in denial for a while, eventually she herself recognized that she wasn't herself. She even started blowing Peter's corny ass off. Claire was growing tired of that unsettling feeling, that funk she was in. She decided to seek counseling. Yes, my people, it's okay to ask for help. It's okay to need someone to just listen sometimes, and to get perspective from other sources. Not to copy them, but to build around what you may have already knew and apply it to your circumstances.

Claire did some research. I didn't think she was clear on what she was searching for when she came across my ad. It read, *"Feeling restless? Feeling like something is missing? Need a boost in areas you didn't know you had?"* It sparked her curiosity and she came to the right place. I had a great track record in rejuvenation and ego boosting. Though my practice was in its beginning stages, I've had nothing but good reviews from my clients. I've been able to unleash lionesses within my clients, giving them the ability to control and maintain pleasure beyond anything they'd ever imagined. It worked in ways YOU wouldn't believe until you've tried it yourself. I helped unleash the power to have the nerve to do the things you only dreamed of. My clients loved me for it and they sent friends. I've even learned a few things about my own sexuality from them.

Starzpen

WET

As Claire entered my office, I sized her up off the rip. She was about 5'9", wearing a 2-inch block heel, maybe 150 lbs. with a praline complexion. She wore glasses, the ones with the thick frames. Her hair was pulled back and wrapped in a bun. She looked like an usher... a librarian, I thought. She was beautiful still, and nervous. Obviously, she was unsure of herself. Claire barely knew how to walk in those heels. "This might be pretty easy," I thought. She just needed me to readjust her crown. Well, maybe start from scratch and get her a new one. She was a little rough around the edges.

"Hi, I'm Cccc... Clai... Claire," she spoke, stuttering softly. "Hi, Claire. I'm Cynthia Ryan, you can call me Cyn," I replied in a loud voice. She noticed and looked up at me, seemingly in awe of my confidence. I knew her. "I saw your presentation at Andrew Jackson high school." She giggled like a shy child. "Tell me a little bit about yourself and why you came here today," I asked, recalling seeing Claire at a few business luncheons and conferences in the community. As recognition settled in, she seemed more comfortable knowing I wasn't a total stranger.

"I've just been feeling strange lately," she said. "Strange? Strange how?" Claire began to tell me how something wasn't right in her spirit. Something seemed to be missing, she said. "I only feel like half of me," she admitted.

That was powerful to me. She talked about her love life as if it were non-existent and she spoke of that damned Peter like he was a bobble head on her dashboard. She complained of boredom and talked a lot about things she wished would happen, which I interpreted to mean things she wished she had the nerve to do. It was almost like she didn't believe anything beyond what she'd experienced thus far could be possible. At least, up until now.

I thought to myself, "this bitch just needs some dick." Make no mistake, I knew she loved Jesus and I did too. I didn't encourage anyone to fall short of his glory. However, what I did know was, every time I fell short, I liked it! Forgive me Lord, but I knew exactly what Claire needed.

I was the queen of, *"I'm going to be happy regardless."* Yes, that would be me on the set saying, Sin, Claire. Sin. She was going to be just fine and if I had anything to say about it, Peter's lame ass would be history, a thing of the past.

Claire had come to see me once a week for about six months now. We've completed trust building and confidence building exercises. We've broken down her fears and explored areas of interest completely outside of Claire's norm. Each visit, Claire told me a bit more of the secrets feeding her misery. She let go of things she'd never thought she'd say out loud. She trusted me and we've somewhat become friends. I learned to listen to the things she didn't say along with her reaction to certain subjects.

I wanted to get her out her comfort zone, somehow, hopefully she could feel free enough to let her hair down… literally. I had a plan to dangle possibilities of her wildest dreams in real time. I wanted her to believe the things she felt were normal and within her reach. So, I scheduled a session at this dope art museum on 5th Avenue.

The art there was quite seductive and really made you think. There were no faces, no pictures of the ocean or a horizon at sunset. This art was eccentric, mind boggling. It usually had me asking questions like, "W*ould I do that with one leg up or both legs up?"* Or wondering if I could take that size D propped up on that rock in the middle of rain forest... never mind. I wanted to open her up. I was practically screaming, "Sin Claire! Just sin! Get your back blown out and join the mile-high club. Take off them damn glasses for one night!"

Just as I thought, Claire was quite intrigued by the genre of art. She stared at the figures and paintings oddly, just as I did my first time there. She was wondering just as I did, exploring the real desire to enjoy life immensely. As we walked through the gallery, she began to open up. While staring at each painting, studying them, she twisted her head to get a better look or a different perspective. She laid her hand on my shoulder and to my surprise, she said, "Cyn, do you know how many times I thought of fucking the shit out of deacon Brown at church? He is so damn cute."

My eyes opened wide in astonishment. I even burst into laughter. She went on to say, "One Sunday, I was leading the choir. I was singing *Yes Lord* and I started crying. Everyone was shouting and praising God, not knowing I was crying because I couldn't believe I was leading this song and fantasizing about fucking somebody's husband. I felt so bad and dirty. But my body was praising a different spirit. Cyn, I just knew I was going to hell that day."

I frowned. "Claire, are you serious? You mean to tell me, you think it's something wrong with going with the feelings running through your body? Isn't that why you're here? What do you hope to accomplish from our sessions?" Annoyed as fuck, I questioned her repeatedly. I wanted her to answer my questions and ultimately answer hers too. She was getting there, though. I was going to have to get a little tougher with her. I needed to go harder and dig deeper. Didn't Claire want to know what it felt like to just get fucked? Didn't she crave some TLC from time to time? Lips on ya' pussy, a dick to massage your insides?

My lips formed a hard line as I stared at her. "Honestly, when you were singing and lusting after the deacon, what were you thinking of? What would you have done had it just been you and him, naked and wet? What would you do to him?" I whispered in her ear. "How about somebody nibbling on your ass cheeks while you watch your favorite movie? Or, someone to massage your clit while you read your favorite book?"

Claire's nose scrunched. "That sounds nasty, Cyn. I don't know if I could do that... Sounds nasty." She repeated. "Well, it is and nasty is good. Sex and sustenance are a man's greatest needs."

Claire had already told me she never had sex. She was really trying to live up to the stock she was bred from. I totally understood that. But I wanted to scream, "Bitch, how you think you got here? Mary wasn't ya' mama, right?"

This chick was funny, but sweet, though. Nevertheless, it was another successful session with Claire. I got her thinking. The seed was planted. Now that her mind was wandering through the land of Cyn, I figured I'd go in for the kill. Amused at Claire's innocence, laughing and hugging her neck, I said my goodbyes... not without teasing her first. "Well, doll, get ready for next week. I have something fun in mind." I rubbed my hands together like an evil villain.

I knew Claire was pondering on all those freaky questions I hit her with. I was hopeful my strategy would help her to allow her pussy to erupt and would send Claire into the land of the living.

***

WET

At our next session, I asked Claire if she wanted to try and let someone eat her pussy. To my surprise, she shyly shook her head yes, but I could see her shame and embarrassment. She was thirty-five and still a virgin. She would feel awkward the first time. I figured I had a solution for that too.

"Why did you ask that?? Cyn, what we are doing today?" Claire was growing nervous. "Well, I have something planned. But, you gotta be completely on board or it won't have any effect." I told her. "Well, what you want me to do?" She asked suspiciously.
"First, take those glasses off." Hesitantly, she did. Claire had beautiful, dark brown piercing eyes. "Now, take your hair down." I instructed. She did, pulling a brush from her purse. Her hair fell down into her face on one side as she swooped the other side behind her ear.

I handed her that new nude Fenty lip balm and gestured for her to apply. She did, giggling softly, with and unsure childlike confidence. Next, I handed her a sexy red Victoria Secret lounge outfit I'd picked up on one of my shopping sprees. I handed it to her and she asked where the bottoms were. "They're attached." I replied, laughing and showing her how to put the lingerie on. She went into the bathroom and changed, hollering things like, "lawwwd, have mercy" and "forgive me father". I could hear her through the door. When she came out, there was a chocolate piece of perfection sitting on my desk with nothing on but a pair of all black boxers that went well against his deep sexy brown skin. His name was Brick. *Dear God,* I thought, smiling devilishly. "Don't you wanna share, Claire?" I asked.

Brick was a little cutie from the strip club I went to every now and then. He was sweet on me, so he'd do anything I asked, even slide up in another chick at my request. Claire ran back into the bathroom, like she had just run into a lion's den, screaming. "Who is that? What the hell? Cynnnnnn?"

I pushed the door open and aggressively pulled her onto the chaise lounge that sat at the edge of my desk. She looked amazing in that little number. I could tell by the bulge in Brick's pants, he agreed. Now we just had to make her believe it. I calmly explained that nothing was going to happen that she didn't ask for. By the end of the session, I was sure she'd beg for the D.

I poured a shot of Hennessey for all of us, a little extra in Claire's. She took it to the head too, rubbing her hands together, anxious to see what was to come. I turned on my flat screen and inserted a flick. She covered her eyes and looked away, secretly glancing from time to time. She was getting hot, I could tell. So, I poured her another shot. While watching the threesome on the screen, she took the potent liquor to the head, her eyes never leaving the screen. Claire was intrigued, something got her attention. She really couldn't stop watching now. I grabbed Brick by the hand and walked him over near Claire.

"Claire, put your glass down." I instructed, grabbing it from her hand. "Now, lean back and close your eyes." She complied, hilariously laying down, opening her legs in a V-shape. I couldn't help but laugh.

"Brick, take your left middle finger and rotate it clockwise on her left nipple, then counter clockwise on the right nipple, slowly." Claire didn't move. She stiffened. I smelled her fear. I also smelled a cherry that was so ripe it may have just burst on its own.

I instructed Brick again. This time, telling him to tell Claire how sexy she was, while I knelt down to her ear and whispered.

"Sin, Claire. Sin! Use him. Use his dick like a toy. Just play with it, girl. Stick it in ya' mouth and taste it. Watch his face when you do. It's priceless." I antagonized her, urging her to release the inner lioness. "Nibble on his waist, his belly button, kiss it sweetly. He's yours for tonight. Make him do what you want him to do."

Brick, while still tracing her nipple, removed one hand and inserted two fingers inside Claire. She clinched the sides of the chair and jumped back a bit. She tried to shut her legs tight and Brick fell back a bit. I gently moved in and removed the hairs that had fallen and stuck to the small beads of sweat on her face. "Claire, Sin." I whispered in her ear while gently spreading her legs apart for Brick. The couple on the flick became louder and more intense. I turn it off suddenly and asked if Claire was okay.

"Yes, Cyn. But, I'm not sure about this. Do you want to stop, Claire? How does your body feel?" I probed with a raised brow, all the while pulling Brick's fine ass closer to her. She didn't respond. She just sat there looking fucking retarded. So, I asked again. "Claire, do you wanna end this session?" She looked at us both. Brick, then me, him, then me again. "Will you stay and make sure I'm okay?" I was shocked and pleased, knowing my nasty ass was staying anyway. "Sure," I exclaimed with a smile of comfort. I immediately stepped into director's mode. "Brick, sit down in my chair."

I took Claire's hand and walked her toward him, coaching her body into another world. I almost wanted that nut for myself, but I'd had several, so I decided to let my girl get hers and be happy about it. "Claire, sit on it. Just slide right down until you are sitting on his lap." I coached. She attempted to sit on him, face to face and I objected. "No, turn around. Let him admire you from the back. This is all for you. In my experience, an orgasm is at its best when completely controlled by the recipient." Hesitant and clearly scared to death, she sat right down on it. I was secretly dying laughing inside. This was so funny to me. I was glad I finally found my niche and I was enjoying it to a fault.

Brick had a long skinny dick. It was cute, though. No scars or nappy hairs and shit. However, I preferred rugged and not so pretty boyish; long, fat, black and a little pink at the tip. Oh yeah, I didn't mind a little curve, either. She could have this one.

Claire sat down and took all of what appeared to be about seven slim inches of manhood, but she just sat there; no grind, no bounce, just not moving at all. Brick held back a snicker or two, grabbing her shoulders and pushing her body downward.

"Ou... ou... ouch!" Claire screamed. "Cyn! Cyn," she cried.
I replied, "Yesss, Claire. Sin... sin, Claire. Sin." She was moving her body wildly up and down now. I walked over to her and put my hand on her neck, slightly rubbing it. "Slow down a little. Move your body like you are on a swing. Sway. Sway sweet, slow gallops in between each swaying stroke. Imagine you're on the beach, sitting on a swing. Mhmmm... yeah, just like that, Claire."

"Cynnnn," she whispered. I couldn't help thinking, *why this bitch calling my name?* I took Brick's hand and made him stroke her clit while he rammed his dick inside her sloppy wet pussy, repeatedly. She went crazy like I knew she would. That slow grind shit was over, she jumped off Brick's lap and onto my couch, spread out like a butterfly in mid-flight and said, "Fuck me like this, please sir."
We all laughed hysterically. He flipped, slammed, and swung her every which way. Then, he went in for the kill. He slid his dick out, slowly massaging himself with both hands, dropped

down on both knees as if to hail the queen, wrapped both lips around her whole pussy and went in. Claire's mouth hung wide open; like that mask from those dumbasses *Scream* movies. She never had her pussy sucked on. I could hear Brick's lips swimming in the Claire pond. It sounded like somebody was eating baby back ribs.

"Mmhmmm, hell yeah, boo. Get you." I shouted from across the room. He ate and ate and ate like her juice box derived of fruit from the tree of life. I knew this wouldn't take long, so I waited until I saw Claire spew literally and sin undeniably. It was breathtaking and I was honored to be a part of it. She scratched Brick's back like an alley cat would a threatening dog. I could see her eyes rolling back and forth as juice began pouring from between her legs. Brick knew she was coming, so he looked up at her, gripping her thighs and aggressively planting his face in her pussy.

Oh, that face she was making. "Mhmmmm, yesss, Brick!" I shouted, congratulating him on the win. I could hear her teeth grit and the love noises she was making ensured me my work was done. I cut off the lights and slipped out the elevator entrance. I figured they may be a while.

A few weeks later, I get an e-mail from Claire. She wanted to thank me for "dusting her crown". She said she had a friend in Trinidad that she thought I could help. Something about river and staying "WET" sounds crazy, but we'd see. In my reply along with an invoice for my services, I agreed to speak with her friend. I wished Claire the best sex ever and told her to stay in touch.

I reached out to her referral a few days later. "Hello, Claire referred you as a prospective client. I'm Cynthia. My friends call me Cyn." I introduced myself as soon as she answered the phone.

"Hi, I'm Najmah. My friends call me Najee and here is my contact info. Let's set up an initial consultation and then we can discuss flying you out to Trini. The Rico Seco waterfall is beyond anything you'd ever experienced." *The river*? Oh, this chick was looney! What had Claire gotten me into now? I could use a vacation, though. Plus, I'd never been to the islands. Najee booked my flight about a month later. I was due to leave the following weekend. It was an adventure I was ready for. I might even snag me some island dick while I'm there.

WET

The Deity

A conversation with the other woman never goes well. Somehow for me, it wasn't so bad. My mindset was somewhere between, Thank-God-somebody's-fucking-him Avenue, and I'm-getting-knocked-off-on-the-low Lane. It was quite comical though.

This bitch had the nerve to tell me, "He love this pussy!" I couldn't have laughed hard enough! "Honey, he a man; he loves pussy, period!" That's especially truly when it's the only hole to dump in at the moment, I wanted to add as I thought to myself, *how about I go kill this bitch!* The thought lasted for all of...hmmm...30 seconds before I quickly came to my senses and realized I was about to catch a charge over something I really wasn't even mad about. This relationship had grown old before it had even grown. Obligations, mortgage, kids... all that shit makes one tolerate more than they would under different circumstances. I loved my family and wanted it to work. However, the lack of trust, compatibility, and good sex is a recipe for failure in anyone's house.

Somewhere, somehow, this shit had to change. I needed a different walk in my life, the type of walk that being broken back from 8 or 9 inches of violent stiff flesh would produce. You know, a slight limp to accompany a wide smile? That's what I needed in my life! I was no longer settling for miserable.

I started working at the Label shortly after I discovered Chase was fuckin' around. I needed a lane of my own to cruise in for a change. I was trying my best to hang in there for the sake of doing the right thing, but every time I looked at Chase, I got sick to my stomach. Simple shit like hearing him breathe irritated the fuck out of me. I needed to feel alive. Hell, I deserved at least that, didn't I?

Arriving at my office one morning, I ran into this beautiful chunk of man. He was about 6'2" and 200 lbs. of sweet, rough butterscotch smothered in fine! Yes honey!!! He had light brown eyes and thick ass brows perfectly shaping his face. He was clean cut with just a little fuzz on his cheeks and chin. Perfect for scratching that itch from my mid-thighs on up to my fruit basket. I pictured my nipples fitting perfectly into his dimples. Inspecting him closer, I zoomed in on his hands. They were huge and rugged with well-manicured fingernails just like I liked. I pictured those hands smacking, palming, and squeezing this round ass like a grapefruit, squeezing all the juice out.

"Good morning, Gorgeous," he greeted in a silky baritone. He said gorgeous like it was my name, all confident and sexy as fuck. My pussy immediately began jumping and shit. As the words left his mouth, I locked in on his lips? Damn!! They looked like they could just wrap themselves around my clit and allow me to move my body until I reached a satisfactory level of pressure on my spot. Mmm hmmm... all he had to do was lend me his face and I would do the rest.

Oh hell, snap out of it! I told myself. "Good morning," I replied, cold and unbothered, as if there wasn't lava dripping in my panties from the sight of this specimen. He chuckled, knowing I noticed how gorgeous was. "Ahhh... I think I'm lost," he said. "I'm looking for Ayesha Storm. The Storm is what they call her." "What is it that you need with Ayesha?" I asked.

"Well, we are here to set up her office equipment and data programs. I also have the contract ready to be confirmed and signed." I figured I'd play with him a little and get some more info. So, I twirled a lock of hair in my finger and told him to have a seat in the reception area and someone would be right with him. I closed the door to my office, pulled out my mirror and adjusted my crown a bit. Lips popping, hair on fleek, outfit dope... yep, I was ready.

I hopped online and googled the CEO of his company. To my surprise, his picture popped right up.
"Oh, hell yeah!" I hissed. Jackpot! I could rock wit' it.
I stepped back out into the hallway and said, "Hi, I am Ayesha "The Storm". I was under the impression Mr. Smalls would be meeting with me personally."

I pretended to not realize who he was. We both laughed, somewhat relieved that we at least had the chance to be in each other's presence a bit longer. I allowed him to see my eyes roam over his body. I was silently telling him to run it cuz' I'm wit' it.

I saw his eyes fall on the sparkling diamond on my left hand and he seemed to fall back a bit. I didn't push him though, that's not my style. He walked closer to me and extended his hand for me to shake it. I gave him my hand and he smoothly raised it to his mouth and pecked the back of it.
"Hi Ayesha, I am Chink Smalls, CEO of Smalls Corporate," he said in that damn baritone again. I swear, my juices were percolating so hard, I thought my panties were going to slide down my legs. "Well, it's very nice to meet

you, Mr. Smalls," I replied all cool and innocent, as if I didn't damn near check his credit score.

"Please, call me Chink," he requested. "Okay Chink, please come in. Would you like a cup of coffee?" "Yes, please?" As I hit the intercom for Lisa to bring coffee, Chink sat down in front of me. Just before he sat, I noticed the bulge in his slacks. *Baby! Ain't nothin' small about that!* I started daydreaming about what it looked like. He probably had a curved dick, long and thick with just a few meaty veins in it. A smooth, round hot-pink head with a juicy eye in the middle of it. Mmm hmm... I couldn't believe myself. I was salivating like a rabid damn animal thinking about this man and his member. I wondered if he saw right through me. I wondered if he knew I was fantasizing about sitting on his face eating a banana split while feeding him the cherries?

I didn't have to wonder long. Just like I knew he would, Big Sexy went in for the kill. Once we finalized the paperwork, he decided to test my temperature a bit more. Chink asked me if I was just wearing my ring, or if I was *wearing* my ring. I laughed. It was kind of cute though. It was his subtle way of asking if he had any chance of fucking me. Honestly, I thought he represented very well. He looked amazing and smelled fuckable. He also had his shit in order with more than just a few coins to throw around.

I looked him in his eyes and was straight up with him. "Let's be real," I said. "At this point, you know you don't give a damn about me being happy. You wanna know if I'm ok wit' you getting happy. Right?" A crossed my arms and waited on his reply. The diamonds in my wedding band beamed from the overhead light. "It's a beautiful ring I'm wearing, isn't it?"

Chink took two giant steps toward me. "That it is... just beautiful," he replied, as he reached down and kissed my hand. He reached across me and grabbed my phone off the desk. The air from his movements sent the hint of Jimmy Choo from his neck airborne. I inhaled the scent and nearly became intoxicated. His vibe? Yeah, I was rockin' wit it hard and he knew it.

Once he had my phone, he dialed his number from my cell, then put the phone back on the desk. He stared at me for a second, boring his strong gaze into mine, then he walked away.

Mmm... so fucking sexy. He left me knowing exactly what it was, yet still wondering exactly what it was. He left my mind racing with thoughts of... Well, hell, truthfully just his dick game. I didn't need him for anything else. Nevertheless, my pussy thumping was all the confirmation I needed right now. I was maaaad curious, but I'd wait. Pretty sure he would be back. I already knew I was gonna let 'em taste my pussy, but I was in no rush to do so. I loved the foreplay of the mind even if it took months. The climb to the top is out of this world but remaining there— even after reaching its peak— is the desired end game.

Chase couldn't make me cum even if I helped him these days. I was no longer turned on and was on the prowl to share some of this new pussy.

My juicy hotbox and I had a new mindset. We had a new goal, a new promise to ourselves. We were determined to have all the sex they say we shouldn't have. Karma is sweet as candy, but payback is a bitch on her period, and she move fast as hell too! You won't be able to stop her. She can and will only be tamed by her own desires, as twisted and unconventional as they may seem.

Just thinking of Chase eating some other bitch's pussy and bringing his ass to my dinner table hungry and shit, repulsed me. I did hope his dick could stay hard long enough for her easily opened ass to at least get wet. I damn sure wasn't swimming in love juices fucking him. Sadly, by the time my pussy even got wet, Chase was pulling out, going to sleep. He was done, dick dead as fuck, looking like a little fucking gummy worm; me pissed the fuck off. Another waste of time – the story of my fucking life. I was sick of it. Every woman deserved a good nut. Why was I so convinced I didn't deserve that? Why was I content for so long with deprivation of the "D"? No fair!!

Well, no more. I was going to get me some damn dick for real! No more flirting and playing around to see if I still got it. None of that shit no more. This pussy was up for grabs and that butterscotch babe Chink from the office was on my radar.

***

It was a week before my birthday. Chase's boring ass hadn't celebrated my birthday in years, so I knew he didn't have shit planned. Surprisingly, I got a text from Chink's beautiful ass. It read: *"Me &u lunch, today, noon. A car will be out front your office to pick you up."*

I smiled wickedly in anticipation of some excitement in my mix for a change. Yet, I waited about five minutes before I replied. I answered with a seemingly unbothered, *"Sure, see you then."* He replied back with a thumbs-up emoji.

The door man called up to my secretary about fifteen minutes before noon and informed her that my car was waiting downstairs. "Stormy," she whispered while peeking out the window. "Who dat in the back seat?"

I hopped up to see what Lisa was babbling about. I looked out and saw that it was Chink. "Oh, just my business lunch waiting," I answered. "Business lunch? Since when does business lunch look that damn fine and pick us up from the office?" "Us?" I replied. We shared a laugh.

I gathered my things and walked toward the elevator. When the doors opened down in the lobby, Chink stood there with a bundle of amazingly scented lilies. Lilies were my favorite. I wonder how he knew.

"Hi," I said, a little too cheerfully.

"Hello, you look gorgeous," Chink complimented. "Gorgeous flowers for a gorgeous lady."

I blushed. "Thank you! They are beautiful, and lilies are my favas. How'd you know?"

"I pay attention to things I wanna know more about. You also have pictures of lilies all over your office," Chink recalled. "Your screen saver is a lily. You're wearing lily-scented lotion too. I saw you moisten your hands with it the first time we met."

"Wow! You are observant. I'm impressed!" And even more intrigued, I wanted to add.

"Good! Mission accomplished," Chink said, as he opened my door to the car.

Chink sat down and I smelled that sexy-ass Jimmy Choo cologne again. This time it was mixed with just a hint of weed. *Hmmm,* I thought. *We've got that in common.* I smoked a joint socially from time to time, so I wasn't tripping. On top of being sexy as hell, Chink owned his own business which meant he called the shots in his life. A quite prominent business too. He supplied companies like the Label I worked for with computer surveillance and recording equipment. He also designed the internet programs to go with the equipment they provided. Major labels and large corporations used them, so he was a big dawg within the business world. His ambition turned me on as well.

Chase was content writing articles for papers every now and then. He never exhibited the drive to have his own column or his own paper. I hated that about him. He was happy just ... being. I wanted to be happy being happy as hell about being happy!!! You understand me?

Chink whispered sweet shit in my ear, tantalizing my hot spots and giving a major boost to this damaged ego of mine as the car coasted down the highway. He could've been talking about golf and it would've sounded erotic the way he was blowing that silky shit in my ear.

We pulled up at a spa. I'm automatically thinking... Ummmmm, hell, what was I thinking? Oh yeah! We getting mani-pedis or some shit? It didn't matter though. We could've been getting crucified in that bitch and I would've still followed Chink's ass.

We walked inside and the host led us up a flight of white marble winding stairs to a private room. The room was a beautiful, calming deep purple, so deep that upon first glance it appeared black. However, the sunlight beamed through the huge bay windows and manifested its true colors. The room was dressed in lavender lilies and Knick knacks were positioned all around. The furniture was a soothing, cool white leather with huge backs. It mirrored a royal feel. The ladies serving us wore fluffy white robes with fluffy slippers to match. The fellas wore white linen shorts or pants and tan suede slippers. Everyone was sipping on power drinks and mimosas; some even drank Bloody Mary's. It was a pretty upscale place. I likeeeeee!

Jazz instrumentals piped through the surround sound softly, the kind you'd hear in a yoga studio. Sweet melodies surrounded by birds chirping and waves splashing. It was very relaxing.

Two individual king and queen style pedicure stations with two massive leather massage tables were centered in the room. A nook filled with croissants, smoothies, and every fruit in the garden were placed in the corners of the room. A server passed Chink and I our robes and directed us to the changing stations.

Inside the room, I slipped out of my office attire and into the cute little swimsuit they provided and draped the fluffy white robe over around me. Stepping back out, I saw Chink already waiting at the station. His feet were soaking in tub of steaming hot water filled with bath salts and oils. "So, I love your idea of lunch," I complimented him as I walked over to my seat.

"Ohhh, you like huh?" Chink replied. "Yes, I do. Very thoughtful of you. Thank you."

"You're welcome. Let's say it's my thanks for you endorsing my contract."

"Well, you have something I need desperately."

"Oh really?? What's that?" Chink asked, amused at my candor.

"Those data programs are the best thing since a hard dick. I desperately need the service your company provides," I said. "So, thank you."

Chink looked a bit annoyed at my response. I'm sure he was expecting a more needy answer. Some little girl shit like, *'It's you baby; I need YOU!'* Nah niquaaaaa, wrong woman. Bottom line, I don't give a damn about you. Know that!

Chink cracked a few jokes and we both laughed awkwardly. That laugh was enough to steer the convo back to the right a bit since it was veering left quickly.

I adjusted my pillow and got comfortable while I slid my feet into this soothing water. My head fell to the side and I noticed Chink had the most amazing arms. I could see them because the women wore robes and the men had a choice between flannel pants or shorts, many wearing no shirts.

"You down to soak in the mud tub with me?" Chink asked hesitantly. It's almost like he was nervous. I thought it was cute. He was intimidated by my, *I gots this shit and don't need you* swag.

"Now, that sounds great," I replied. "Is it warm?"

"I don't know, is it?" He asks softly and cuts his eyes down at my legs. "Ohhhh, you meant the mud bath? Yes, it's warm," he says. "You'll love it." He gathered himself and queried, "So, what do you do for fun, Stormy?"

"Well, lately, I've been concentrating on getting my book done, so not much time for fun."

"The husband's no fun? If its ok to ask that," Chink pried.

"No, he is a great guy. I just don't like him anymore," I answered honestly, while still saving face. I wasn't into the man bashing stuff. Chase was a good man; he just was not the man for me. Talk shit about my fam? Nope, not gonna happen. I may tell *him* he's a stupid, inconsiderate, erectile dysfunctional asshole. But YOU better not say it.

"Soooooo," I said quickly diverting attention away from myself. "What are some of your hobbies?"

"I love to relax. Just take time out for myself. I travel quite a bit for work, and I love it. If you could visit any place tomorrow where would you go?" Chink asks.

"Hmmmm... I would go to an island somewhere or maybe the Dominican Republic."

He snickered a bit and said, "Pick one. If you had *one* wish to visit one spot anywhere in the world, where would you go?"

"I read a story called, Wet, once. It was about a river. It was a beautiful waterfall turned sexual entity, it took place in Trinidad and Tobago. It's called the Rico Seco."

"Wet huh? Sounds good?"

"It is," I assured him. "I wrote it."

"Ok ok, I see you. Can I read it?"

"Yeah sure, when you buy the book," I replied sarcastically. "I would love to do a shoot there for that chapter. Wow! That would be hot. Can you swim, Chink?"

"I can. How about you?" He asked.

"Like a mermaid," I replied. "I love water. I spend a lot of time at my dad's cabin on the ocean."

The hostess entered and asked if we were ready for the mud bath. Chink looked to me for approval. I liked that. He was a gentleman and was thoughtful enough to check with me first. Chase's lame ass would have said, *hell no, I'm not getting in no mud.* Or just got up and hopped his ass in and yelled, *Come on baby!* Ugggh! I guess that was a red flag he's always been that way.

I removed my robe wearing the bathing suit provided by the spa. Chink looked unmoved. I almost felt embarrassed that he didn't start drooling at the mouth or something. Like, oh you don't see all this? You gonna sit there and act like you don't see all this? It was a ten second attitude. In all reality, the woman in me knew he saw this shit. I also knew that the MAN in him wouldn't allow a reaction. Boys did that. It also told me Chink was interested in me.

Little girls listen... pussy comes dime a dozen. Dig deeper and someday you'll be a keeper. Okaaaay!!! Just a little nugget for you little girls.

Anyhooo!! Stepping into the mud felt amazing. It was smoothly thick, nice, and warm. It smelled like coconut oil. Really rich and earthy. I began to smell a hint of hazelnut and chocolate too.

Chink began tasting the mud from his hands. I looked at him, puzzled. He laughed and told me it was edible.

"I knew I was smelling chocolate!" I screeched. "Wow! How'd you hear about this place?"

"One of my clients actually own the place. We service all of the equipment you see. I've been here a few times— ALONE. I see one of those relaxation sessions you so crave."

"That's great, Chink. Must be nice to have these kinds of friends."

"Yeah, it really is though," he says.

The hostess brought out a fruit platter. I immediately began dipping the strawberries in the tub. I realized I was looking greedy, but this shit was good as hell.

After some laughter and great conversation, I decided to cut this short, but before I could get my words out, Chink beat me to it.

"So Stormy, I'm a go ahead and be honest. I like you a lot as a person. Not to mention the size 7 ass you wear over your radiant, caramel-coated skin. Your big brown eyes simmer like the sun at dawn, and those perfectly shaped lips... On top of your down-to-earth childlike womanish personality, its irresistible," he concluded. "I want to be in your company again. I want you as a friend. If you let me, I want you to sit on my face every chance you get and don't dare move until I make you move. Literally."

My mouth seemed to be watering like a wolf in the wild just spotting a bunny rabbit. Chink went on to tell me. "Listen, I got a bucket list I've been working on and I'd love to take you with. You should know I'm married also. Been married 8 years. I'm turned off, bored to death, and I wanna share my free time with whatever free time you may have."

I was sitting there sucking the mud off my fingers while he pitched his game. "Ok," I began. "So, I only play games on my terms and this is a dangerous one."

"So, you wanna just stay friends?" Chink asked.

"No!" I said, abruptly.

Chink rushed toward me, gliding through the tub over to all this sweetness and firmly planted both lips on mine. He sucked the mud off them like they were a cherry popsicle. Then, he glided back to his spot in the tub.

I was speechless, to say the least, but I felt a jolt of excitement in my universe when his lips touched mine. Hell yeah, I'll bucket list wit' yo ass. Let's go!

"Well," I said, blushing, somewhat stunned by his commitment and honest loyalty to being dishonest. Yet, I was desperately intrigued by his sexiness and his clear interest in me. Run it, playboy!

"Well what?" Chink replied.

"Well, I don't mind making new friends but let's just hang out, get to know each other, and ride the wave from there."

"I like waves," he says softly. "Yeah, let's make a few waves," he suggested, moving his hand through the chocolate mud filled tub as if he were a fish.

"This was a great lunch. Thank you for thinking...like I would?" I said, surprised as I realized we were on the same wavelength.

He smiled and said, "Let me be the calm in your storm, Ayesha. Let me be for you what I wish somebody was for me. Let me give you something you clearly crave."

"And what's that?"

"Your smile."

I smiled and walked toward the showers. I gave him a slight wave and blew a kiss. "Till next time, boss man!" I yelled, while fading into the changing area. I heard him yelling back.

"When? Tomorrow? Stormy?"

I didn't reply. I snuck out the side door and hopped into a cab.

On my way home, I received a text that read, *"Hope to see you sooner than later."*

I hit right back and said, *"@sooner"* with a thumb's up emoji and a smile.

When I got home, Chase was sitting around looking dumb as hell working my last nerve.

"You hungry?" Chase asked.

"NO!" I snarled.

"Well hell, I am," he said sarcastically.

"Go tell that bitch to feed you!" I yelled.

Chase simply sat there like a scared puppy. I knew it was unfair of me to hold on to something I'd already let go of.

In my heart, I really didn't want to be with Chase anymore, but I loved him. Does that make sense? He was part of my life, embedded in my spirit like a blood relative should be. I felt a loyalty to a fault to my vows, even if I wasn't happy living with them. I loved him; not in love. I didn't have that can't-wait-till-he-gets-home-from-work so excited about my man type of love. I chose to love him. Think about that. The choices we make in life... The choice to bend for others. The choice to put individuality in a box for the sake of "US" was the most powerful selfless choice one could make to me. So, that's why I stayed through his side chick dilemma, and all his other bullshit. In all reality, she wasn't the problem; WE were.

So, fellas, you know how you just bought those fresh new kicks, and somebody steps on ya shit!? You never look at those shoes the same. You keep them because you paid a coin and a half for them. Hence cheaper to keep 'em. That's how I felt about Chase. He was the fucking stained shoe in the back of the closet. Chink was a breath of fresh air. New meat. Got his own issues, so I didn't expect any childlike or clingy type behaviors from him.

Wait, was I a fucking side piece? No! Right? Chink was married, happy or not, and I definitely considered him a side drop of chocolate. So, I guess I'm a damn side chick.

Well, whatever the hell was going on it was going to be all on my terms. Take it or fucking leave it. I didn't care. Let's see what Mr. Corporate had to offer. I always told myself I would never mess around with a married man, but that was when I was single. It seemed different now that I too was somebody's wife. Different in that I didn't want a real relationship with Chink. I just wanted to fuck 'em. How am I a homewrecker if I had my own damn home? Besides, the way I see it, neither I nor Chink were happy or we wouldn't have ended up sharing mud baths and shit.

Chase would have just died if I even mentioned a mud bath. I could hear him, *"Why am I gonna pay money to sit in some damn mud? This some gay shit!"* Chase was just "ignant" and closed-minded most times.

I had convinced myself that two wrongs would make it right. Drilled into my head that I deserved to enjoy life. And I did; we all do. Was I selling my soul to the devil by

Starzpen

stepping outside my marriage? Was my pussy speaking for me? It was quite deprived. Fuck that!!! I thought. Chase been slinging his sour-ass gummy worm around for a minute. I can't let him get away with that shit. Pure hate for what I ultimately allowed was what was driving me. I had no plans on pumping my brakes anytime soon though. Unless it was to slow my grind for some little hottie.

Let's face it, if it wasn't Chink, it'd be somebody. My pussy was on fire and I had chosen Chink to douse my fire.

***

I arrived at the office the following morning and Lisa handed me a package.

"Open it, open it, Stormy!" Lisa urged.

"Why you so excited?" I asked.

"Oh well, ummm... I opened the first envelope it came in."

"Really Lisa?"

"I'm sorry, Boss. I spilled coffee on it," she lied.

We both laughed knowing her ass was just nosey.

"It's from that gum drop that took you to lunch a few months ago ain't it?" She asked, nudging me for info. I opened the envelope and there were two tickets to Trinidad and Tobago, First Class. Attached was an itinerary complete with amazing excursions, oceanside massages, and what??

"Oh my goodness Lissssss…"

"WHAT, Stormy??? WHAT?"

I paused, shaking the paper in my hand. "It's a confirmation slip for a full photo shoot at the Rico Seco

Falls. Make-up artist, stylist, equipped with wardrobe and a personal assistant of my choice," I relayed.

We both screamed like two schoolgirls just asked to prom by star athletes.

"You taking me, right boss?? Right?"

"Well ummmm...of course, bitch! Who else? Let me holler at Chink before we get all excited and see what this is really about though."

"Ok, I can dig that. Call me as soon as you know something so I can go get my hair did," Lisa requested. "Oooh girl, I'ma get some wet n wavy! Oooh, or maybe a bone straight 22 inch... ohh yeah, and my nails wit' some island shit on 'em."

Lisa was going in. I laughed at her as she babbled her way back to her desk. I was hiding my excitement, trying to be cool about mine. Inside, I was floored by his thoughtfulness. Intrigued by his bold interest in me. I decided to give him a call.

The phone rang twice, and I heard that deep, soft, rough, sexy voice say, "How's your morning going ma'am?"

"It's great, thanks for asking. How about yours? Working hard, are we?"

"No, not really. I'm packing, about to head to L.A for a few weeks."

"Oh! Business trip?" I asked.

"Yes. We are expanding so I'm going to close this deal and begin our West Coast chapter."

"Oh wow! That's awesome. Congratulations."

"Thank you. I'm really excited! It's a huge move for the company," he explained.

Chink changed the subject and asked if I had received my early Christmas present.

"I was wondering when you were going to take your trip," he asked.

"Ummm... well yeah, I kind of wanted to talk to you about that."

"What's to talk about? There are two tickets for you and your assistant, which I'm assuming is Lisa, considering she made sure I knew you would not go on this trip without her."

"Oh, did she now???" I asked, surprised at her incredulity, and irritated simultaneously at her nosey antics. But not too deep down inside I was saying, *Yes bitch, good job!!*

"Don't be mad at her," Chink advised. "Besides, you'll have more fun with a familiar friend around."

"Wait, so you're not going?"

"No, I mean I can, but I figured you may think it was too soon for that," he explained. "This is something I wanted to do for you. I want to see your book do well."

Ooooooh! I just wanted to jump through the phone, hop on his dick, and squeeze my pussy walls around him until he popped. *Who the fuck is this dude?* I thought to myself. He was too good to be true. He must cum quick. Can't eat pussy. Dick big and awkward with no motion control. Something had to be wrong with him.

"I'll be in L.A., but I can always get a chopper and fly over for the shoot and dinner...and maybe breakfast," Chink plotted, talking that BIG talk, choppers and shit.

"That sounds fabulous! I'd love to have you share this experience with me," I said, letting him know how appreciative I was. "So, I'll text you when we arrive."

"Yeah, do that. And please, if you ladies need anything, just ask. Anything. Oh, I also left some cash for you both at your villa."

"You didn't have to do that. We have money."

"I know, I know, love. But now you don't have to spend it. Enjoy the rest of your day, Stormy."

"Same to you, Chink," I replied.

I ended the call and looked up to see Lisa tiptoeing back to her desk after eavesdropping on my whole call.

"Lisa!!" I yelled.

Lisa ran in my office. "Yeah, ma'am?"

I looked at her with my angry bird look for about five seconds.

"What???" Lisa said, annoyed at me for playing too much.

"Go home!" I yelled.

"Huh? Go home?"

"Yes! Take your behind home now!!!" I repeated, then screamed, "AND GET YO HAIR DONE BIHHHHHSH! WE GOING TO THE ISLANDS!!!"

We jumped around my office like two fools, screaming and laughing.

"When we leaving, boss?"

"Well it's an open-ended travel package soooooooo... let's see when the next flight is," I suggested.

Lisa ran to my desk toward the laptop, then she stopped and turned to me. "Oh wait, is this some I'm gon' be the third wheel type situation?" she asked.

"No, actually Chink will be in L.A. on business for a few weeks. He said he would fly in for the photo shoot, dinner, and maybe even breakfast though."

Lisa frowned. "Eeeeesh, see if he got some friends maaaaaan dang!!!"

Starzpen

Lisa rubbed my back as if to console me right before she took the picture of Chase and I and slid it in a drawer. We both stared at each other in a moment of clarity. She knew, and I definitely knew, my marriage was over. Not because of Chink, specifically, but because in that moment I realized life wasn't life unless you were living it. That was more powerful than any orgasm.

Lisa and I spent all night surfing the web for info on Trinidad looking for the best places to eat, nightlife, transportation services, etc. They had one place that took you everywhere by horseback. I thought having a horse at the falls as a prop for the shoot would be dope.

We finally found flights for that Friday morning. We decided to take Chink's advice to save our money and shop when we got to the island with the cash he left at the villa. I'd never been outside the country, so I was so excited to see another culture. Not to mention being able to see and experience firsthand the location I wrote about. It was a chance to bring my story to life. It would also be great promo for the book. The trip was a win-win, and I couldn't be more excited.

***

The following morning, Lisa and I boarded the plane giddy as a teenager with star athletes at the prom.

Just as I sat in my huge seat, I received a text from Chase. It said, *"Have a safe trip. I love you."*

"Love u too!" I replied.

I almost felt bad for living my life, for initiating happiness, for doing whatever made me tick? I quickly backed off that bullshit this time though. Chase was off my radar now, husband or not. Maybe if we had gotten some counseling or assessed and addressed our issues before he betrayed me, we'd had a chance. It was too late for reconciliation now. I was flying to live my best life.

Lisa and I boarded the plane and took our seats directly behind the cockpit. I snatched the window seat, no doubt. Luckily for Lisa, there was an empty seat across from mine and the flight attendant allowed her to float back and forth.

It was a long flight, but we couldn't sleep in anticipation of our arrival. We filled our time playing cards, doing some online shopping, and watching movies on our phones. Oh, I can't forget the unlimited amounts of alcohol we were able to consume. We knew we were getting closer before the airline staff announced it. We could see huge beds of water, beautiful greenery, and lots and lots of sandy terrain. About twenty minutes after we spotted the terrain, they announced our descent.

We deplaned and upon exiting the airport we noticed a huge sign with what appeared to be Christmas lights that read: *A storm is coming with a girl named Lisa.*

Hilarious. Lisa and I both pulled out our phones to get selfies with the sign.

"Hello Ladies," the driver said as we snapped away. "Your chariot awaits."

Chink reserved a black Lincoln Navigator for us with the option to switch cars if we wanted. He was unbelievably considerate. The fact that he wasn't pressed about coming along or trying to ease up my wet windy road was confirmation that he was *that* man, or a very good play.

As the driver took us to our villa he told us about the island, pointing out certain landmarks to punctuate his point. He talked about the Rico Seco being the most amazing place on the island.

He leaned his head back and said, "Your villa is on the fall."

"Really?" I yelled. "You mean we are staying at the river? Not down the block or five miles away?"

"No ma'am," he confirmed, shaking his head vigorously. "There are four private villas on the property, which are extremely difficult to get, I might add. You must me somebody pretty special," he said.

Lisa nodded in agreement.

"Ok my beauties," the driver said in his deep Trini accent. "We reach pon ya space, eh?"

"Wow!" Lisa exclaimed. "This is beautiful!!!! Eeeeesh!" Lisa teared up and thanked me profusely for bringing her. "I hope to God I get to test out one of these fine citizens. Oooh chile! Yes, I must find me a playmate for this vaycay."

"Go 'head Lissssss! I really want us to have a good time, so if you don't find you a stick to get in gear, I'll find you one."

We laughed and high-fived each other as we approached the villa. We entered the villa and saw a large yellow envelop attached to the table in the foyer. Inside the big envelope was another envelope addressed to Lisa. She ripped it open like a child on Christmas morning and dug her hand inside. She pulled out a stack of hundred-dollar bills and several meal gift cards, confirmation slips for our excursions, and a voucher for a scheduled helicopter tour of the entire island. Mr. Smalls definitely knew how to plan a trip. The fact that it was tailor made to suit me made it even sweeter.

Lisa and I headed over to the bar while the housekeepers took our bags to our rooms. We both needed a minute to gather ourselves, still in disbelief of the opportunity that had just fallen in our laps. It really was a dream vacation for the both us. No one had ever even thought of doing anything like this for me. He believed in my book and in me. I knew that no one would go this far for potential pussy. So, his vested interest in me was obviously deeper than physical.

Wait..."wayment!!" Was my self-worth in doubt? Was I unsure of my ability to attract real interest? Why didn't I know why HE was going all out? Some shit I had to figure out within, I guess. For the time being, I was going to put my foot into this shoot, slay this video, and kickback and enjoy myself. We were here as long as we wanted to be, and since I pretty much ran the label from my phone and Chase knew to leave me the hell alone, I figured we would stay for at least a week.

I regrouped in my room then found myself with Lisa at the bar sipping on some red wine and nibbling on cheeses and various flavors of bread from the basket left by guests' services.

Lisa looked around and surveyed our surroundings. "Girlllll, we about to turn the fuck up! Listen, don't nobody know us, we got all this fucking money," she said while thumbing through the bills, kissing and blowing on them and shit.

I laughed, "Girl, you are nuts," I said, shaking my head. "Ok, what should we do first?"

"Well, I saw this ad for boat charters. We could rent a boat and ride out to the exact spot of the falls. I know you'd love that. I emailed the captain and he said he would pick us up here and sail us through the caves directly to the spot where the water falls. He said it takes about 45 minutes to get there."

"Wow! Really Lissssss?" I said, shocked that she was even thinking of me. I was also a bit puzzled because, again, no one had read the book yet. How did she know what the perfect spot would be? "That would be great," I told her, curious to see this thing through.

"Ok good. I thought so, so I went ahead and scheduled our ride for 10 am. Brunch, wine, and some island weed will be on board," Lisa shared.

"You've been busy I see. When did you have time to do all this?"

"Oh, I made a few arrangements from the plane via email boo. You know me!" Lisa sang. "I'm always on top of my ish."

"Yes, you are. That's why I love you, girl."

"Ok, so I'll order dinner. We can shower and watch some movies from the hammocks in the sky box. It was so peaceful there. The view was almost as if you were watching the stars dance with the wind from the moon. Amazing clarity, a breathtaking calm."

We watched a few movies, laughed up a storm, and had a grand time. After a few minutes, we both grew sleepy.

WET

Lisa stood and announced, "Ok boss lady, bedtime. Let's get some rest tonight."

As we headed up the narrow staircase to our rooms, I had a startling image. Or was it a daydream or a premonition? Whatever it was, it was an image of someone who seemed to be drowning. Just a flash though, a woman frantically fighting... the water? Perhaps she was trying to swim maybe? It was somewhat alarming, so much so that I stumbled backwards.

"You alight?" Lisa asked.

"Yeah, I'm good. Just tired from that flight I suppose. Good night Lissssss, I'll see you in the morning."

"Night, girl."

The window in my room was open. You would have had to be there in order to believe the breathtaking hold the breeze had on me. It was slightly frightening. It paralyzed me for a good ten seconds. Then, a single swift wind blew and suddenly I was free. Standing there, I wondered if I'd had too much wine or if the jet lag had affected me in unexpected ways.

Tired as hell, I brushed it off and went to shower. The entire time I could have sworn someone was calling my name. *Ayeeeesha...* the voice whispered eerily. *Ayeeeesha.* I didn't know if I was drunk or what, so I just laid my head on the pillow and closed my eyes.

The wine must have had me out of my mind because I dreamed of Chink's fine ass. The dream was so vivid it was as if he was in the bed with me, fondling me, coaxing me into the abyss of a deep orgasm. I could feel his lips nibbling on the back of my thighs with both his big, strong hands wrapped around my waist. His hand slid between my thighs and gently parted my legs. His fingers trekked up my flesh and squeezed my pussy lips together, applying just the right amount of pressure to my clit while running his tongue up and down and around and around both my ass cheeks.

"Oh wow… unnnnhmmmm!" I moaned. I placed his hand firmly in the center of my back forcing me to bend, holding myself up with my hands palming the wall. I arched my back toward him, and without warning, he thrust himself inside me and began to move to a rhythm I craved since my cherry had busted. It was like dancing to Maxwell's, *A Woman's Worth*. I heard the song in the recesses of my mind, the beat prodding me to move to a nice and slow rhythm, speeding up at the perfect moments. He went deeper and harder in perfect alignment with my body. I moaned uncontrollably, sweating and aching for some relief. I felt that silky sweet, torturous feeling rising to the pit of my stomach. Heat settled there and swirled like the beginning of a typhoon. I arched my back and rode the wind until…

My eyes suddenly snapped open. I awoke with one finger inside my wet heat and the other in my mouth. Oh shit! Was this a dream? My pussy was dripping wet—I should know, my damn fingers were all up in it!!! Quite disturbed and confused as to what the hell was going on, I tried my best to just get through the night.

The next morning, I awoke to the smell of Belgian coffee Lisa was up preparing for the day.

"Good morning!!!!" I greeted cheerfully.

"Good morning," she replied.

"Did you sleep okay?" I asked.

"I did. I had the weirdest dream though."

"Oh yeah? What about?"

Lisa stirred the coffee and stared off as if she was trying to recall the dream. "I don't remember much, but I do remember something about a river and somebody fucking in it, or on it, or some shit. I don't know girl; it was craaaazyyy!"

I found her dream crazy too because no one had read any parts of my book yet. However, the details she described sounded somehow familiar. *Oh, girl, get out this suspicious morbid funk you're in,* I tell myself. Eventually I shook it off and enjoyed my coffee.

There was a knock on the door that startled us. Lisa yelled that she would answer it.

"It's probably the captain," Lisa figured. As I grabbed my bag for this ride, I heard Lisa say, "YES THERE IS A GOD!"

"He fione girl??" I called out.

"Yesses. He is beautiful!" Lisa snatched the door open and showed all thirty-twos.

I dismissed her antics and thrust my hand out to greet him. "Hi, I'm Stormy and this is Lisa. You'll be driving us today?"

"Yes ma'am," he said, his eyes never leaving Lisa. He grinned from ear to ear. Apparently, he was just as horny as her. Lisa *was* a baddie though.

Lisa stood at a stacked 5'4," and weighed about 160 pounds. The weight was in all the right places too. She had naturally curly, bronze-colored hair that was cut in a short hair style reminiscent of Anita Baker in her heyday, and she was funny enough to make a corpse laugh. Lisa was a good girl. She worked hard and definitely helped me out in major ways. I felt like she deserved a little me-time, so I wasn't going to throw salt in her oatmeal.

"He is a cutie! Go for yours," I encouraged her. "Maybe this is what your dream was about."

"Mmm hmmm, I didn't think about that. Hell yeah, girl let's go!!!"

"Guess I'm on some third-wheel shit, huh?" I pretended to be upset, but I was really rooting for Lisa. She deserved to get her back broke in by this Adonis of a man.

We both laughed as we boarded the boat. The boat was a beauty. It was all black with gold trimming. Her name was *The Morning Star.*

As I read the words, my eyes widened from fear. I looked over to Lisa and she looked as if she had just seen Pac. Lisa and I made eye contact immediately upon noticing the boat's name. It was inscribed across the front and sides of the boat, outlined in a beautiful green with a star inside a crescent. We were both tripping on the coincidence of the name of the boat. My name was Star— MORNING STAR, to be exact. My dad had given me that name as a child, but mom stuck with Ayesha to make him mad. She said she called me Stormy for a reason. She said in her mind it was the total opposite of his Star. So immature, I thought.

After a moment of silence, Lisa and I ignored the coincidence and shrugged off these almost wicked but sensual feelings we were both experiencing. We chalked it up to it being confirmation in a big way.

Lisa and I both boarded the M.S. and inspected the vessel more thoroughly. It was pure royal. Everything we saw or touched was either leather or marble. There was a hot tub, pool table, and a huge entertainment room with every game imaginable, from glass chessboards to twister. There was a lavish seafood platter enough for at least twenty-five people, it seemed. It was loaded with huge king crab legs, lobster tails, and the biggest shrimp and scallops I'd ever seen. The shrimp were prepared in three different ways: fried, boiled, or scampi style. There was a minibar on the upper deck stocked like a Brooklyn liquor store. Lisa was acting as if she was used to this shit, but truth be told, we did fit right in.

We never followed the rules and always thought we deserved the best. This was no different in our minds. Well, maybe a little. We were dope queens, and no one could tell us we weren't. We were rightfully where we were supposed to be

***

It didn't take Lisa long before she hopped on the captain's dick and he let her. Meanwhile, I was sitting on the deck below enjoying the breeze and the scenery. It was truly a dream come true to be here at the Rico. The exact location my book was based upon. I was getting crazy ideas for the shoot the next day. Maybe I'd charter the boat again and take a few shots on the deck. Lisa would love that I'm sure a second chance at getting next to the hot little knotty Dred that just happened to fall in her lap.

I began to hear the Falls somehow in my soul. I could feel it. I felt as if I were about to visit a close friend. A familiarity that was out of this world. I had a feeling that I had been here before, knowing I hadn't. It was weird. The water splashed into the river forcefully.

Suddenly, I felt hot and tingly all over. I could see the water turn green as it hit the river and blended in with its contents. I felt horny as hell for some odd reason. The temperature between the walls of these caves and my thighs had changed. It was hot as hell. My nipples were so hard they ached. This feeling seemed so familiar... like déjà vu. *I'd been here before,* I thought to myself again. This time the feeling was a thousand times more intense.

Out of nowhere, I felt something sliding up my leg. Fingers? It felt like hands and fingers gliding its way up my legs. I called for Lisa, but the words wouldn't come out. Something had my mouth covered. Terrified and trying to figure out what the fuck was wrong with me, I heard footsteps. Somebody was coming...

Lisa? Thank God!

I still was unable to say anything. The very moment Lisa's foot hit the deck, the hold on my mouth was released.

I stood and fixed my clothes while I gathered myself. Lisa noticed my disarray and stared at me curiously.

"You okay, Stormy?" Lisa asked.

"Yeah, yeah, I'm good," I lied. "Just a harsh strong wind scared me a little."

"Are you sure? You look like you just saw Pac. And I didn't feel no damn wind."

"No, no, I'm okay," I insisted. "Besides, you know I'd be naked by now if it was Pac. I'd be over here hailing Mary and shit," I joked, attempting to infuse some humor into a tense moment. I wanted to shift the subject. "Have you been feeling strange, Lisa?" I asked.

"Hell yeah, gurlllll!!! My pussy in overdrive; that hottie up there sexy as hell. His name is Spragga. He was born here. He single too girl."

"Oh ok."

"Oh ok? What the hell is wrong with you, girl? For real, for real, you look like you just woke up from a nightmare. One wit' Freddie or Jason's ass in it. What's going on with you?" Lisa asked, genuinely concerned.

"I'm ok. I'm just tired."

"Ok. If you sure you're okay, I'ma go ahead and get back in the Captain's seat if that's alright, boss."

"Yes, go have some fun."

"Thank you!!! Call me if you need me."

After Lisa left, I sat staring out at a beautiful, but ghostly scenery at the Falls. It felt just like I wrote it. It had that same out-of-this world aura about its atmosphere. This was the strangest feeling ever. Was I living the story I wrote? Was I going crazy? Confused and scared out of my mind, I decided to shoot Chink a text:

"I could really use your vibe in my presence. Can you fly in ASAP?"

To my surprise he hit back immediately:

"Thought you'd never ask. Ordering a flight plan right now."

I replied: *"Great we are on a boat in the Rico."*

He texted back: *"Cool! Have your captain send me you guys coordinates."*

I forwarded that info to Lisa so she could tell Spragga.

The boat coasted to a spot I thought would be great to sit and wait for Chink. I figured I'd get some work done and let Lisa have her way with Spragga. He was a cutie though.

WET

After a few hours of working and exploring the island a bit, I sent Lisa and Spragga back to the boat to get lunch. Sitting on those same rocks in the book, colored of earth draped in the most beautiful vibrant green-shaded moss, I was in great anticipation of…something. I couldn't quite put my finger on what. I was so excited to see Chink, but it was something else. This must have explained this euphoric feeling showering me.

Looking out at the Rico I felt this overwhelming need to touch the water. Slowly and somewhat hesitantly, I moved closer to the edge of the river. It seemed as if something was pulling me toward the water. I reached the river's edge, removed my flip flops and stepped in. The water was quite warm and seemed to be rising. It was already covering my entire foot. *Is this water getting hotter?* I felt heat and the water began to spin in circles. I was shocked into paralysis. My panties slid down my legs and I screamed in silence. I ran in horror, yet I was not moving at all. I was terrified but my pussy was craving thrusting, begging to be penetrated.

Suddenly, I heard Lisa laugh as she rounded the corner. Oddly, the very minute she was visible to me, the hold on me lifted. I could finally move and speak, but I chose not to. I was still stuck and wallowing in disbelief because I couldn't tell these two this mess I was experiencing. They'd think I was crazy. Hell, *I* was feeling crazy, so I'm sure they would feel that I was crazy too.

I snapped the fuck out of my stupor and pretended to just be a bit emotional about being here. I gave them the story my Aunt Najee told me about this place I'd never heard of before.

"Her husband was a Marine, so they traveled all over the world," I explained to them. "She visited this area quite consistently. I never asked why. One year she was here with some friends on vacation when her husband Don died in combat in Kuwait. She never left. She died here. She told me stories of how beautiful the Rico Seco was. Writing about it helped me keep her memory alive."

I told them my story and it seemed to do the trick. Lisa quickly changed the subject, as she was clearly preoccupied.

"We got you some food, Boss Lady," Lisa said.

"Thank you!" I gushed. "I'm starving; what do you guys have there?"

Spragga was carrying the most amazing platter of traditional West Indian dishes. There was roti, Aloo pie, corn soup, Pholourie, bake and shark coconut jelly with warm fresh coco bread, cassava pone, Toolum. You name it and it was there.

"When did you do this, Spragga?" I asked. "All I saw on the boat was that wonderful seafood spread on the deck."

"Secrets of the island," he replied with a sinister laugh.

"Girl, his homeboy brought it in on a speed boat. Listen gurlllll, it was like some 007 stuff," Lisa chimed in.

We all laughed.

"Oh, no secrets with this one around. You just learned a valuable lesson today, sir," I informed Spragga, referring to Lisa's runny mouth.

"Wait! Listen, y'all hear that?"

We all got quiet and focused on the sound.

Spragga said, "It's a chopper. Must be your friend. His ETA at the time he sent coordinates is right about now," he estimated, looking down at his watch. "I'll go get him.

You ladies enjoy lunch." Before disappearing, Spragga looked back at *me* and said, "Oh yeah, don't go in the water without me, Lisa."

But why was he looking at me? I had the strangest feeling, a vibe that seemed out of this world. I made a mental note to go see my girl, Cyn. She was always good at inserting some clarity in my mix. For now, I decided to shake off my apprehension and enjoy Chink's fine ass while he was here.

I looked up and saw a silhouette of what appeared to be a giant in the shadows appearing on the walls of the cave. The arms were huge, and the frame was perfect. The walk was confident and sure. As the figure walked closer, I heard Chink's voice.

"Just in time for lunch, I see," Chink said.

"I hope that's not all you get to eat," Lisa said, mischievously. We all acted as if we didn't hear her.

I hopped up to greet Chink when suddenly my knees buckled and I began to feel faint. Chink reached out and caught me inside his beefy arms. He swooped me up just in time to keep me from hitting the ground. Lisa rushed over in despair.

"Boss Lady! Boss Lady! Eeesh!! What the hell is going on? Girl, are you preggers? You've been on weird since we got here!" Lisa yelled.

I panted in panic, and in this instant, I realized I had been summoned here. I was drawn to this place somehow. Lisa and Chink rushed over to see what was wrong. Spragga didn't move. He stood there watching the water. His reaction confused me, so I quickly caught my breath and ran to him.

I grabbed both his hands and fought him for eye contact. "Explain Spragga!" I begged. "Explain! Please?!

You know this place; you haven't reacted to anything. You're not surprised at any of this."

"Stormy," he says. "Mi nah tink ya raddy! Come! Sit!" He pulls out his phone and shows me a photo of a woman. A woman with my face! She looked exactly like...ME! Lisa and Chink curiously rushed toward me to see the picture.

Lisa gasped and said, "Eeeeesh, that's you...but you on that rock over there!"

"Huh?" Chink looked closer at a specific dent in the rock formation. It was identical to the one in the photo.

Spragga stood still with his feet spread apart rotating the beads on his bracelet while gazing out at the river. Lisa stood transfixed in a state of fear, her mouth still open, looking at me. I couldn't make sense of anything at this point and I'd had enough.

"Let's just go," I suggested.

As I walked toward the boat, I heard a voice whisper, "Ricooooo..." Now, I knew for sure I needed some damn sleep and a definite therapy session.

We boarded the boat in silence with a fearful vibe amongst us, all except for Spragga. He was calm, cool, and somehow, I suspected, connected? To this... hmmm... this? What the hell was this? I didn't know what to call it.

I decided to head down to one of the cabins and get some rest. The view, the glass of red wine, and my feet propped on a pillow was doing wonders for these damn mental health issues I was experiencing. Ledisi was belting out higher than this on the sound system. Her smooth sounds rocked me quickly into this dreamland and I began to feel water sprinkling me. The water felt nice. It was all around me now and I felt as if I was a part of it. Slowly, I glided through this amazing garden filled with big fish, little fish, all types of fish. Oooh shit! A stingray swam right by me too!

I swam with blue fish, golden fish with orange stripes, beautifully vibrant-colored sea creatures as if I were one of them. Floating through the water I felt like I was in heaven. I felt at peace, loved beyond measure and my body never felt this good. That climb? I was on it and I didn't wanna come down. Not yet anyway. It was like sucking the strawberry flavor from the last slice of cheesecake, holding it just a little longer before it was all gone.

Out of nowhere I heard a loud boom. I jumped up and heard a slight knock on my cabin door.

"Come in!" I yelled.

"It's Spragga. Whaa gwan baby gull? Your friend Lisa fell asleep and ya man friend dem working on his computer. You alright?"

"Not really, Spragga. What's going on?"

"You know something strange is happening to me here, Spragga."

"Ahhhh! My queen! Everything is nah whaaa it seem! You must believe in all you've ever dreamed of; you must look into your heart and see what you really desire. But most of all, my love you mustn be afraid. Mi gon' leave you wit ya destiny," he says while stroking my forehead. "You mustn be afraid! Now get some rest; everything you need is right here."

He gently pushed my head back onto the pillow and I laid almost in a trance staring out at the horizon, slowly dozing off. I woke up from a jolt in the boat and noticed an old photo album laying open at the foot of the bed. It was me again, or my twin I suppose. The page had pictures of my Aunt Najee with this lady that looks exactly like me. Out of fear, astonishment, and just sheer disbelief.

I dropped the book and ran to the deck to see Lisa asleep sprawled out on the deck sofa. Chink was at the table in the lounge area, laptop still open, drink half gone, and his food slightly picked over. He was laying with his head down also appearing to be asleep. I ran to the Captain's wheel where Spragga sat. He wasn't there. Someone had tied us on though. Someone had docked the boat.

"Lisa! Chink!" I screamed. They both woke immediately. Both of them were really groggy and trying to wake up from their deep slumber.

"What happened?" Lisa asked.

"I have no clue. Has anyone seen Spragga? Chink, are you alright? I found this book in my cabin," I explained, still rattled.

"What book, Eeesh? What the hell is happening around here? I never thought I would say this, but I wanna go home. My pussy not even idling no more!!!" Lisa complained.

Chink laughed at Lisa while walking toward me. He put his hands on my shoulders and asked, "You good, beautiful? You look a little shook. Can we see this book you found?"

"Yeah, Boss, where da book??" Lisa added.

Terrified, I walked back to my cabin. They followed silently behind me. Chink sat down on the bed gazing back and forth between me and the picture. They turned the pages and there was a picture of a man. He was the only man anywhere in the book. They thumbed through the book all the way to the end where they found a story.

The story in the back of the album was about a water goddess called, Mami Watta. Since the eighteenth century she had led a cult of followers who believed wholeheartedly in her spirit. In some instances, she was known as the guardian of nature, a protector. The story went on to talk about a human son who was killed by non-believers. People were afraid of him and his powers. Though he lived in the flesh, he dwelled in the spirit. They said he was burned alive on top of another man's wife. The legend had it that before he died, he sketched the words, *"WET"* with the blood of the woman under him on a pillow that sat neatly on the bed. Legend had it that the whole house went up in flames, and everything burned except for that pillow. The story talked about how those lacking love and compassion for others dared not touch his waters.

The story went on to speak of mysterious deaths across the African ocean for decades. All of breathtakingly beautiful women. All married, all seemingly unhappy. Then suddenly, the story stopped. No more entries, nothing else written. There were twelve empty pages. It was said that the spirit finally fell in love. The last page read: "A storm is coming..." Beneath the words, my picture was sketched into the paper.

I fainted and fell straight back on the bed. Lisa rushed to my aid, gathering cool rags and water. I heard Chink say, "Ok, I'm getting the helo ready."
A wave of relief washed over me at hearing Chink's words. I was suddenly craving Stateside air.

"Ayesha, Ayesha, can you stand up?" Lisa asked.

"No worries," Chink assured her. "I got her."

Chink picked me up and carried me up to the deck. Placing me on the sofa, Lisa sat beside me and we all looked like we just saw Pac, Biggie, and Whitney. Chink got on his phone and ordered up a helicopter to take us home. He did that shit like he was ordering a damn pizza. As we waited on the helicopter, Chink and Lisa gathered our things.

"Lisa?"

"Yes boss?"

"Get the album?"

"You sure you wanna take that semi Ouija board home?"

"Yes, Lisa, please get it."

"Okay, okay, Ayesha."

I stepped back into the villa and the whole atmosphere was different. It was calmer. I felt safer. I was convinced in my soul it was the water. The pictures, Spragga and his unexplained disappearance, these amazing feelings of lovemaking throughout my entire body, this intense connection to the river, and to my book... I didn't know what to think. What to do?

We all plopped down on the couch, anxiously awaiting our ride.

"I'm sorry this didn't turn out like it was supposed to," Chink offered. "None of this was in the plan."

"No Chink, you're wrong. All of it is in the plan. We are all exactly where we're supposed to be at the right moment," I said.

"I believe that, Eeesh," Lisa said softly. "I'm over the moon about being able to come here. How long before the helo arrives Chink?"

"Oh, it's gonna be about an hour before they can get a flight plan, and twenty-five minutes to touch down."

"Ok, so you both know I've been working extremely hard on this book," I shared.

"Oh yeah, the one nobody can read until it hits the shelf?" Lisa mimicked me.

"She won't let me read it either, Lisa. Don't feel bad," Chink chimed in.

"It's been written for a year! Lisa belted out, then clasped her mouth.

"Lisa!!!"

"Sorry Eeesh!!"

"A year, Stormy! Why?" Chink demanded.

"Just a few mishaps and loose ends I need to tie up. It's no big deal," I replied dryly.

"Ummm, she ain't got the money," Lisa exposed, breaking Girl Code.

"Lisaaaaaa! Ok, now you are talking too damn much, 'bout to be fired," I threatened.

"For telling the truth, Boss? You *don't* have the money. Well, not all of it anyway."

"Money?" Chink said. "You gotta be kidding me! Why didn't you tell me?"

"Tell you WHAT? It's not your problem or your business, for that matter, what goes on with my book. This is my project! I don't need no damn body talking about they helped me do shit! I got this."

"Really? Really, Eeesh? This man just made one of your wildest dreams come to life. He didn't even try to fuck you," Lisa pointed out. She leaned over closer to Chink and whispered so loud I could still hear her. "Ummmm... did you?"

"No, no, I didn't come here for that. I could've gotten my dick wet where I was at," Chink assured us.

"Well, why the fuck didn't you then playboy?" I exploded. I couldn't even explain the rage of jealousy that ripped through me.

"Because you asked me to come to you. So, I did what my heart said."

That silenced the room. I felt a little bad for accusing him of being anything but genuine. I knew he was genuine in my spirit. Somehow, I just knew.

"I apologize for being a bitch," I said.

"As you should," Lisa mumbled.

"I'm sorry! All this stuff has my mind going 'round and 'round in circles," I said, sincerely. "Well, since we have some time before our ride gets here, I want to read something to you. It should explain why I've literally been going out of my mind."

"Oooh yeah! Something from the book!" Lisa yelled.

"Yes, it's a chapter called, *WET*."

"Wait! What?" Lisa said.

"*Wet*... isn't that what that Mami Watta sketched into a pillow?" Chink asked suspiciously.

"Yes."

I began to read, starting off telling them about the Sangre Grande, the city in Trinidad and the exact spot we'd just left.

WET

Wet

WET

Sangre Grande, a beautiful city in Trinidad and Tobago, is home to one of the most amazing waterfalls I'd ever known. It was named The Rico Seco, and it was on the northeastern coast of the island. The water fell white but turned a vivid green when it settled into the river. Huge, smooth, round rocks in various shades of earth's color piled on top of each other, nestled in their own corner surrounded by huge leaves and moss, colored in envy. You dared to wish you were that beautiful, that still. You'd never ever become anywhere near as perfect. It was as magical as it was breathtakingly calm and peaceful. I'm Najj, and I would know... I was born there.

Somehow, I had always been drawn to it. I'd come here as a child and sit for hours. We moved to the U.S. when I was in my teens. I vowed to visit often, and I did. After my love passed on, I remained here. Staring at the water falling and changing colors as it crests within the river. This day would change my life.

It was a cool day. Still, the sun's rays warmed the river. Kneeling down closer to the sea, I trickled the water between my fingers while I watched my reflection in the water. I saw me but it was a different me. This image was wearing nothing but a pair of lavender lace panties. I moved my hand back and forth in the water in an attempt to whisk away the image. It didn't move. I stood to my feet and stepped in. Suddenly, the wind began to circle my body. With one forceful wind, my panties mysteriously blew off into the water and I couldn't move. The water seemed to be rising. It started out about ankle deep, then it went up to my knees. I was terrified but my body was in another place. I felt hands caressing my whole being. From my head to my toes, a gentle kiss covered me. Infused with passion, I began running my hands through my hair. Swaying my hips from side to side. Kissing and squeezing on my titties. I stuck one finger in my mouth and slid my tongue round and round and round. Slow and sexy, as if I was sucking on his dick, moving my head in an outward motion, lips to throat gently so I didn't bite. Mmmm...I was in awe of this thing, this feeling that came over me. This shit felt wonderful! I knew it was a dream or a vision, and I begged not to be awakened.

I felt like someone was watching me. I didn't care. It gave me a reason to be sexy as hell. I liked it. I welcomed the moist humidity coming from my pussy. Even submerged in water, she stayed sticky and extra hydrated. The river was turning me on. My mind racing like an out of control locomotive. *What the hell was this?* It wasn't of this world; I was sure of that. There was no one here! What was happening?

I felt hot and jittery all over, as if I'd just stepped inside a sauna. Uncontrollably, my hand was moving. Something was making me touch myself. I tried to move my hand in another direction, but this thing whispered in my ear seductively.
"Najjjjaaah..."
How did it know my name?
"Where are you? Let me see you!" I cried frantically.
"Najjjjjj! Take three fingers and slide em' inside you," he commanded.
Oooh myyyyyy... something was moving my hand. I no longer had control of my limbs. I wanted to stop out of fear of the unknown, yet I wanted this nut like chocolate needed chip. Can you imagine the most amazing feeling to

ever come over you? You can't explain it but can't live without it? That's what I felt. Lord help me, I was tripping out! My hand was reaching hidden spots inside me I didn't know existed.

I moaned and whispered, "Please, please, please! Fuck me! My pussy so wet. Who are you? Where are you? Who... what are you?" I mumbled. "Touch me there," I pleaded.

I snapped out of it for a second and looked around embarrassed, wondering if I'd really just said that out loud to a river.

Suddenly this force, this entity, moved my fingers onto my clit and tapped on it swiftly. The water assisting my fingers and its motions in the glide from my asshole to my flower bud back and forth, just like the waves surrounding me. I felt my nipples harden and my mouth watered in dire need of something to suck on. I was desperate for some lips to wrap around mine. The spongy sweetness from the head of his dick resting on each cheek is what I pictured while licking my lips. I needed that. Oooooh my my my!

The river's bottom flipped me to my knees in the most peaceful way, then up again. Then ahhh!!! Whoever— whatever— it was, slammed me down. Without notice it aggressively slammed me on my knees into a doggy style position. Hands planted firmly on the water's surface. My knees planted on what felt like a fluffy cloud. My ass swayed to the water's rhythm. Wait, if it was water, why wasn't I sinking?

Was I fucking dreaming? A wet dream maybe? If so, I didn't want to wake up. I wanted the end game to be my pussy on swoll and clit laid to rest.

WET

While straddling the river it felt like there was something sliding underneath me. At first, I thought it was a fish or some type of marine life. Whatever was under me was causing me to ride this amazing wave in great anticipation of its crest. I began bouncing my ass on the water, slapping and grinding on it. it created pulses of ecstasy throughout my entire pussy. No intimacy was present, this was just a straight up get mine and go. Ummm umm hmmm!

I began to call out for him... it... this thing. "Rico Secooo..." I whispered softly. "Ricooooo."

At this point, I was riding the D like it was real, wondering if I was still alive. Wondering if this is what sex felt like in heaven.

I bounced on the D. Pap... pap... pap... pap pap pap... pap pap... mmm...

I slid out with water splashing on my titties, feeling like lips nibbling on my nipples. I grinded harder on this masculine image beneath me and laid my head on the river bed as if it were a shoulder. My hands gripped the waves as if they were fingers while my body stroked the river over and over, up and down. In and out, round and round and round, slowly speeding the beat of my flow. The waves crashed and I lost it.

Ahhhh...yeah!

"Ricoooooo... mmm hmm..." I screeched as I filled the river with liquids of my own. *What the fuck just happened???*

Suddenly, I belly flopped into the water. Completely submerged and lightly treading water, I felt its presence. I saw a silhouette, a cloud like motion in the water. Without warning, I popped to the surface like a clown in a Jack in the Box. I looked around nervously and anxiously, praying no one saw what just happened. The Falls were empty, thank

WET

God. It was quite eerie, silent, but still spoke volumes. Me? I was loving that shit! My pussy never felt better. Somewhat fearful, I'd convinced myself that I'd simply just masturbated in the water. After all, I really was the only one at the Falls. Yet, knowing in my heart someone or something just fucked me like never before.

***

A few weeks after I was molested by the water, I was sitting on my patio enjoying a pretty, comfortably cool evening, sipping on some brandy. I heard a voice whisper on the wind.

"It's Rico," the voice said. "Seco... Seco... Seco..." the voice echoed repeatedly. The whisper grew closer and closer, and I realized it was *my* voice! It was my voice, my spirit, my body calling... longing for... the waterfall?

The Rico Fall was lusting after me and I was lusting after it.

I hopped on my horse named Beauty and rode towards the river. Beauty galloped through the forest in a subconscious hurry. Me on top with just the black silk sheet from my bed flailing in the wind. My whole body was exposed by the wind and swift galloping movements of Beauty's glide. The wind caressed my body and enticed me beyond reason. I wrapped both of my hands around the back of my neck, my titties bouncing in the wind, and my pussy hitting the saddle, stimulating myself secretly. I couldn't get there fast enough! I pulled Beauty's mane as her tail softly brushed my ass cheeks as it swayed.

Beauty was in full speed and we reached the Rico in record time. Before I could jump off, she flung me right into

80

Starzpen

the water. I swam for a few seconds, not knowing where I was headed or what I was looking for. Then I saw the most beautiful cave. It had a mind-blowing coral reef. Yellow, green, and blue sea life covered the cave's entry. Amazing seashells and gorgeous rock formations. Still under water, my master appeared out of nowhere, spontaneity at its finest, along with some roughneck shit. He pushed my body between the rock and the water, making a surface to rest my body—his body—on. Still, I didn't see anyone else. *Was I making love to an alien? Was it really all in my imagination?*

I was confused as fuck! Nevertheless, I felt safe. I knew I would leave here completely satisfied, yet still wanting more. I was okay with that.

Somehow, I was still submerged under water, as if I were asleep, floating on a love cloud. My feet left the river's bottom and my body was slammed onto this hammer-like object wiggling its way inside me. I felt a huge, long hardness with pulsating veins. It was stiff as a board. It entered slightly, just about halfway up inside me, making swishing noises from the moisture. He was teasing me.

"Go deeper!" I cried, as I tried to squirm my body into a better position to throw it back and finesse this nut like I knew how to do. This thing, now getting closer to invading my belly button, thrusted softly inside me. My hands waddled in the water with my face pushed up against the smooth mossy rock between it and this thing, this lover. This invisible king of mine, Dear God!! I wanted to cum so bad!

"Mmmm..." I moaned and begged for it to make me cum. I begged and pleaded, "Ricooooo! Eat my pussy."

"Eat who's pussy?" A voice replied.

"Yours!" I answered frantically. I was afraid that he wouldn't blow the bones from my back if I didn't reply.

"I'll play in this pussy how I wanna play in it," the voice said "Shhh..." My mouth suddenly shut tight. I couldn't part my lips. "Shut up and say no more. I know what this pussy need."

"Mmm..." I groaned. "Yess Daddy! This hot box belongs to you, my king!!" I screamed. "Please, please take away this ache. Touch me there with your lips."

He reached downward to caress my thighs, then reached up and massaged every ache, throbbing, and dripping part of me.

Suddenly, he wrenched my hands up over my head. Mysteriously, a string of seaweed wrapped itself tightly around both wrists and locked them together. I felt this weight on me, a gentle giant kind of weight. Huge, fierce and totally in control, yet submissive, protective, and amazingly satisfying.

My pussy hole was throbbing, beating like drums, awaiting Rico's full reign. My body began to float, still submerged beneath the water. I laid face down on the water and the wind swayed the water side to side, spreading my legs wide open. Legs open, Rico slid in completely and stroked me like a musician playing a fast, sexy beat on a guitar. I felt like I was swimming without moving. The water was so serene, sending electrifying shockwaves through my portals.

Oh shit! Without warning, my pussy spit!

"Mmm... mmm... yeah... yeah yeah... Damn! Ooooh!! Uhhhhh..."

I came hard. Twice. OMG! I never wet two times back-to-back in my life.

WET

Still in mid-orgasm, I heard this giant commanding voice say, "This is my pussy always... say Rico Secoooo... my king."

He fucked me harder and slower, then softer but faster, then still, slow grinding movements, squeezing out all my love. I didn't need anything else. I was on another planet when it came to the Falls. They say sustenance and sex is man's greatest needs and I couldn't disagree at this point. I didn't wanna come up for air. Drown me in this shit for eternity. I would become a permanent fixture at Rico Falls from now on. Honestly, though, I was curious to see if anyone could match up. I needed to be sure that feeling was more than the mirage I'd convinced myself it was.

I wanted to fuck a man—a real one. I needed flesh to flesh, skin to skin, lip to lip.

After the incident at the Falls, I invited an old friend to meet me at the Falls for a late dinner. I knew there would be no tourist there that late.

As Beauty and I arrived I saw Kenny sitting on a rock pouring wine in our glasses. He looked amazing! His dark, chocolate skin draped in cream-colored linen shorts with no shirt. He wore a gold Cuban link that graced his abs and his grey eyes pierced through the forest brush like a beautiful black panther's eyes under the moonlight.

I slid off Beauty while Ken stood to greet me. I wrapped my arms around his neck and squeezed tight. He wrapped his arms around my waist then swooped me up off my feet and twirled me around. We said nothing; no conversation was needed. I didn't feel like the small talk and phony shit. I hoped he knew I just wanted him to fuck the shit out of me and then he was free to go the hell home. I extended both hands and lured him toward the water.

I untied the drawstring on his shorts and slid them off. I kneeled and removed each foot one by one. From my knees, I massaged his calves, thighs, and then his balls. As I massaged his balls, I tantalized the head of his dick with the tip of my forefinger. Kenny squirmed in my hands, but my mind raced and told me that I needed to get wet.

I rose to my feet and slowly slipped my T-shirt over my head, leaving me completely naked. My honey brown skin glistened from the lavender coconut oil I moistened myself with. The nipples on my firm D cups were at attention and my size 8 ass looked plump and inviting. I took his hand, kissing and sucking on each finger as I walked backward enticing Ken into the river. With his fine ass, it was just something about that bottom lip though. I could picture it resting on my mine, both sets of lips.

We began to slow wind wit' Kellz's music ringing in my ears. *I just wanna slow dance witchu... Heeey Mr. DJ...* Grinding to the music, getting sucked into the warmth of each other, we lost ourselves in bliss.

Ken snatched my head back by the ponytail I had hanging to match Beauty's mane and gracefully sucked on my neck just below my earlobe. *Oooooh he hit a spot!* Then he kissed me right behind my ear. *Yesssss, I'm weakening.*

Ken took both hands and secured them under my ass cheeks. He lifted me onto his waist, and I felt his dick was hard as hell. Like a slinky, it wiggled its way toward my entry way.

Oo

oooh almost...

I pushed my body downward and tried to assist in the penetration when suddenly I noticed a chilly draft. It was freezing all of a sudden. I looked at Ken and his face twisted up as if he'd just seen a ghost. Ken stared blankly out into the river as it turned colder by the second. It turned so cold I heard it crackling as it turned to ice. We tried to move, run – something! But we couldn't move. We were stuck! Ken's feet were stuck. He was freezing. He was literally turning into a block of ice. As I screamed in horror, I heard a loud noise. I turned to see an enormous wave seconds before it crashed on me and swooped me up high onto the apex of the wave and sat me there. I was so high I could reach the clouds. It was as if I were on top of Mount Everest and the view was out of this world.

In the blink of an eye, Ken shattered like glass breaking.

I screamed, "Ken!!!! Kenny??" Screaming and crying, I was helpless. Ken was gone.

What could I do now? I should have never brought him here. I felt terrible. Sitting on this wave completely naked, feeling like a freak, a goddess, and a mentally challenged individual all in one.

Then, oh hell! Something shut my mouth. It literally locked my mouth shut. Huge, gently rugged hands, that familiar sea-like scent with a hint of jasmine, like the smell of the river, that demanding entity. My king, that thing that had me feeling nasty as hell. I was glad he was here.

"My pussy... always!" He demanded. "My pussy only!" He yelled.

WET

What? Are you kidding me? He was fucking jealous. The river? Smothered in envy?

Magically, a vivid shade of green coated my body frame. He didn't want any other man inside me. He wanted to be the only one to make me spew honey-scented passion throughout his world... our river. In his jealous rage, he ended Ken. Ken, now turned to ice particles, sprinkled and glistened on the river's surface. I couldn't believe my eyes. He killed him. He was angry that Ken was about to slide up in my honeycomb hideout. Me, still rooted on top of this tsunami-like wave Rico had created.

I felt firm hands on my thighs prying then apart. Yeah right, as if they needed prying. In truth, my legs gracefully slid open wide. He placed one lick, then two licks. Oh shit! He gripped my clit between his lips and pulled on it. Then he licked some more, poking my juice box with his finger. I was about to bust, but the climb was so amazing I didn't want to come down.

"Don't stop, Rico!" I cried.

"My pussy!!" He demanded, licking and sucking and sliding his tongue across my asshole.

"I'm gonna cum my love, but I'm not ready. Lick some more right there. Mmm hmm... a little to the left, please?" I begged.

The licks slowed up a bit as he obeyed my every command and I obeyed his. I palmed what imagined to be his head and pushed up and down, directing its lips across my clit.

"Ahhh yesss, my king! How do I taste? Suck the tip of my clit and massage my ass," I instructed. He did just that.

WET

Swooosh!

Uncontrollably, I spilled a beautiful pure white stream of passion into the river. It poured out of me like a waterfall.

"Uuuuhh uhhhhh, hun, say my name," the voice yelled angrily.

"Ricoooooo baby, fuck me now! I... I... I need you in my space. Invade this pussy like it was war and we were in the trenches."

Fighting through the waves, he rammed his snake-like dick inside me once again. This time, he wiggled it wonderfully making just the right moves. In and out, in and out...

I felt sucking on my flower bud, but the "D" was still inside me. Yes, my king was fucking me and sucking on me simultaneously like I was a mango. He choked me lightly like it had several hands and several sets of lips. My whole body was being loved up on all at the same time. I was in that other place again. That other world. Fuck it!! I was gonna savor the moment.

I pleaded with Rico to slow down. He did and it was sensual and romantic. He touched me differently. He was making love to me this time. Kissing my forehead and wrapping inside his safeness. Whispering eternity in my ears. Mumbling that my sweet pussy belonged to him.

"You like that, my love?" He asked.

"I love it, my king!"

"Don't bring another here to me. I'll keep you wet," he promised.

"Yes daddy," I vowed, as he continued to stroke me slowly. He was definitely still inside of me. Each time I

Starzpen

reached my climax it was different, each one more intense than the last. I had to have it. I was hooked like it was a bad drug.

Magically, the next morning I woke up sprawled out across the rocks I was found on where my mother drowned herself after I was born. I was beginning to think this was my destiny. This jackpot I hit was my birthright.

Rico... mmmm... This... he... it... was my home.

I slid off my little pencil skirt and undressed for a bath. As I turned on the water and tested the temperature with my hand, I heard this faint whisper. It came to me almost in a song-like melody. I couldn't make out the words. As I removed my hand from the water, the sound faded.

Ok, so I'm losing it again. Maybe I should get some counseling. Maybe I should call my girl Cyn in the morning. She can shed some light on what was going on in my pussy area.

I peeled my size 8 caramel booty cheeks and my pretty puffy melon-shaped girls out of the rest of my clothing and reached for my Armani body wash. It smelled of lilies and chamomile. I switched off the lights and lit some candles. Then, I stepped into the water and slid myself down into the tub. The steam rose with Lauryn Hill's voice through the speakers. It was the sweetest thing I've knoooownnn played softly in the backdrop. I laid my head back on the bath pillow and quickly fell into a trance. The humidity coming off my body created a slight sticky dew that covered me as I stared into an abyss. Mysteriously, the rope-designed tie backs from the curtains loosened in the blink of an eye and bound my hands together in front of me. Terrified, I tried to jump out of the tub, only to be pinned down. Water splashed everywhere as I struggled to break the holds. The candles doused from the swift wind of my hands while the remainder of the tie backs secured my feet. Sitting upright, hands and feet tied, I tried to speak or scream. My mouth moved but no sound escaped.

Suddenly, a wave of pleasure washed over me as a feeling of ecstasy gripped me. Someone was sucking on my nipples like it was a sour apple jolly rancher. Then I felt another set of lips on my other titty.

"Wayment!" How in the hell were there lips on both titties simultaneously? That shit was freaking me out the most, believe it or not. Did I fall asleep in the tub? I wasn't at the waterfall anymore so how was this happening.

Suddenly, I heard that familiar whisper, "Ricooooooo Secoo. My pussy always. Oooh, you're so wet!"

My king! My king was here.

The water from the tub turned on full blast. My body slid toward the streaming water. Rico bent my knees and positioned my honeycomb directly under the stream. It was forcefully perfect, gently taking my breath away.

"Uuuunnn...whooo! Right there baby. Yes, yes, yes!"

I clamped each hand around what I imagined to be his ears and pulled him closer. I began fucking what I saw to be his head, not the water stream. What the hell?

The water trickled at the perfect speed, the perfect rhythm. His hold wrapped tightly around my waist in a bear hug but sexier. I was exploding inside.

"Oh, hell yeah! Fuck this pussy!" I moaned. "Baby, go harder!" I screamed.

Now my voice was no longer muffled. He must have wanted to hear my nasty noises because he drove me insane with his moves. I screamed in disbelief of the level this shit

WET

kept taking me to. Higher and higher, he went deeper and deeper.

The water turned off and the room went silent. I was still coming down and Rico whispered again.

"Mine. My pussy always. Wherever you are. Say my name, my love," he demanded, while stroking one side of my face with one hand and slowly scanning and calming my clit with a finger from the other hand. It was like sticking a pin in a balloon and releasing its trapped air. That enormous kiss covered my entire body. Then this deep, sexy voice echoed inside my ears and instructed me,

"When you need me, just turn on the water and say 'Ricooooo... daddy... slide up inside me... NOW. I'll be there before your pussy gets wet."

I woke up the next morning on the floor of the bathroom wrapped in a towel and the bath pillow considerately positioned under my head. I jumped up quickly to compose myself. Sitting on the edge of my bed I thought, *"Let me call Cyn!!!"*

WET

Beauty's Beast

WET

Romello was about ten years old when the Colombian Cartel murdered my mother and both her parents. Her name was Bonita. It meant beautiful in Spanish! Guess you can figure out why they named me Beauty.

I was 8 when my mother was killed. My memory of her was vague but I had them nevertheless. We had a few pictures and some jewelry and a few other keepsakes she left in a box for me just in case anything ever happened to her. Daddy had one too. What I remembered most of all was her touch gentle, but her voice was stern and rugged. My mother was killed by some wannabe cartel members trying to take over. A hit on her father— my grandfather—prompted the war. They fought hard and even shut shit down for a brief moment, but a few years later they were killed in my grandparents' home. The guards were ambushed and hit with silenced bullets. The maids found Nona and Papi in bed with three shots each. One in each of their heads and two center-mass. Classic execution style. They never saw it coming. Mommy went over to fix them breakfast that morning. She did that from time to time. She was found with a bullet in the back of her head slumped over in the pancake mix she was preparing.

A year or two after that hit Daddy decided to get us out of Colombia. We were going to be leaving behind everything we knew. Our school, friends, family... everything we'd ever known. He knew we would be next if we stayed. We were the last of the bloodline and they wouldn't stop until we were all dead.

One night, Daddy said we were going out for dinner. However instead of arriving at a restaurant, we arrived at an airstrip. Daddy and Romey went inside while I waited in the car.

Soon, Rome came out to retrieve me. "Let's go, B," Rome said, gathering my things.

"Go where?" I asked.

"Daddy bought a plane and hired his own pilots to bring us to the United States."

"Huh?" I was thoroughly confused.

"Just come on, B," Rome repeated, yanking me by my arm.

"What about my stuff? School? I mean, we just leaving?" I cried. I knew they were talking about leaving but I thought they were just meaning an hour or two away. The United States though?

"Look Beauty, Mommy, Papa and Nona... the whole damn family... they all gone, Beauty! We gotta do what we gotta do!" Rome stated firmly. "Now get ya ass on the plane!"

Daddy did the best he could to give us the life we were accustomed to. He worked hard to provide a life for us, and protected us at all cost, including getting us to safety in the States. Unfortunately, Daddy died a few years after we arrived in the States due to complications from pancreatic cancer. We never even knew he had it because he never said a word about it.

After his death, we remained in the U.S., no doubt. Daddy's sister, our aunt C.C, and her daughter, Deena lived there. They didn't have much money – if any at all sometimes. Even though we were young, Romello and I never remembered having to share food or clothing. We never remembered wanting for anything. We came from money and power. We were riddled in pride, unaware of the part about falling. We never wanted to burden anyone; it didn't matter if it was family or not. We just weren't built that way. At an early age we learned that surviving and sustaining was mandatory. Living with my Aunt C.C. was like going from the womb to the wild. We took hit after hit. Disappointment after disappointment. Bad luck or some shit, I used to say. Nothing seemed to go right.

Aunt Cecilia died from cancer shortly after Daddy died. It was really just me, Rome, and Deena now. Everyone else was dead, sucked into the pipe, or in love with the needle. Permanently buried in misery, destruction, and the end game... death.

Our very existence was rooted from the gutter. We lived to just live. We were bred from drug dealers, gangsters and killers then forced into the wild alone. We were starving! Not for food though. For the power and respect we'd known as little ones. The lifestyle we believed to be ours. Bottom line, we knew there was nowhere to go but up.

Our purpose, according to us, was to TAKE what they said we couldn't have. Love where there was hate and to fight till our last breath for each other. That's exactly what Romey did and taught me to do before he too took his last breath.

Romello, Blue and Speedo were on the way back from D.C on a drop run. I knew they smashed the hell out some seafood. We always hit up the pier before we came home. The officers on the scene said they found 20 lbs. of lobster and crab in the car, no doubt. They were bringing them home for me. Speedy said they were coming through the tunnel when traffic seemed to stop. Three dudes jumped out of a car behind them and sprayed bullets until their clips were empty.

Speedy said Rome tried to pull off but they were trapped because traffic wasn't moving. Then Speedo pulled out his piece and fired to shatter the back window to get a better shot. They bust back, hitting Blue in the back of the head. Romey hopped out of the driver's seat in an attempt to end the war and try to stay alive. He sprayed repeatedly, hitting one of the dudes, but still he went down too. Speedo darted from the passenger seat and let off repeatedly...

Pap... pap pap... pap, pap

WET

Then he saw Romello go down. He let off two more shots and clipped him but it was too little too late. Blue died instantly with one shot to the head. My brother was hit 6 times in the chest and head. He bled out waiting for EMS to get through the tunnel.

My brother was compared to Nikki Barnes and Frank Lucas at times. We (yes, WE) claimed the streets we grew up on before we grew up. When I turned eighteen, I received a settlement I had no idea existed. It was a substantial amount of money and more to be disbursed on my 21st birthday.

I was already in a great financial position. Hell, we had most of Brooklyn on lock. This money would seal the deal on the other four boroughs. Maybe me and Deena could take a little break and hit the islands for a few weeks. Seems like we hadn't had any fun in forever. It was always a funeral or some business more important. We figured we'd sleep when we die. Stack and move wisely while we were alive. I decided when we touched down in New York City, as a little one, that I wasn't gonna get lost in all this concrete. I would stand my ground at all costs and take my place at the top of whatever mountain I climbed first. By that time, we had learned to take whatever place available.

We didn't have Christmas so we bagged up tress. There were no birthdays, so we packed cakes with coke and moved 'em through the bakery on Utica which I now owned. We couldn't boil Easter eggs and color them with no electricity, so we threw them shits off the roof and popped niggas upside their heads. Those same streets that beat us down daily. These streets that kept us wondering why Daddy brought us here, we would eventually run. *I* would eventually run!! I wasn't taking no shorts. I was built that way. It seemed even when I tried to be the "bigger person," I'd feel fake, untrue to myself, and something in my blood just wouldn't allow me to live.

95

WET

Something in my spirit would fuck you up!! One, because I knew my brother would kick my ass if I didn't, and second, I just wasn't gonna not fuck you up!! My brother and the few we called family were all that way. Deena would put a hole in ya head if you rubbed her wrong.

Romey was that shoot-first-and-never-ask-questions guy. Speed was loyal to the bone for his, pop off at the smell of beef. Then, there was me. I lived what I learned. Shoot first, fuck the questions. My daddy would say she's as cute as a button, yet deadlier than a boa. She's a beauty though, he would add.

They trained me like a Pitbull preparing for a fight. They fed me hot sauce daily like I was a dog to piss him off! They installed survival into my soul. It was my God-given right to live, to lose, and to love. My family taught me to protect, preserve and defend that right by all means necessary.
    In Romellos' words, "DIE TRYING "B," DON'T LIVE FAILING."

Romello and Blue would slap box the shit out of me. For a while I would cry and ball up in corners or hide in closets. At first, I thought they were just being boys. Just bullying me and being mean. It wasn't long before I started hitting back and I learned to hit hard. Quickly, everyone especially me, would learn exactly what seed they were really planting. What lessons they were really teaching. Rome knew I really wasn't a fighter and pretty much stayed to myself, but in Brooklyn that sometimes was worse than running with a crew. The loner was the target.

One day, on my way from school. It was "the high" aka boys' and girls' high school in Bed-Sty where you literally did or died. I was just about to jump on the train when some gutter rat and one of her frumpy disciples walked up all slick and dusty looking. Almost as if they were sure to take the "W." One asked where I got my earrings from. The other said, "they cute too."

Oh lord! Not now! I didn't feel like fighting, but I automatically slid into my beat-this-bitch-ass costume. I don't know this bitch, so I'm gonna treat her like this was some stranger-danger type shit. It was self-defense in all realty. Nevertheless, I got scared.
Now let me explain my scared and how it differed from the world's definition of scared.

You see fear shows up when we don't know what to expect, what's coming next. For me, fear was fuel. It's your get up and go! Fear is the highest gear that automatically moved me into survival overdrive. Romello kept me fly once I started high school to help avoid people picking at me. He said it would be one less reason for him to have to kill a nigga for fucking with me about looking busted so he bought me all the dopest gear. Kept me in all the latest shoes and all that. Anyway... I don't think he thought about the haters that wanted to try and take my shit. It didn't matter in my book. I was Jane!! Fuck Tarzan, this was my jungle.

I recognized this loudmouth from Breevort projects, but I didn't know her.
Loudmouth turned to her friend and asked, "You like those door knockers in her ears boo?"
"I love 'em the girl!" Her friend replied with a roll of her neck.
I said nothing as I turned to walk away. Then, *Baaam!* This bitch just snuffed me.

My nose immediately began stinging and throbbing. I thought I felt drips of something sticky and wet. I wiped it away and saw that it was blood. In a flash, I transformed into Go Mode. Rage bubbled up inside me that I didn't even know existed. I felt mad disrespected and mad fucking violated. My brother taught me, nice girl or not, don't take no shit off nobody ever!!

She reached her hands toward my ears I assumed she thought she'd be taking something from me. Before I could blink, I pumped two slugs in her with the .22 I kept in my waistband. Preem gave it to me when I turned 10. I popped one bullet in each knee. Amused, I watched them buckle. I watched her head spin around and giggled while her whole body hit the floor. It felt like the blood I saw ooozing from her legs was the same blood pumping in my heart.

That pump... it excited me. As I looked down at her squirming on the ground, screaming for her friends to get me away from her, I slowly took off my earrings one at a time and dropped them in the blood spilling from her body, sarcastically asking if the gold door knockers she so admired were worth her legs.

Her friend backed up with her hands out in front of her, practically begging me not to shoot her stupid ass too.
She screamed frantically, "Debbie, Debbie! Oh shit, Debbie! God, she shot her. She *shot* her!"

As I admired my work, I saw the rest of her crew rushing down the block. I hopped in a cab before they reached me. Not out of fear of beef, but fear I'd shoot another one of these hoes. Romes dying just intensified my rage. Increased my desire to avoid vulnerability. I would seize the moment and take my brother's legacy to a whole other level. I would be all they taught me to be times a thousand. I would become Beauty's Beast. I would truly live up to my name.

WET

After Romellos crew was dismantled, so to speak, things got extra tense in Brooklyn. From Giwanas projects to the Polo Grounds, territory was up for grabs. Everyone wanted to claim something. I wasn't having it!

I called Speedy and we hit the round table. We came up with a strategy to leave the mark of the beast from Brooklyn to Staten Island, the city that groomed us to move about this life in beast mode on purpose. The streets that taught us to wreak havoc on any obstacle threatening our stability. The bloodline that bred us to die trying.

We decided to start with the young boys. They were raw, hungry, and ruthless as hell. We formed alliances from East New York to Far Rockaway, from the Bx to Staten Island, throwing money around rounding up soldiers. Grooming them for what would be Beauty's reign on Brooklyn. The Haitians in the 90's were my biggest threat. They thought they ran shit that side of town. Ok, they did run shit. As far as I was concerned that was over. All bullshit carried a shelf life, and it was time to expire they asses. I had to eliminate that problem completely. Permanently! It wasn't no going up and hittin' a few. I had to wipe out his entire crew.

Later on that night when I knew the Haitian crew would hit the block, I snatched up Speedy for the assist. He was wit' it, dressed in all black sweats and black Timberlands. He pulled his skullie down over one eye like Romello used to do. It was a welcomed memory. Needless to say, the queen was beyond fly for her debut. I was screaming bad bitch in silence, wreaking confidence from the inside. I hopped into my little red leather shorts with a low-cut button-down blouse. Slid into a pair of red thigh-high leather boots. I figured I'd top it off with my diamond studs and Gucci watch. I packed up my Louie duffle with some sweats, my makeup bag, of

99

course, a burner phone for emergencies. I pulled my hair up in a ponytail, assembled my armor and vested up.

Chaos was concealed at my ankle. She was this sexy little nine milli my brother gave me when he thought I outgrew the .22. My boo was baby blue with platinum trim. It was inscribed with the word, "BEAUTY" in big pretty cursive writing. I never left home without her.

"Change of plans," I said to Speedy as we prepared to make our exit. Instead of pushing the truck I wanted to pull up on the Ninja on two wheels. We decided to leave early so we could stop at the underground and pop a bottle or two before I went to make my point.

I pulled up on set on one wheel, poppin' a wheelie and looking like the Colombian goddess I was. My peeps came out and sat with me and Speed's bikes. Ballers were scattering to get the perfect view of my lil' size 8 ass and face like a princess. My smile, like the sunrise after a terrible hangover, was piercing, blinding those that were lucky enough to make eye contact. They made a path as I made my way to the bar.

Shooting over the music was shit like:

"What's up, gorgeous?"
"Yo, who dat?"
"Lemme buy you a drink ma!"
"Damn she fine!"

Deena was the bartender. She was a baddie too. Deena had always been my roadie. She knew me like I knew me. She always had my three shots of tequila ready and waiting. I'd pop back each one, ten minutes apart.

Speedy was at the pool table looking like he was feeling nice, slapping himself in the head for that shot he just missed. I rushed over, strutting through the crowd, making my way to the table where Speedo was at.

I grabbed the stick, slightly bent my body, then propped myself up on the table for the perfect shot. I slid the stick between my fingers in and out, then in again out again. I swiftly rammed the stick into the shiny 8-ball effortlessly. Gracefully, the ball rolled right into the side pocket.

I remained in my position, arched across the table for a second or two. Then I looked back at speed and smiled. He smiled back, pumping his heart with his fist.

I rocked to the beat a for a few minutes, hollered at some of my peeps, and just chilled. After about an hour, I threw my hands up and the DJ shouted out Preem and Blue.

"Rest in peace to my fam Preemoooooo the Don!" The DJ roared into the mic. I grew saddened in my heart as the crowd went nuts. The DJ roared into the mic again, "Shout out to my man, Blue! We miss you, my nigga!!! Speedo is in the building wit' us by God's grace!" He yelled, then he must have spotted me too. "Holla Bonitaaaaaa!!!!" he shouted, and the crowd went berserk. I did a little dance, raised my drink in the air, and saluted the love they were all showing. Then I signaled Speed with one finger to the door.

As headed for the door, ready to take my rightful place on the block, guess who walked in? That clown Xavier. He ran the Haitians' crew. It was just a few of them but I figured I'd go ahead and make some noise right here and now.

I sent out a text to my bodies posted up in and around the club. Then, I stood by the door sucking on a sour apple blow pop bobbin' with Pac's, *I Ain't Mad at Cha*. My phone buzzed with a text that read all stars. Translation: it's a go.

I walked over to where my target stood and stepped up in his face. "Sweetie, you are going to pay me 90% of your corner boys' daily bag," I demanded. "The alternative being... umm... I let you live, and I'll allow you to relocate across the bridge somewhere."

Xavier threw his head back in laughter. His boys moved closer, laughing also. He looked at me, amused and confused. I stared right back at him, saying nothing, still sucking on my blow pop.

From somewhere in the crowd some dude yelled out, "Yo, is that mello little sister? Beauty? Maaaan, go sit yo little stupid ass down!" They all laughed.

I remained silent, walked right up to the loudest one (hence the weakest one). I attached chaos to his temple, curled my finger around the trigger and pulled it. His thoughts splattered all over my outfit, not to mention my damn boots.

Nobody moved for about four seconds, then people began moving toward the door slowly. Nobody panicked or took off running. They knew I hit who I wanted to hit. They knew who I was, and they knew I wasn't alone.

No one dared to buck back though. I told Speedy to make the call for my squad to expedite and execute the hit on the Haitians' block. Take them all out was my order. Speedy tapped my arm and ushered me out the door. Before I stepped, I squeezed off and emptied my clip, all head shots for the rest of his crew.

Speed yanked me out the door, yelling, "Yo B, you wildin'! Let's gooooo!!!"

"Ok, ok," I replied, while swiftly heading for the door. I grabbed some paper towels off the bar and tried to wipe the blood off my shit! "Ugggh!"

"Beauty, fuck them boots!" Speedy yelled, annoyed at my carefree attitude regarding the numerous bodies I left bleeding on the floor of the club. I hopped in the jeep Pop was driving with Deena. Meanwhile, Speedy got on his bike and Pop drove my bike.

I rode to queens and hid out at AJ's house for a few days, knowing no one would talk but just laying low.

An hour after I arrived at the chill spot, I received the text from Ghost. It read: *100*. That was the code for a successful execution. All alive, nobody locked up. It meant they were safe! Next, I had to get Crown Heights on lock. I had a different plan for them though.

June ran that crew and he been tryna scratch n sniff for a minute. I was gonna work this a little different though. I hung around niggas all day long. I knew how to stimulate and manipulate their minds. I never messed around with June because Romello was knocking his baby mama while June was locked up. They knew each other and were civil but didn't really rock with each other. Romello respected June coming home and stepped off, but there was just a wee bit of static there. He never held it against me though. On the contrary, he always let me know he wanted to spoil me, keep me, fuck me... all that. I knew it was really just the fuck me part, so I never took him seriously. Now it was different though. *Hmph, gimmie a week and I'll have him his crew and his spot bowing down royally*, I estimated.

I called Speedy over to talk to him about my ideas. He was mellos' best friend and like a brother to both of us. The day Rome and Blue died, Speedy was the first person I saw when I got the call. He looked at me as if to say, *we all we got now.* He just grabbed me and told me how he tried to bust back but they were ambushed. We were actively seeking info about that hit. Just on the low. I was taught knowledge is key. So, I believed it would be to my advantage that they had none!!! They would never see us coming. We would get what we needed soon. I promise to God the world would remember. Before I put my gun in his or her mouth, right before I squeezed, I wanted to hear them say, *Yesss, she was a beauty though.*

Speedy did anything I said. It was like I took over my brothers spot instead of him. He let me. Honestly, I think he knew I would slay this shit. I was bred for it my whole life. I was built like Romey but created from sweetness. I was smart, no nonsense, but somewhat timid at times. Only because I didn't want to shoot you if you said or did some dumb stuff. I stabbed a 9-year-old boy in his leg when I was four because he put gum in my hair. I was afraid to be agitated, sure that I would react until my comfort level revived itself. Until my phobia of being uncomfortable receded. I wouldn't let you make me uneasy.

I finally got to holla at Speedy about June. He was down with whatever. I knew that I just had to keep him on his toes. Let him know when to talk too much and school him on when to shut the hell up. I wanted to establish a few new code words in case I needed something in the clutch.

Speedy claimed he parlayed with this lil hot box on June's block that would help him stay close. Her name was Cash. She was a stripper out in Bushwick somewhere. I heard she handled her biz though. Worked, went to school, took care of her mother and her little brother. She had a wild side though, like me. *Hmmm we'd get along just fine*, I thought. I told Speedy to hook up with her Friday and bring her to Queens. We had a session with Bill Blass and Cool G Rap. I figured she and her groupie friends would love that. We would be off to a wonderful start.

Now June, on the other hand, I had to play smart. He was a semi goof ball, granted, but no sucker. He would spot bullshit a mile away. The good thing was I was kind of digging him anyway. I just never really played this close to home. I usually preferred to dabble in Hempstead or across the bridge in Chelsea when I needed a honeycomb hide out. For a chance to lock down this side of town I'd make June fall in in love with me, breathing the air from my forest and suffocating without it. Mmmm yeah, I could do that. June was 6'2" and about 230 lbs. cut up. He was just enough pretty, and his swag was suave. Laid back, quiet... one of those fine-and-I-know-it type dudes.

June was a killer though. About a year ago, he kidnapped some low-level clowns from the Dominican crew in the Bronx. They say he held them in a basement in Jersey for a week. They never found any of their bodies. I knew he wouldn't hesitate to eliminate a threat.

Speedy was taking Cash to empire this Wednesday. It was reggae night so I bet money June would be there. I figured I'd hit the mall and get fresh so I could pop up, red carpet worthy.

On the way to 34th Street to hit up Macy's, I received a text from Speedy. I told the driver to let me off on the corner by the pay phone.

"What's up baby?"

Speedy was amped. "Yooooo, guess who I'm at the seaport wit'?"

"Who?"

"That rooty poot nigga, Jigga. We about to hit the skating rink," he answered in code. He was speaking in a form of pig Latin we used to use.

"My nigga," I said. "See, that's why I love you, bro. You hear me when I ain't said a word. Yes boo, plant some seeds."

"I got you, B" Speedy promised.

I was confident that he knew exactly how to set the stage for me so I headed into Macy's on a mission. The incident at the underground was the first time anyone had ever seen me dressed like that. I usually wore sweats, Timbs, and a polo shirt. No makeup, no heels, just rugged like Romey. I knew I turned heads entering the club that night. Dudes were looking like lions and I was the little doe lost in the forest. They were probably more surprised than anything. I quickly became well aware of the power within. I saw how men *and* women reacted to me. I could feel eyes fixated on me as I entered a room. It was like the world stopped and paid homage to my presence. Still, I remained humble and didn't let it get to me. Even June showed some casual interest but to pull this off I wanted an irresistible, breathtaking bulge in his pants type of reaction.

From Macy's, I selected this cute black leather skirt with the jacket to match. I picked up some fish net stockings and a new Gucci clutch to accessorize. I called up Nikki so she could do my hair. She had been dying to color it, so I decided to let her. All this long pretty Colombian hair, I just threw a rubber band around it and called it a day. Well, Nikki was about to spruce me up. We went with honey blonde tips, middle part, cut in a bone-straight bob. She killed it too! I didn't even look like me.

"Come on, Beauty. Let me do your face," she begged.

WET

I fought her for a minute then gave in, figuring that would add that extra thing I was looking for. That pop. Pop it was too! I felt like J Lo. People said I looked like her, but I never thought so.

Instead of going all the way home I went ahead and showered and changed at Nikki's. when I was done and dressed, Nikki couldn't contain herself.

"Sssssssss… Caliente bebita! Bonita!" Nikki screamed as I twirled around for her to see all my angles.

I was eagerly waiting to make my debut, and after about ten damn minutes, Speedy finally called me back at Nikki's.

"Where are you all at? I'm on the way. Keep him there."

"We at Trudy's in the pier popping bottles. Come on!" Speedy yelled over the music. "We ain't going nowhere til' you get here. But listen, B, there's some chick pressing up on ya boy hard. She bad too. Not badder than you, but yo ass ain't here. Hurry the fuck up and come put a dent in this shit."

"Got it! On my way," I replied, not worried at all. I was raised to believe no bitch was ever a threat to me. If I wanted June TODAY, I'd make that happen. I just prayed I didn't have to shoot a bitch tonight.

I arrived on set in my pearl-white Benz looking like a porno waiting to happen. The valet opened my door and I hopped out with my stilettos clicking as I walked. Speedy spotted me off the rip and threw up two fingers, which meant it was all is good.

I approached smiling as I greeted everyone. "Hello hello, good people," I said cheerfully. I hugged Speedy and stared June dead in his eyes.

From my peripheral, I saw this thirst bucket looking like she wanted to say something slick, but I knew she knew better.

107

Starzpen

WET

"June, you remember Beauty, don't you?" Speedy introduced.

"Mellos' Beauty? You Romellos' lil' sister? You look different."

I wondered at times if I should get t-shirts with that saying on it. *Damn, you Romey little sister?*

"Yeah, but I'm Beauty's Beast too, ya heard?" I reminded him.

I heard this man-like voice snicker and say, "That's your real name? Beauty?"

My initial reaction was to pull chaos from my ankles and make this bird suck on her tip. Instead, I answered.

"Yes Doll, and a beauty she is," I said.

"Hmp," she whispered.

"What's your name, sweetie?" I asked.

"Treasure," she replied.

"Nice to meet you, Treasure," I told her. "Speedy is my brother."

She looked somewhat relieved, assuming that was my reason for being there. Then I bust her bubble.

"I'm thinking about letting June start playing in my pussy," I said.

Everyone had their mouth open. Speedy damn near choked off the Henny. June was looking like, *Hell yeah, I'll play in it* but he remained silent.

Treasure stood up. I remained seated.

"Is this your girl?" Treasure asked June.

June didn't know what to say. What he did know is that if the tramp kept talking I would push her ass in the Hudson River.

Treasure looked at June and then looked at me. "What the hell is this? You not gonna say nothing? You just gonna let her dis me like that?" Treasure ranted.

"I just met you, girl! You ain't my girl."

"Oh, it's like that?"

"It's like that!" June assured her.

While June dissed her, I was at the bar sipping Henny with Speedy paying her no mind.

Treasure gathered her things to leave. As she walked away, she mumbled, "Puerto Rican bitch."

That comment set off my rage. It came on when I felt the intense need to feel respected. I took the bottle of Remy I was about to crack open and bust her in the side of her face.

Glass shattered, skin split, and blood spewed. I reached for Chaos to finish her ass off but June grabbed me and threw me over his shoulder and took me to his car. Speedy ran behind him to make sure I wanted to go with him. He wouldn't have hesitated to blow June's head off if he thought I was in trouble. I threw up two fingers and Speedy U-turned and went about his biz. Probably headed to meet Cash at Empire.

"Yo, you wiiiild, Shorty," June said in disbelief.

"I'm not nobody's Shorty, first off. Second, she was getting on my nerves, so I had to dismiss her. Didn't see you tryna defend her," I pointed out.

"I just met that girl yesterday. She work at the Donna Karen store downstairs. She was having lunch when she spotted me. She came over and said hello," he explained. "Well, that's dead now so what's next beautiful? Since you ruined my lunch, come take a ride with me. I'll bring you back to your car when you're ready."

Reluctantly, I paused for a minute before I answered. "Aight, cool. I don't have nuttin' else to do anyway."

We rode up towards Redhook. He was going to the edge of Brooklyn I bet. His car smelled like bud and Drakar Noir cologne. He had some booming speakers playing slow jams loud as hell. Babyface sang *Sunshine* as if he was sitting in the back seat.

WET

June turned the music down when we reached a red light and cut his eye over at me. "So, wud up, B. Why you come through blowing up the spot like that, doe?"

I shrugged, "I told you that slug was getting on my nerves. You saw her looking me up and down and shit, don't front."

"Yeah, yeah, ok. She was but so was I and you didn't hit me with a $150 bottle of Remy."

"Whatever! She was running her mouth too much. She wasn't for you anyway, papi!"

"Oh word?" He said, lauging and blushing at the same time.

We pulled up and parked at the cab stand. We walked about two blocks laughing and remembering some times on the block and stories about my brothers reign on Brooklyn. As we reach the cliff I could already see the water. My mood changed. Melancholy crowded me. I loved the ocean. It was peaceful yet territorial. Forceful at times but calm and soothing at others. Silent but spoke volumes. The sun was going down over the bridge was always the most amazing view. So close you felt you could touch it, yet still so far from your reach you'd dream, one day 93 million miles away, I'll fly away. By now we were pretty zooted. We put about three in the air and killed a 40 ounce of OG— ole gold, that is.

June said, "So B, back to my question you so eloquently avoided. What's up? What's this?"

"I don't know, June. What your gut telling you? Mine says, 'let's just run it.' I snickered at my candor. It was so refreshing from my sweet demeanor. I was soft-spoken even when I pulled a trigger. I squeezed like it was the head of a dick I was about to polish. Finesse at its best, not to brag or anything. It just came naturally.

June walked closer to me with his hands clamped behind his back. He leaned forward and rubbed his nose against mine. My heart skipped two beats.

Starzpen

WET

What the fuck?

I gasped for air. He took one arm and pulled me to him, just rubbing his face across mine. It was the sexiest gesture I ever encountered. I was literally floating on a magic carpet across the Pacific with eagles leading the way. *Bitch pull yourself together,* I said to myself. I felt vulnerability creeping up. I felt something I never imagined I could feel. Hell, I didn't know this existed.

I had to keep my head on straight. I knew mixing business and pleasure was toxic. I couldn't help it though. I liked him. I genuinely liked being around him. Convincing myself I could still handle business and have some fun at the same time I carried on in the moment.

By now there was just a peek of orange coming from the sky as the sun was almost entirely invisible.

"I always wondered about you and me, Beauty," June claimed. "What made you come around so suddenly?" He asked, suspiciously.

I kicked into Go Mode knowing I had to make this good. Using a few tricks my squad taught me about a man, I turned on my natural pheromones and said, "I don't know, June. It's just something about you. I wanna know more, so run it Papi."

He melted his droopy, puppy dog eyes and she sucked on my top lip like it was covered in fun dip. Then he sucked my bottom lip and placed his cool hands on each cheek. He tilted his head a little to the left and kissed me. Both of our eyes opened and looked right at one another, wondering what the other was thinking. I gripped the back of his head with one hand while he wrapped my other hand inside his. Both of our eyes were now closed and something else had taken over. Passion? Lust? Authenticity? Fear? Or all of the above.

Starzpen

WET

I kept my eye on the prize even though I wasn't sure what the prize was at this point. I backed up and told June I had to go. He asked if I wanted him to take me home.

"No Speedy," I said. "I will have my car picked up and I'll take a cab."

"You sure?" June said, puzzled.

"Yup, I'm good. Later June."

I left like men do after getting confirmation that getting the P is a sure thing. Like they don't give a shit. I left June standing there literally with his hands in his pockets. I hopped in a cab without even looking back.

Pooch was sitting on my stoop when I arrived home. Pooch was a homeless man that had been around since I was a little girl. He became my snitch.

"Wuz up, Pooch? You hungry?"

I handed him a twenty I had stuffed in my bra. Rome taught me to always keep at least that much on me and the rest in a stash spot only I knew about.

After I gave him the money, Pooch belted out some info about my brothers being ambushed in the Tunnel. He said some bitch sent all her brothers to get em'.

"WHAT? WHAT BITCH!???" I yelled frantically. "Pooch, Pooch who did this?"

"I don't know her name, Beauty. I just heard them at the bus stop."

"Heard who at the bus stop?" I asked.

"It was Rudy and his boy from 40." He meant 40 Projects. Romello and his crew had beef there, but it was simple stuff. Nothing worth murder.

"Aiight Pooch, go get some food."

112

Starzpen

WET

Something was missing I thought. What had we missed? Rome told me everything. The answer was in my head. I just had to figure this out. I couldn't help but remember pooch say *she* sent them. Who in 40 would want them dead? Or was it them? Maybe it was just one of them. Speedy was always messing with somebody but I couldn't find any reason someone would want him dead.

I called Speedy for the update. Speedy said, "They shot Blue first as he popped out the back window to get a better shot."

That sounded accidental. One shot to his head from that far back. Romello fired six shots in all. Someone was angry. His piece never aimed anywhere else. Now my brother was the target. And SHE... whoever she was, was about to meet the most beautiful beast.

I told Speedy what Pooch told me. For some odd reason he wasn't surprised.

"What?" I asked.

"Well, he was sliding up in this little tender roni over there and her man came home from Rikers," Speedy recalled.

"Yes!! June was her man."

" Romeello backed off. He didn't give a fuck about her ass and all was squashed. A few months later I heard him on the phone saying, 'I'll give you 300, but ain't no me and you.' Then he was like, 'Hello hello.' She must have hung up."

"Now that I think about it he kept getting mad vexed 'cause somebody kept paging him 2 - 3 in the morn. Do you have Romellos' pager?" Speedy asked.

"Yeah, I got it. It's at the brownstone in Fort Greene."

"Aiight bet, I'll go get it tomorrow and we can go through the numbers."

"Ok," I agreed.

I took a long hot bath and prepared for bed when I heard my door buzzer going off. *Who the hell is that* I thought? Peeking out the window I saw June standing there with a pizza from Tony's and a Pina Colada icee. I laughed and told him to come on up.

"It's open!" I yelled. Quickly fascinated by the night air I waited for him on the fire escape. When he arrived, I greeted him, "Ahhhhh, my faves! What you are doing on this side of town?" I asked.

"I was checking out some shops over here looking to open a barber shop," he explained.

"Oh ok, I see somewhere to wash all that dough huh?" I replied sarcastically.

"I hear you making a shit load of dough out here yourself, Beauty, he countered."

We both laughed and slapped each other five.

"Nah, on the strength though, I waited till I thought you were home so I could bring you dinner."

Sweet, I thought. June was that way though. As rugged and thugged out as he appeared, he was a sweetheart. I got my boom box out my bedroom and popped in a tape. It was a mix of the quiet storm and some R&B. June lit the L. We kicked it for a while talking about what we wanted out of this thing called life. June was a deep soul; he was compassionate and cared about people. I could tell he would fall for me... like I was falling for him. I didn't want to complicate things. I was on a mission. When it came to June, now my mission was unclear. Honestly, he was just a piece to this puzzle I was completing. My heart was hardened so even if I did move forward with a me and him scenario, if he made one wrong move, I would end him.

There were rumors that June's baby mama got busy with Rome at a party while June was on Rikers. She was pregnant a few months later. No one ever saw the baby though. Before she had him, she and June fell out probably about messing around while he was lock down. She moved to Yonkers just before the baby was born. We really thought little of it, besides Romello never seemed to give a fuck so we didn't either. He always denied hitting that, claiming they were just rumors and he didn't have a baby. That brought me back to what Pooch told me. Figured I'd do some subtle digging.

I asked June how his son was doing.

"Oh, he aight," June replied.

"Let me see a picture."

"I don't have one on me, but I'll be sure to bring one next time."

"Ok cool," I answered.

The radio played our song and we started dancing on the fire escape while the block joined in. Suddenly I felt a drizzle, so I pushed the radio back inside and climbed in as well. June followed and shuts the window behind him. I stood there with some boy shorts and a wife beater on. June was looking quite edible himself. I reached for his hand and he gave it to me.

I lead him to my bed and sat down on it while he stood over me. We were both silent, just staring at each other.

Suddenly, June grabbed me by the throat and snatched off my shorts. I let him. He pushed my head down, still semi-choking me and went straight in. His dick was brick hard with a fat soft little mushroom on top.

Still gripping my neck, he started fucking me like I knew he did in his dream. Like he did in my dream. I just watched his sexy abs puff up each time he went in. Then his face each time he came out. Before I knew it this nigga had nutted all over my stomach. My pussy wasn't even wet yet.

"Damm baby!" June hissed. "Why you make me wait so long?"

Oh, hell no!! I thought. I saw I was going to have to get me before he ran out of gas.

I got up, pushed him down on the bed, and told him it wasn't no fun unless we both got one. I climbed on top and sat on his face.

"I got you, B," he moaned. "Slide that shit over here."

He grabbed my ass cheeks and sucked on me like I was a mango. His tongue game was fucking great; I didn't have to coach him or even grind harder. It was sweet and gentle. He was hitting my spot automatically. As I came all over his face, I felt like I was supposed to be there. Like his face was my pussy's home.

My body collapsed with half of me on his face, the other half on the headboard. Drained. Yes... I could work with this. Intoxicated by the good loving, I did something I had never done I let him sleep with me. Like really sleep. That wasn't my M.O. I would normally do my thing for my pleasure only. That drove men crazy. They liked it when I took control, but they couldn't handle my demand to remain in control. I wasn't in control this time, my heart was. I didn't like that one bit.

The next morning, I was cold and distant. I had to make myself act that way. In all reality I wanted him to kiss me and say good morning. I wanted to feel his heartbeat in my ear as it rested on his chest. Nevertheless, I rejected all his advances to remain close to me.

"What's up, Beauty? Having regrets?" June asked.

"Nah, I'm good. Just have a long day. Besides, I'm not a morning person."

"Oh, aight as long as you're good I am too. Call you later?"

"Yeah. I'll be in late, so I'll call you," I replied.

As he walked away, I saw the confusion in his eyes. I felt sad for myself as well. I deprived myself of an amazing feeling.

Quickly I remembered my mission and told myself to shut the fuck up and get back to business. I wanted that block more than I wanted June's ass. I needed that paper and I was not about to let this bumpy make me lose focus. Back to business for me.

I headed out to pick up some dough from a few of spots. All was well, product moving like the wind and money was stacking like I couldn't believe. I dropped off some money to Nikki so she could clean it up through the salon. Then I headed over to the underground to do the same with my girl Deena, the bartender at the club. She was my sis from another miss. She would flip it through extra bottles at the bar. She was fucking the owner, so he didn't care.

Leaving the club, I saw Cash, the girl Speedy was pushing up on mostly for information. She was arguing with some dude in the parking lot. I didn't want to get all in her business, so I just threw my hands up and asked gestured if she was good?

"Hey, Beauty," she said, trying to act like they weren't arguing. "I'm good!" She yelled.

I wondered what that was about and started having this weird vibe about Cash. I stopped at the barber shop on Fulton to holla at Speedy. Yup, we owned that too.

"Hey fellas," I said cheerfully as I walked into the shop.

"Looking good, Beauty! I hear you out here beasting in these streets," someone said. "And looking like a goddess. You got any Colombian sisters running around?"

They all cosigned his comments and agreed, kissing my ass as usual. I donated a lot of money within my community. I made sure no child was hungry within miles of our area. No child I knew about went to school without what they needed. Everyone I knew ate.

"What's up?" Speedy said.

"Come to the car and chat with me for a sec bro," I urged.

WET

We got in the car and Speedy already had what I needed.

"Yo B, listen, I got something to tell you, but you can NOT spaz the fuck out," Speedy said.

My eyes wide open, I said, "What the fuck? Talk to me."

"Promise me you gonna take this and keep ya head about it," he insisted. "So, listen, me and shorty was on the roof kicking it after we left Empire the other night. Man! She was drunk as hell. She fell asleep and her beeper kept going off. I was like nosey and shit, not really giving a fuck about who was paging her but just bored. This motherfucker sleep and shit so I picked it up and checked out the digits."

I interrupted him, "Ok so what happened, Speed. I ain't tryna hear all that crap! Like, come on, nigga! What's up??

June waved his hand. "It was June's baby mama."

"Cassey June? Ok so what!!" I said, agitated as hell at this point.

"Let me finish, B. So, you know June baby mama left for Yonkers right before she had the baby. Right?"

I answered, "So, June baby mama and Cash are sisters right?"

"Right!!!"

"Speeds?" I said, wanting him to spill it already.

"Ok, ok, I followed Shorty to Yonkers one day just for GP. To see if I stuck my dick in a sink hole and I saw this kid, B. B, if that ain't Romeys' son, you can shoot me."

"Wait? So, Cash knew all along that baby was ours?"

"Yup, she knew something? How about June?"

"For some reason, I don't think so, B? But you don't know do you Speed?"

Wheels turning, rage on a thousand, I knew I needed more details and I was damn sure going to get them. Anyone who whispered knowledge regarding the hit on my family would leave this world because of it. I missed my brother and if there was any chance I had a blood nephew out there I was going to find out.

"You aight, B?" Speedy asked.

"Yes, I'm ok?"

"What's the next move, Queen? I know Beauty is ready to beast," said Speedy.

"Yeah I am, but I need to do something first."

I wondered if June knew that boy was not his. We had a distinct look in my family. Me and my brother looked like twins. If Speedy said he saw Romey in that boy's face, then he saw him.

I made some calls to some peeps I had posted up at the DMV and a few hospitals. I needed info about this bitch and this baby which, by the way, was 4 years old now. Waiting patiently, I got the call from my connect giving me the address to where Casey lived. I was also able to get a copy of his birth certificate. Rome's name wasn't on it. I didn't really think it would be, but I had to be sure. I had to see this little boy. His name was Miles. I had to see whatever Speedy saw.

I popped back a few and put one in the air on my fire escape listening to Lauryn hill sing the sweetest thing I've ever known. My mind was wandering but somehow lately, it was always wandering back to June. This was too much. There were too many what ifs. Too many questions. He kept paging me, but I was zoned out and didn't feel like messing with him right now. I snuggled up to my Versace sheets and joined the dreamers.

Speedy was still getting close to Cash. She wasn't talking much though; at least, not about anything important. I decided I would head to Yonkers today. My connect informed me of his pre-k location.

WET

I still didn't have a picture of the boy, but if he was my blood, I would know it. There was only one pre-school class in the building, so it wouldn't be too hard to find him. I sat in my car across from where the buses boarded and waited.

As they began to come out of the building, I pulled my binoculars up to my eyes, analyzing each child. *All these girls. That can't be him. His head is nappy as hell. Dear God!! Huh? Oh my God. That's Miles*, I thought as I jumped out the car so I could get a closer look. I couldn't believe my eyes. He had my family's whole face. He walked like him, and oh wow, look at him laugh. It was my brother when he was that age. He had Romellos chinky light brown eyes and he walked with left leg dominance, just like Rome.

I walked over to where he was and just stared at him. He stared back, almost like he knew me. I knew he didn't, but I thought maybe he could feel my connection to him.

"Hi," he said as he waved and boarded his bus.

I was stuck watching him until he was out of sight. I drug myself back to the car with a thousand questions. Why the lie? Did Preem know? Casey had to know. She had to take one look at that boy and know who his daddy was. Does June know? Who ordered the hit? I was determined to get to the bottom of it all.

I couldn't let Miles walk around not knowing who he was. *Time to beast*, I thought. It was war in my eyes. Somebody was going to meet chaos… my gun.

I drove straight to the spot on Dean and Nostrand Avenue where Speedy was cooking a batch.

"What up?" He asked.

"I saw Rome's son, Speedy."

"What?" He yelped. "You went to Yonkers?"

"Yeah, I did. I just left there. His name is Miles. He's four years old and he looks just like us."

"What you gon' do, B?"

"I'ma kidnap this bitch and stash her in the Bronx until I get what I want."

"Ok, so tell me what exactly it is you want again."

"I want to know who killed my brother and Tru, then tried to kill you too." I screamed at him, trying to make him understand. He should have known that I would die for mine and kill anyone else that fucked around and crossed us. My crew would die for me too.

"Aight, B. Want me to go get her?"

"Yes, make sure the boy is good, though. I'll meet you at the stash house. Page me when you have her!" I stormed out mad as hell, wondering how it all would end.

Hopping in the car, I got a page from June. It was a welcomed summons. I was down for some rough stuff. I could use his gentle touch and see what info he may have had about Rome and Miles. I decided to fuck 'em and have a little pillow talk after.

It was raining out, not a hard,messy rain, but a soft misty one. June arrived in record timing and we didn't waste a minute. I popped in a tape and sparked up the bud like we always did. Michelle's soft voice rang through the room.

"Before you turn off the lights, let's get one thing understood. If you want to make love to me, you got to do it good..."

"Mmmm, hell yeah." He was stroking my back with his tongue and loosening up my biceps. The song's words were perfect. They fit the moment so well.

"I'm a hell of a woman and for me, it takes a hell of a man. So, don't you dare turn off the lights, unless this you understand."

I could sing a little, so I knew I fucked him up with that one. I wasn't no Whitney Houston, but I could hold a decent tone. It was dark, rainy, and I was feeling freaky as hell. I hopped out on the fire escape, dropped my robe so I was butt ass naked, literally soaking wet from all angles. June climbed out next, fully clothed, which was more fun for me. I got to strip him and make love to him in the rain.

I began with his belt. *Get this shit out my way*, I thought. His pants dropped as he stepped out of them, swiftly leaving his Calvin Klein boxers on. He was anxious, almost as if he couldn't wait.

I crouched down and licked around the head of his shaft, water from the rain dripping in my mouth. "Yo', B. You wanna do this out here?" he asked.

"Yes sir. Make love to me right here." I purred.

He threw my leg up on the fire escape's railing. I held on, gripping the rails with both hands. He glided inside me, hands wrapped under my arms with his fingers on my shoulders. Nose to nose, we made a beat like Run DMC's *Sucker MC*. Rough in stuff wit my afro puffs, rage rock on wit' ya' bad self-kind of love making.

I was all in, throwing it back… and forth. Chest to chest, my legs wrapped around his waist. Damn, he was holding me up as if I was light as a feather, just bouncing my body on his dick. He was hanging in there too, not that minute action like last time. I was hot as hell, but the rain eased that cooled me.

"Omg, I think I love you." I blurted out simultaneously with the juices he forced out.

He knew I was coming, demanding that I stared at him, eye to eye contact. I couldn't. I was at his mercy. He was in control.

I was slipping, but I couldn't stop. All the way there, he sweetly wiped rainwaters from my eyes, forcing my face directly into his. I had no choice but to look at him.

We locked eyes and boom, there was a rush of passion from both sides. "I know I love you," he whispered in my ears while my body quivered.

I was shaking like a leaf. He held me tighter as I came. "Don't turn off the lights unless you love me right." I began to sing even though the song went off. He chuckled his approval and carried me inside.

He went straight to the bathroom and turned on the water. June took my hand and helped me into the shower. Then he removed his boxers. The warm water was refreshing after that cool shower we just took on the fire escape.

June grabbed my loofah, my coconut body wash, and began to wash me. I felt like a baby. That naked vulnerability was creeping up again. I needed this more often than I ever thought I could. I was slipping. Romello would kill me. He would say, "Beauty, to be a beast, you can't give a fuck."

However, after all that sexy connecting we were doing, we laid down and watched *Crush Groove*. The back of my head rested on his head, cradled in his arms. I felt safe, but what really got to me was the fact that I felt love. Not loved, but I felt love and I knew from that point on, I'd crave the feeling and wouldn't live without it.

I had to find out if June knew about Casey's baby. Did the guy arguing with Cash have any part in any of this?

"Hey, when you gon' bring Miles by to meet me?" I asked.

"Who's Miles?" He answered.

I was confused, so I said nothing. He didn't know who Miles was? Huh? Uh oh, something wasn't right.

I quickly grabbed his balls and started kissing him, in an attempt to change the subject. I decided I would hit him off again and put him to sleep so I could think in peace.

I climbed back out onto the fire escape and began sorting through what details I had. Nothing was making sense. I sat there until the sun began to glisten over the river. June snuck up behind me, wrapping me up in his arms.

"Good morning, beautiful."

"Good morning," I replied smiling, irritated at all the drama but still trembling from his touch.

"I gotta go tie up some lose ends at the shop. Call me later?"

"Yes. I will." I told him.

Before he turned to leave, he looked at me. "You know what you in for? I ain't gon' change, B. This is me."

I smiled. "Ditto, love. I was thinking to tell you the exact same thing."

I blew a kiss and told him to make the day count.

He smirked. "It already does."

So sweet like honey, solid like concrete, and sexy as ever. *Please, God*, I prayed. *Don't let June have anything to do with this.* I knew I would cut his throat in the middle of times square if he did.

Later that day, I got a 911 page from Deena. That was an emergency, so instead of calling, I hopped in the ninja and rode to the club.

"What's up, D?" I asked, walking in, alert.

"Take a shot, B"

"Oh, hell." I replied, popping back one of the Tequila shots that she had on the bar.

"You ready?"

"What D?"

"What the fuck? Que pasa, puta? Casey was in here last night with Dre."

"Who is Dre?" I asked.

"Dre is Casey's man."

"Ok so?"

"So, Pooh was at the pool table behind V.I.P. where they were sitting. I took Pooh some wings and overheard him say he still couldn't believe she fucked them niggas. She said she was sorry.

She was just bored. He was gone so long. What the fuck did he expect her to do? He told her to shut the hell up. Then, he told her how she was out here having babies, got him out here killing niggas trying to take his family. Apparently, June didn't know the baby was his and everyone thought June was his daddy but she was fucking Preem too."

I frowned. "Dre killed my brother, D? Casey knows it? Cash?"

D nodded. "I don't know about Cash. Honestly, I didn't want to say nothing, but I heard a few former old heads from the crew moved to Yonkers. They said Miles looks just like y'all.

"He does," I replied.

"How you know, Beauty?"

"I saw him."

"Whaaat? When?"

"A few days ago. I've been on the trail. Just the wrong track."

After a few more minutes, I decided to leave. Telling Deena I'd see her later as I revved up the ninja. My blood was boiling. However, somehow, I remained calm. My mind was racing, but I was moving in slow motion. I had to get somewhere safe so I wouldn't hurt anyone. At least, not yet.

I headed to Romey and Blu's grave to spark a spliff and try to make sense of the foolery. I sat there for hours before I headed home. I wanted to sleep on the new info. However, I got a page with all 6's from Speedy. That meant he still didn't have Casey.

I was unbothered. I laid my head on my pillow, wondering what Romello would do? I heard him as if he was standing right next to me.

"Don't worry about what I would do. You're BEAST all on your own. Do what I taught you. Make it make sense."

WET

The only way I knew how to do that was war! I had it. I was going to destroy the 40 projects. I hit Speedy back on the pager with the number 9. That was code for restock my gear. I needed bullets, grenades, a car and a walkie-talkie. He knew what to pack for me and I let him know I needed it NOW.

I hopped on my bike looking like Halle Berry in *Cat Woman*. I was in all black down to my toenails. Black represented power and I felt powerful. With a vengeance, my heart was hardened, and chaos was by my side, beast mode.

Today, Beauty would unleash beastly hell on Dre, Casey, Cash and the whole 40 projects if need be. Speedy still hadn't gotten a hold of Casey's trash ass. So, I decided to go get her myself. I knew she worked on 5th Avenue at this high-end spot.

I sent out pages to my crew reading all 3's. That meant I needed them to post up at the spot. Once they all assembled, Speedy hit me back at the payphone around the corner from her job.

"Que pasa, papi. Wait 'til we get to the door and spin the bike to get the attention off of us. As we exit, I'll sit and wait in front just in case she leaves early."

While I waited, I saw my squad posting up slowly and quite subtly. I thought, *good job boys. Here she comes*.

I hopped off the bike and put up 2 fingers for my peeps. I waited until she hit the corner and snuffed her, damn near knocking her whole head off.

She went down, hitting the floor, trying to brace herself. I put chaos in her.

"Get in the van." I demanded.

While holding her head, looking around for help, she tried to run. Before she could flinch, I hit her in the back of the head with my pistol, then again on her forehead.

She was out like a bad bulb. I jumped in the van and Pop grabbed the girl. I heard Squid spinning like crazy, laughing, knowing those white folks were about to die.

We pulled off quietly. Nobody said a word. After we drove far enough away from the scene, Speedy asked where we were headed to.

"Poconos," I said, and they all laughed. "You know you about to die, girl?" I taunted.

She said nothing, just crying and looking scared to death. Rightfully so, I was going to end her. But first, I had some questions and I needed access to Miles before she was gone. Or, I'd have to take out her whole family and ultimately, be all he had left. I would raise my brother's son. I swore to God. Everyone in the way of that would die.

I owned a cabin in the Poconos. It had its own private lake and I had two gators in there. I wanted two things. One, to know why she ordered the hit on my Rome. Two, for her to call her sister and tell her she'd be having her friend from work pick them up and bring Miles to the cabin. I would send Deena.

Deena had my back since the sandbox days. I trusted her. Cash would die here with her sister. I wanted to be the one to watch Dre's head spilt in half when I shot him at point blank range with my mini 14. That was sure to be a beauty.

"Why did you have my brother killed, Casey?" I asked. "Pooch said it was some dudes at the bus stop saying that a bitch had them killed. You're that bitch Casey."

She shook her head. "I don't know what you're talking about, Beauty." She pleaded.

"You don't know why or you just don't know?" I asked. "Who is Miles' daddy, Casey?"

"Dre," she said.

I took my lighter and put it up her nose, ignited it, and held it there for about 3 seconds. She looked like she wanted to pass out and I needed this bitch coherent, so I poured some water over her head to cool her off. Squid was in the corner bugging out, praying for her, and asking if she was at peace with God. I chuckled.

"I didn't have Rome killed," she yelled frantically. "I tried to stop them. But Dre was so mad when he came home and saw Miles. He looked just like your brother. I couldn't even convince myself he wasn't his."

"And June. Did June know Miles was our blood?"

"No," she said. "June never even saw Miles. I begged him to just act like he was Miles' dad from a distance. If anyone ever asked him, he was cool, and it wasn't hurting anyone."

"Why? You stupid bitch. Why the lie? If Dre thought June was Miles' father, what difference would it make if he was Romellos? I don't get it. Dre knew the boy was somebody's, right?"

"Yeah, but-"

"But what?" I yelled furiously.

"Dre was already vexed that I was with June. He would have killed me if he knew I'd been with more than just him."

"So, my brother and one of his closest friends had to be buried because of your hoe ass tendencies? Because of you? You are a gutter rat. Face it. Like a penny with a hole in it... no value!"

I couldn't breathe. I couldn't move. My veins began to turn dark purple. My head felt like it was spinning. Like, I was dizzy or something.

Speedy noticed and handed me the blunt. I didn't want it, but I was back from the trance I was in. "I'm going to let you go, Casey. But I want to see my nephew," I told her. "Untie her and get her a shot. Pass her the L too."

Squid and Pop looked puzzled but not Speedy. He knew exactly what I was about to do. He thought like Rome. That's why they were so close. I would eventually grow up to think just like them.

She puffed a bit, then she emptied her shot glass. Still terrified. I was sure of that. She began reassuring me she didn't want Romey dead and how she had no control over Dre and his boys. She also spoke on how she wished we could have been a part of Miles' life.

Really? You dumb hoe? Does she really think I'm gonna let her walk out of here. I had to ask myself that. If she wanted to play dumb, I'd just play dumber.

"Call Cash. I'm going to send Deena to get him. Better yet, tell her to come too so Miles won't be scared by himself. You cool with that? He will have fun up here. We have horses, he can ride the boat, whatever he wants. Relax, boo. I just needed to know who pulled the trigger. Now that I know Dre-"

"Sure, it was Dre. Me and you cool." She cut me off.

"Man, Beauty. What the fuck you doing? I thought you was gonna dead this bitch." Squid gritted.

"It's alright, Squid. She didn't know," I replied.

"She did know," he insisted. "I ain't with this shit," he added as he stormed out. Speed followed him. No doubt, to calm him down and reassure him I had this.

Deena pulled up with Cash and Miles. As Miles walked in, we all just stared. I even teared up. It was my blood, my brother's seed. I felt obligated to his heart. He was the last of my bloodline. I wanted to call him Supreme so bad.

"Tell him who I am, Casey." I demanded.

"Miles, this is your aunt, Beauty. Say hi."

"Beauty?" He asked. "Like Belle?" He added.

"Yes handsome. Like Belle from Beauty and the Beast."

"You look like me," he said.

I couldn't hold back my tears. Squid was crying like a bitch too.

"Mi amore!! Can I have that apple on the table?" Miles asked.

"Yes, my love. You can. You can have the world if I could reach it."

He laughed. "You don't got the whole world."

***

Once Miles played and ate himself to death. I read him his first bedtime story. He fell asleep in my arms. Tomorrow would be a new day, and a new life for Miles and I. I could hear my brother smiling. "You a beast, Beauty. Well done." He said.

I went downstairs and had Squid at Miles' door. I didn't want to wake Miles. So, I directed everyone away from his room.

"Let's go put one in the air by the lake." I demanded. Everyone followed; Cash, Casey, Pop, and Speedy.

Pop sparked the L and handed it to me. I hit it. Then, I asked Cash if she knew Romello was Miles' father. She hesitated, looking at Casey.

"Yeah, Beauty. I knew, but she's my sister."

I became enraged at that answer. I pulled chaos from my waistband and shot her dead in her face. Casey screamed, running toward her, yelling.

"Cash! Cash, wake up!" Cash was over. I didn't feel a thing as her lifeless body hit the ground.

Pop and Speed began pulling out the boat. They tied Cash to the back by her feet so she would drag in the water.

"You bitch," Casey yelled. "We didn't kill Romello. Why you do that to her? Oh my God! No! No!" She cried frantically. "Why did you kill her? Fuck you, Beauty! Fuck you, Rome, and all of y'all. You gon' reap what you sow, hoe!

"I already have!" I stood over her and screamed back in anger. "Bitch, shut up. We're in the woods. Can't nobody hear you."

"Let me get my son, bitch! Beauty? Please!" She screamed.

"No, bitch. My nephew will never know his father because of you. So, now he won't know his mother either. Tie her ass to the boat too." I demanded.

"You not gon' shoot her first? Blu asked.

"Nah, I'm not. Tie her to the boat, Pop."

Casey put up a good fight, scratching my boys all up. So, I shot her in the arm, then her foot. She began to weaken, but she was still breathing… struggling for air, begging.

"Please, Beauty. Don't do this begging."

I grew deaf and could only hear my brothers voice. "Dust that bitch off, B. Be a beast, Beauty." He chanted.

I shot her again, just so she'd shut the fuck up. Still alive and still trying to fight, her body went under the water. Pop and Speed did about two or three donuts and the rope came up empty.

I was sure my gators would leave no trace. So, we left the boat out on the lake, put Casey and Cash's personal items on board and staged a boating accident.

The detectives didn't ask many questions once they saw Moby and Max swimming around. The fact that they were drunk and ignored the danger signs I had posted made things much better. The case was open and closed. Besides, Drew did the investigation. He was Rome's homeboy and informant. He worked for the NYPD for years, then he made detective and cleared a path for us within the department, leaking info on raids for Rome, Blu and sometimes myself. When they'd let me come, I would intercept drugs and dough in transit. He made shit like that mad easy.

My last step was Dre and his crew. *One to the skull*, I thought. We planned an assault on 40 projects like Queens had never seen. We waited about two weeks or so, just to let the noise about Cash and Casey die down. Casey's mom was a heroin addict. She was Miles' only blood relative left. At least, she was the only person I may have to lay down regarding full access to my nephew.

WET

I called Tonya. She was my attorney and my home girl. I had her draw up guardianship papers for Miles, naming me as his full legal guardian, relinquishing any and all rights. His daddy was dead, so there were no worries in reference to anyone challenging the motion.

I decided to offer Casey's mom the choice to accept some dough and sign the papers or we was going to drop her in the middle of the Atlantic ocean; whichever she preferred. Needless to say, her drug habit wouldn't allow her to turn down any money. I gave her twenty thousand dollars, a new Toyota Camry, and had her dropped off in North Carolina. We made sure that she was well aware that if she ever stepped foot in NYC again, orders were in to put a bullet in her throat, on site!

I scooped up Miles and took him to my cabin on Virginia Beach. He was quiet the entire ride up. I could tell he was wondering what was going on and where his mother was. Strangely, he never asked. Yet, he was comfortable enough to tell me he was hungry and had to pee.

I told him he could have whatever he wanted. Deena was flying down the next day to hang out with Miles while I finished off Dre, his grimy ass crew, and if need be, his whole family.

I pulled off on an exit in Delaware to get food and use the restroom. Pulling into a parking space at Texas Roadhouse, Miles asked if I was his family. He looked just like his daddy.

I almost cried and pulled out a picture of Rome and I when we were kid. I handed it to Miles. His eyes widened and he just stared at it. After a few seconds, he looked at me.

"That looks like me!" He squealed. "You look like me."

The tears were coming. He knew. He felt the connection. I truly believed he knew.

"You were at the bus stop," he recalled.

I nodded. "Yes," I replied, laughing. "I was at the bus stop." I pointed to my brother in the picture. That is your father, my brother."

"My daddy?" He screeched.

"Yup, your daddy!"

"Where is he?" Miles asked excitedly.

I paused, not knowing exactly how to answer that. "Well, he had an accident and went to wait for us in heaven." I finally got out.

Miles looked down at the picture. "Like mommy and aunt Casey?"

I bit down on my bottom lip. "Yes, like mommy. Come on. Let's go eat. You're gonna eat vegetables, right?"

"Well, I guess I'll eat broccoli," he sighed and we both laughed.

"Ok, broccoli it is."

"Beauty?" Miles called out.

"Yes, my love?"

"Am I gonna stay with you now?"

"Would you like that?" I asked.

"I guess, he shrugged, somewhat unsure.

"Well, Miles. Aunt Beauty would love for you to stay with her. Let's just enjoy lunch and get ready to have some fun with aunt Deena at King's Dominion."

"King's Dominion? I see that on TV with the big roller coasters." Miles was excited.

"Yup, that's the spot. We have a few more hours before we get there. So, come on. Let's go wash our hands."

I tried to walk him into the girl's bathroom. In my eyes, he was still a baby. However, he let go of my hand.

"That picture has a dress on it! I go to the door with pants on it."

I laughed at his alertness. "Ok, but not before I open the door to the men's room and double check. I called out, but when no one answered, I walked in and peeked under the stalls. No feet.

"Ok, Miles. I'll be right outside the door."

"Ok," he replied.

I decided after I tied up the loose ends, I would leave New York. Nothing was there for me anymore. The few people I loved which were, Blu, Deena, Pop, and June, I could take with me.

Deena finally arrived at the cabin so I could handle the rest of my business. Driving back through the tunnel, I got this weird feeling. My brother's blood stained the wall of the Holland. It was like a tomb and I didn't want to have to go through it again.

I started having flash backs of mommy and daddy. The morbid rain sprinkled me. Or was it the tears that were falling in anticipation of an end being near? Composing myself, sucking it up, I remembered who the fuck I was. Swiftly drying my eyes with my hand, I popped in Biggie's *'Who Shot Ya'*. With the radio on full blast, I sparked an L that I had in the ashtray. I zoned the fuck out and easily moved from lil' sweet sis Beauty to the beast I was bred to be. I was about to light the 40 projects up. GROUND ZERO.

I needed to see June first, though. With all the stress I had been enduring, I could use some lovin'… like some real TLC from genuine arms and tasty lips.

June loved me and I felt like getting some of that loving tonight. With a major plan for my pussy, I headed over to the brownstone on Dean and Nostrand. I knew June would more than likely be at the barber shop around the corner. Yeah, I liked them boys up top from the BK that knew how to flip that money three ways... Beyoncé was on to something with those lyrics.

WET

June got money. I liked that about him. Not that I needed it, but that hustler swag he wore was sexy as fuck and I loved it.

I hit June's pager 911. For me, that meant my pussy was wet.

He replied with all stars, which meant our rendezvous was a go. The next page was a seven, meaning seven o'clock.

So, I had about an hour before June arrived. I sent out some coded messages to my crew about our next move. Then I took a hot bath, listening to my girl Jill Scott.

I must have drifted off because when I woke up, June was sucking on my nipples. "How'd you get in?" I asked.

"I pay attention to the ones I love. I saw you put the key under your bike tire last week. Now, shut up and take my clothes off."

I pull him into the tub with me. "Shit, Beauty. This shit is suede." He fussed.

"I'll buy you a new one, love. Shhhh, just play in my pussy."

June kissed me like he missed me, while I removed the soaking wet shirt from his body. I saw his dick trying to break out his pants. I quickly unbuckled the belt from his jeans, damn near breaking it. He hopped up to allow me to take them off, still kissing and squeezing me all over.

"Hell yeah, baby. You missed me, huh?" June asked.

"Yes, love. I did," I whispered.

"Well, what about-"

"Shh, no. Not now," I pleaded.

Finally, all his clothes were off. He snatched me from the tub and slammed me down on the counter top. Then, unexpectedly, he began to move in slow motion. He took the coconut oil from the vanity and poured it into his hands rubbing the oil into my shoulders, then my back, kissing me softly on my neck and forehead.

He massaged each arm, one by one. Then, he gave attention to each foot, one by one. Subtly rubbing his hands up my thighs and

135

Starzpen

between my legs, they began to spread apart on their own. He teased it, blowing on my clit, then raising back up to say hello to my melons, slightly sticking his finger inside me and removing it. I began to snap down and grind on his magical fingers.

I wanted his dick inside me so badly, but he was making love to me and I liked it. "Take your time today, babes." I whispered.

"Oh, I plan to," he replied. "She's soaking wet like she's been neglected. I can't have that." June declared, stroking my cheek with one finger and twiddling his dick between my thighs. The harder it got, the wider I opened up.

Oooh, I feel it. Yes God! He was about to ram that shit inside me. I was ready. However, he backed up about two steps, lifted me up off the counter, and took me to my bed. It was the best fifteen steps I'd ever walked.

My body was melting, not only was his touch bomb, his heart also seemed to beat just for me. I could feel his love for me coming out his pores. That, mixed with what I was feeling right now, was an eruption waiting to happen.

He sat me in the bed and commanded me to sit Indian-style. I did it. I'd do any... well, almost anything for June.

He began to pour more oil, this time streaming it directly down my neck. Its warm drip was easing down to my nipple. Ummm, it was edible oil. So, he caught every drip with his tongue and slowly worked it into the spot it dropped on.

"Tell me what you want, Beauty." He whispered as he kneeled in front of me.

"You. You babes. I want you." I whispered back, gently sucking on his bottom lip that hung slightly pinkish in color. June had sexy ass lips.

"What you want me to do, Beauty? Talk to me? Tell me how to please you."

"Oooh. Hell yeah, Papi. Can you make me come with ya' finger?" I asked, weakening. I tried to spread my legs, inviting the friction in and wiggling the feeling around before I busted.

June wouldn't let me. "No, stay just like that. Sit straight up and close your eyes. Don't open them until I tell you to," he demanded. I closed them, trying to imagine what was coming next.

June placed my hands behind me palms, gripping the mattress. I was trying my damnedest to keep control and enjoy the moment. I could have come in that moment, but I wanted to savor the feeling and enjoy the ascent.

June took an orange and began feeding it to me. It was sweet, juicy, and cold until it rested on my tongue for a second or two. He slid slices in my mouth with his. Mmmm. I try to reach for him to ring him closer so I could touch him, kiss him, squeeze him, and suck on him… I needed to breathe in his scent.

He declined, pushing me back in place, into this crisscross, applesauce shit.

With one strong forceful hand planted on the small of my back, June took one finger and slid it in my mouth. I sucked on it like a well-seasoned T-bone steak. He snatched it out abruptly and used it to massage my clit.

"Mmmm, I want to open my legs," I cried.

"No," he said aggressively. "Hell no. Shhhh, shut the fuck up, Beauty."

Now normally, I'd shoot his ass in both his wrists for talking to me like that. However, I almost spit all over his hand when he said that shit.

Shut the fuck up? Listen, shut the fuck up is what I did.

"I'll open 'em when I'm ready he whispered. "You said to make you come with my finger.

With my eyes still closed, I replied. "Yes, baby. Make me cum," I whined.

WET

He slid his wet finger across my clit like it was a violin... graceful, yet direct. Every stroke meant something different. Every tap created a new beat.

June gently slid one finger inside me and kept one finger planted on my hotspot, moving them about like keys on a piano, playing a soft, sweet, and lovely tune.

Mmmm, yeah. I was zoning out. I began to move. June kept me still, ensuring that I couldn't move.

"Don't fucking move." June growled.

"That shit was turning me on. "Yes, boo. Make me have to fuck you back. I purred.

He was still rubbing and tapping my pussy. I couldn't stay still much longer. June, no doubt, felt the hardening in my clit. He eased up a bit, still playing in that shit like it was therapy for him. He rolled his neck around with the same rhythm as his fingers. They twirled around my entryway.

June was moaning and mumbling, lost in these wetlands, admiring the scenery from all angles. I was getting more and more turned on just by him watching me... watching him loving me, tasting me, sexing me.

He looked down at me. "Stand up," he whispered aggressively. I paused a second or two, and then I did exactly what he asked. Standing up, totally naked in front of him, he just looked at me. Licking his lips, he stroked his dick with one hand, and reached for the remote and cued track 9 with the other.

"Mmm, girl. The way you do me in the mornin'. Ooohhh, girl. The way ya' love me all night long..."

Hey! Freddie Jackson sang through the speakers and I melted. That song was one of my favorites.

"Dance for me," he said.

WET

I began to wind my body around like a hula dancer, slowly swirling my hips from side to side. Caressing my arms, then my breast, I swayed to the slow jam with Freddie.

June was moving his lips, singing silently. He stood up and moved toward me, aggressive and swift... yet sexy, wild, and somewhat startling. He gripped my throat and pushed me against the wall.

Mmm, hell yeah. I loved that shit and he knew it. He'd come back through later and kiss away the slight imprints his fingers left on my fair skin.

June kissed me hard, smashing his lips to mine. Our tongues danced, and our bodies spoke so only we could hear the words. His heart was moving at least one hundred miles per hour.

I wrapped my arms around his neck and tried to lift myself onto his dick. He wouldn't let me. I was dripping wet and my pussy was throbbing. He was teasing me, making love to my whole soul like he knew I craved him and fucking the shit out of me

"I love you, June. I told him through breaths and tongue meetings.

"I love you back, bae," He replied, moving his lips down to my neck, flipping me around so my face was to the wall as he begun to massage my waist and the small of my back to my upper inner thigh.

"June,"

"Yes ma'am," he answered. "I'm gonna do something different."

"What?"

"You wanna try some toys or a threesome or some shit, baby?" He asked.

I laughed. "No, silly. Ooooh yes, Papi. *Besame ahi*," I pleaded, still trying to get the words out. I wanted to leave N.Y. and start over somewhere else.

WET

But, damn. Yes, June. "Uhm, baby. Come wit' it!! You miss me, huh?" I asked, knowing he did.

"Whatever you want, Beauty. You can have it." June answered, as he started eating my pussy like a homeless man at the community Thanksgiving dinner.

My knees were shaking. Fuck the small talk. What we were not about to do was fuck up my own end game.

I spit all over June's face. He loved it when I came. He said it was like peeling a perfectly ripe mango and sucking the juices slowly.

June went nuts over my facial expressions and the cute little purring sound that he said I made when I was in midstream orgasming That was the icing on his climatic cake.

He was twirling his forefinger around my booty, watching me change from power to powerless. Like, beast to beauty. He had me like a genie in a bottle. I was feeling enslaved; like submissive as fuck. My wish was his command type night.

Then, out of the blue, June slammed my palms, so I was gripping the wall. My cheek firmly pressed against the paint. I could smell it. Arms spread, legs apart, he slid himself inside me, gently working his dick completely into place like driving a stick shift. Getting it in the perfect position for gear changes, he glided in and out, securing my hands on the wall with his breathing on my neck and back, whispering my name.

"Beauty," he cried. "This pussy juicy."

Laughing lightly and watching my lil size eight ass bounce with each thrust in out, he went gracefully streaming through my river like a drifting log.

"Yesss babes, wan' me to take my time? Let me paint every inch of you onto me. Will you let me love you?" He asked.

"Yes," I purred.

"I can't hear you." He growled, stopping his movement, forcing me to answer. "I can't hear you. What you want?"

140

Starzpen

WET

His hands forced mine to grip the wall harder and bounce on his dick faster. Oohh, yesss, boo. There you go," he whispered. His hands were on his hips, amused, watching me work this shit because he knew not to be playing wit' me.

My pussy was speaking for herself at this point. We'd made enough love faces and now I needed him to ram that shit inside me and tie up the loose ends.

"Huh, what the hell?" I looked back and June was backing up

"Where you going?" I asked, slightly annoyed and confused as fuck.

"Come here," he demanded.

I swiftly went to him. He moved toward the pool table and I followed. I walked over, throwing one leg on the table, and leaning over, wet dripping, and my throbbing ass in the air, as if to shoot the eight ball in the corner pocket.

June stared silently, swiping his fingers across my pussy and tasting it. Then he grabbed the back of my neck, pushing me slightly forward. He wiggled his dick inside gently at first. After a few slow, sweet, and deep loving strokes, he finally went in; one hand on my neck, the other smacked my ass repeatedly.

"Don't stay gone so long and not call me, you hear me?"

 Slap!

"Yes, sir." I replied submissively.

He slapped and thrusted again and again. My ass cheeks stung, and my pussy was on fire. He was beating this box up. I couldn't breathe. My neck was swinging wildly, back and forth.

"Beauty," he cried.

"Yes, babe?"

"I'm about to nut."

"Well, come on, baby. Come inside me. I replied before I began to massage his balls. His breathing on the back of my neck got hotter and moister. He was drooling, swimming in my love lake seemingly willing to drown with me.

I subtly scratched the paint off the side of the pool table. He was going so deep and poking all the right spots. Both hands were gripping my waist.

June pulled me into him harder and harder, holding my titties to keep them from bouncing too wildly. One, up the hill he went. Two, he was climbing higher. Three, he was s teaming my name. Thrusting harder and harder.

"What are you doing to me," he stuttered, smacking my ass lightly on both cheeks. "Yes, ma. Bounce that shit on my dick," he commanded.

"Get you, baby. It's here for you," I replied, bouncing and grinding, singing along with Usher who was now playing in the speakers.

Grabbing both my titties and sucking on my ears and neck, he was still stuck inside me, grinding slowly from behind. He was on the decent coming down off this high. Euphoria at its finest.

Resting his body on mine, my body laid smashed pleasantly onto the pool table. Both our legs were still shaking and trembling in passion. I was satisfied, but secretly never satisfied… kind of greedy too. In my mind, I was already preparing for round three with June tonight. But I knew I had to have a conversation with him as well. I figured once both our bodies settled, I'd talk to June about the real reason for my recent disappearances.

I had to spill all the tea tonight regarding Miles, Virginia and this new love for life I had been blessed with. I wanted him to agree to be a part of my life, but I was ready for whatever. Truth be told, I loved June to death. He had everything I ever wanted in a man. However, I wouldn't lose sleep if he decided to do something different. Whatever worked for your heart, that's what daddy would say.

***

Waking up the next day, I was ready to get it all out in the open. I fixed us breakfast and started the conversation by trying to get a feel for what he was feeling.

"You seem like you got some stuff on your mind, Beauty. What's up?"

Because I didn't feel like playing and beating around the bush, I just came out with it. "I took Cash and her sister out. They killed my brother and stashed his son, my nephew, in Yonkers. He's four years old and his name is Miles. I paid his grandmother, the only living relative, to sign over her rights to Miles and leave New York. Deena has him in Virginia. I came back to tie up a few loose ends."

"Loose ends? Loose ends, B? Am I a loose end?" He asked angrily. Before I could answer, he went in. "How long have you known all this?"

I shrugged. "A while," I replied. "What information did you have, June? I know you and Casey messed around. Everyone was under the impression you were Miles's father... until we saw him. He was the spitting image of my brother. I asked you about Miles and you had no idea what I was talking about.

"I knew about the baby, the beef, and your brother sliding through shorty on occasion. I never saw him. I just agreed to play along because I knew she was leaving and who the fucked cared anyway? I can't believe you been fuckin' wit' me all this time and looking at me sideways. Who the fuck are you?"

"June, listen. Let me say this. I didn't know what part you played in this. You can't fault me for wanting to find out. I never thought ill of you or looked at you sideways. I was praying to God you were on the right side. Loyalty is not a luxury for me. It's a necessity. I had to be sure. So, I waited until I had my facts straight, and here we are."

"Yeah, here the fuck we are. Now what?"

"Now, you pack up and come to Virginia with me and Deena. I love you and I want you in my life. I totally understand if it's not what you want. So, I'm asking you to come with me."

He was not even looking at me. His eyebrows were raised beyond his forehead. June was pissed off. *Uh oh,* I thought. What was he thinking? I couldn't read him. All the lines read anger.

June got up and walked to the window. He stood there a good five minutes in complete silence. I walked over after a while.

"What's up, babes? What you thinking?" I asked.

"I'm thinking you should go and raise your nephew. You should go and do what your heart is telling you to do."

"What's your heart saying, June?"

"My heart? My heart is saying I crave you. My heart is saying I need you near me. But my head is saying who the fuck are you? You murdered two people in cold blood. Do I love you more for going that hard for your family? Do I run because you're that fucking ruthless. I don't know, B."

I didn't know how to respond, so I just stood there thinking to myself. *So, what the fuck you gon do? I'm good either way.*

He turned and walked out. My heart fell to my feet and my body went numb. My eyes began to water. For all of ten seconds, I felt something. I gave a fuck. Nevertheless, when I got to eleven, I got my shit, got in my car, and went on about my life. I was a firm believer in no fucking worries. If it was supposed to be, it would be.

***

By the time I got back to VA, Deena and Miles were asleep. He even slept like Rome.

I didn't want to wake them, so I went up to my room and laid down for a while. I woke up hearing Miles playing his game and Deena fixing breakfast. The table had four settings instead of three. I looked around for that fourth person, but I didn't see anyone.

"Deena, why you got an extra place set at the table?" I asked.

"Ummm, just wishful thinking, I guess."

"Huh? I replied, puzzled as hell.

I heard the toilet flush upstairs. As I run to the stairs trying to see who it was, someone was coming down the steps. That smell. I knew that smell. As the figure began to move down the steps, I saw the biggest brown eyes and a smile that I'd die to see every morning.

It was him. "June! June! Deena!" I yelled.

"Beauty, shut up and kiss him, Sissy." Deena chuckled.

I fell into his arms. We hugged so tightly that I almost couldn't breathe. I had to go over it all in my head.

"B, when I looked around and you weren't there, I realized that a piece of me was missing. You gonna have to trust me, Beauty. I'd never hurt you."

"I believe you," I answered.

We all sat down to have breakfast and it felt like… home.

WET

Harlem's Heiress

WET

I'm Harley, short for Harlem, and I literally went from the womb to the wild. I was born into struggle, born into sin, as grandma would say. Since the highchair days, all I knew was Daddy, Preem, and my city, Harlem.

Mommy left when I was four years old. She and daddy fought constantly about money and her hanging out so late. Eventually, her needy addictive personality drove her to drugs. She hid it well for quite a long time. She kept a job and at least she didn't look like a crackhead.

Needless to say, the pipe began to speak a language of its own. We would see her from time-to-time for a while. However, that memory quickly began to fade. She became just another slab of cement embedded in that concrete jungle that we called home.

I loved New York. It was all I knew. The buildings that blocked out the sunlight from corner-to-corner, the cold hard image it possessed and rightfully so, it was automatically embedded within each and every soul that dwelled there long enough. I loved the ruggedness that taught you, "*only the strong survive*". It wasn't just a cliché. It was my home and I even craved it sometimes when I was away.

After a few years, we didn't talk about Mommy at all anymore. Once it set in that Mommy was really gone and more than likely wasn't coming back, things began to drastically change. Daddy, always a hard worker, he had two jobs and did a little hustling on the side to compensate. He tried to keep it on the hush, but Harlem raised me and I wasn't slow by any means.

WET

Look. Listen. Observe. That was what my environment had to offer. The loudest in the room was the weakest in the room; at least, that's what Preem would say.

I always knew what time it was. I noticed the manner in which people began to treat us. They showed mad respect, even to the point of kissing major ass. They were kissing behind and overcompensating daily, but I got any and everything I ever asked for.

Manny at the corner store was my favorite. He often allowed my friends and I to come and get snacks and play with Izzy's' dollhouse. She was his daughter. She had the most amazing doll house. It had wooden floors and stairs, furniture in every room, the toilet flushed, lights turned on and off, and she even had dolls.

Izzy's family had loot. They owned clubs, bodegas, and laundromats across NYC. He was like a brother to Mommy and stayed close, even after her "breakdown".

My brother, Preem, he was my brother from another mother, as they would say. Literally, we just had the same dad. His mom died at childbirth. He was about fifteen years older than me, so he treated me more like a daughter than a baby sister.

Daddy somewhat checked out when mommy left. But, Preem got mean, angry, and hungry as hell. Not for food, though. He was on a major mission. He stayed on his grind like no one I'd ever known. Oh yeah, and let's not forget, overprotective on a thousand! He swore I'd break if it rained; melt like sweet white chocolate when it was too hot. He was my hero. Preem, Daddy, and Harlem, in that order.

I was at Izzy's one day after school and Preem came to pick me up. On the walk home, he brought something up that I never paid attention to.

"Why you always over 'dey crib? She don't come see you?" He said.

I thought about it for a few seconds and replied, "If I had a dollhouse like hers, I'd stay home and play with it."

Preem glanced down at me. "Right on, Shorty. God bless the child that's got his own." He grabbed my hand. "Yeah, Harlem raised you."

I woke the next morning and went to the kitchen for breakfast, on the table sat the newest edition of the Barbie Dream House. The pool, the car, and Ken! Two black Ken dolls and accessories like you wouldn't imagine. The Brooklyn barbie even had a little yorkie on a leash attached to her hand. I was so happy that I cried happy tears. I couldn't believe my eyes.

From then on, Izzy and all her homegirls were coming to my house after school. I took the lesson there to not so much be about having the *"material things"*, but him wanting me feeling confident enough to know I could. If you wanted it, go get it. He loved me enough to want me to believe I was worth it. For that, I was forever grateful.

From then on, I began to see more and more money. We were eating steaks, shrimp, lobster tails, and fresh baked bread. I was confused. But, in a way, I wasn't really. I knew Daddy and Manny had gotten tighter over the years. I also knew that queen-sized bed with the canopy on top didn't fall from the sky.

Supreme was spending lots of dough, too. He had the newest Jordan's and fresh polo shirts in every color, for every day of the week. Even though Preem wasn't Mommy's, she was all he knew. She loved him too, as much as she loved me. Slowly, I could see my brother's heart breaking when Mommy left. Deep down inside, I think he knew without her, Daddy would fall apart, and it would all be on him. He knew his childhood was over. Preem knew he'd loved me enough to stay here and raise me like I was his; even if I didn't understand it at the time.

I would eventually grow to see all the pieces fit. Make no mistake, Harlem, as cold as it was, it also taught me to love hard when warranted, remain loyal to the bone, and to protect and preserve your life and that of your loved ones to a fault. Preem would say, "Fuck that, Shorty. Go for yours."

I learned to use every tool to my advantage. I had to. It was my 12th birthday and Preem and Daddy planned a huge birthday celebration for me. I was a preteen that was a big deal, apparently.

Izzy kept hinting around about it not being a party. I had no idea what they were up to. I got home from school that night and there was a package on my bed. I tore it apart, excited to see my gift. It was a red and white Adidas jogging suit with the red and white shell tops to match. I showed it to Preem at Albee Square Mall a few weeks before. Inside the shoe box was a note that read, *a car will pick you and Izzy up in one hour.*

Just as I went to try on my outfit, I noticed another package. It was a license plate that read **Heiress**. I figured it was something to hang on my wall. I was twelve, not quite old enough to drive. So, I shrugged it off and proceeded to get ready for my night.

"Harleeeeeyyy!" Izzy screamed with her Boricua slang. "The Puerto Rican goddess is here. Oh, your outfit is fresh." She added.

"I know, right? It's a gift from Preem." I smiled.

"Where we going?" Izzy asked curiously.

I shrugged. "I have no idea. Preemo said the car would be here in an hour."

That was about fifty-three minutes ago. We raced to the fire escape and there was a black stretch limo out front… in Harlem, on 126 Street. *Fresh to death*, we thought.

We jumped on the elevator, headed for our ride. As we exited the building, the street was flooded with neighborhood people. They had balloons and candy, screaming and shouting. They wished me a happy birthday and let the balloons fly up into the clouds as we got into the limo. It was so sweet, even though I knew Preem probably paid them to do it.

I knew some of them genuinely loved my mother and wanted to see us happy. I blew kisses and waved like I was Whitney Houston singing, *'Dance with Somebody'*.

After about a forty-five-minute ride, we pulled up at this building.

"It looks like a skating rink," Izzy said. It kind of did. I'd love to see it lit up. It had so many lights on it.

Maino opened my door, then Izzy's. We hopped out in anticipation of something over the top. That it was. The marquee on the front of the building lit up and it read, *Harlem's.*

Izzy and I were speechless. Preem and Daddy came running out the front door with lilies, my favorite and Mommy's too. There were more balloons and a set of keys.

"Hey, is this where my party is being thrown at?" I asked. Preem and Daddy laughed.

"Come on in girls." Daddy said.

As we walked in, lights began to flash, music played and my friends from school and from around the block came out of nowhere.

"Surprise! Surprise!" They shouted.

Daddy took the mic. "Baby girl, I love you. You've grown to look just like your mother." I did. I was the spitting image of her, in a smaller body.

He began to tear up and slowly limped his way to Preem. Daddy handed him the mic. "Harleyyyyy, happy birthday, lil one. This is not just where your party is at, it's your spot forever. I bought you this rink so you never have to get kicked out of another. I love you, lil sis, and don't let nobody ever tell you that you ain't Harlem's heiress."

I was stunned into a state of shock, but on cloud nine at the same damn time. Oh, and by the way, the plates I found earlier were for my convertible Mustang when I turned sixteen.

***

As time went on, we seemed to get richer and richer. Preem even put me in private school and a year later, he convinced Manny to let Izzy come too. However, Preem loved Harlem, so we never moved, except to a larger, more expensive high-rise. It was still in Harlem, though.

Harlem was our root and we were the branches. Our foundation was there. To leave would be like leaving a piece of us there also. We'd lost a lot to Harlem. Knowing Harlem would eat up our souls, we stayed anyway.

I was about to turn sixteen when I realized that Preem had run away all my friends that were not girls. All the things he made sure I learned, he never taught me about the birds and the bees. Izzy and I talked a good game, but neither of us had actually done anything with boys, yet. She was dying to be like her sisters, but I somehow believed she was waiting for me. Preem on the other hand, he was a male hoe. He had heifers running in and out of the house regularly.

I got a little curious and decided I was gonna see what all the hype was about. Preem came home about midnight with this lil slut bucket named Kia, he frequented her from time to time, so I hid in his closet.

I know. I know. How rude and nasty, right? But I wanted to know and no one would dare talk to me about the "D".

Times like that, I missed Mommy. After all, I had started my period years ago. Shouldn't I have known more than what I read in health class?

Preem went to the shower while Kia rolled up some weed for them. She rolled up, turned on the WBLS *Quiet Storm*, and took off her clothes; which didn't take long because she was barely wearing any to begin with.

She hopped in the shower with Preem, singing along to En Vogue's *Giving Him Something He Can Feel*.

You nasty hussy, I thought to myself. I liked the song, though. Damn, she closed the curtain. I couldn't see anything. I could hear, though. So, I crept a little closer to the bathroom door and slid to the edge of the bed. I heard Preem.

"Lemme lick that pussy clean," he growled.

"Hell yeah, daddy. That's what I came here for." Kia responded.

It got quiet, then suddenly, I heard skin slapping against water and water slapping against skin.

"Grab my ass, baby." Kia moaned, letting out these wondrous sounds. I could tell she was in another world, speaking another language.

"Mmm... mmmhm, Preem. Damn, baby. I need you to beat it up now. Beat it up! Oh, shit." She was practically screaming now.

Is he gonna hit her? I thought. Before I could catch my breath, I heard the shower curtain rings pull back and then the water shut off. I ducked down and slid under the bed, as far as I could.

Preem slammed her onto the bed facedown. Pinning both hands beneath her breasts, he grabbed her waist, and pushed her head down on the mattress. Ass completely in the air, he licked it for a few seconds. Then, he rammed his situation inside her.

The sheets started coming off the bed and Preem began to holler at her. "Throw it back." He urged.

Apparently, she was throwing it because the bed was moving back and forth, hitting the wall harder each time. I started to feel funny. My belly button was tingly or something. I noticed my breasts becoming more sensitive, all the while still fascinated by what I was witnessing up close and personal. I had never even watched a flick.

It must have felt amazing because both of them were moaning, groaning, and calling each other's names. At one point, I could have sworn I heard Preem beg her to fuck him back and he called her a bitch.

"Fuck me harder then, niggah." Kia responded.

Laughing to myself, but secretly wondering what was so good to them, I began to get the urge to touch myself. Down there! I started to rub my fingers across my pussy to a rhythm it seemed to like. With each movement, I learned a new and more pleasing way to tantalize my own body. I started getting warm all over and my panties were getting wet. I had no idea what the hell was happening.

Suddenly, it grew quiet and the both of them were just laying there, still slightly humping, as if to get the last little bit of cream out the cookie.

About three minutes went by. *Damn, I'm stuck.* I thought. However, Preem got up and headed to the bathroom. Thank God his strumpet followed, giggling.

"Damn, daddy. You make me wild. Let's do it again. Oooh, my pussy so wet." She purred.

Of course, didn't he just dump babies there? Ewe. I thought of what I just witnessed and cringed at the fact that I was still curious as hell.

I didn't want to take any chances of being caught. This was my way out. So, I slid from under the bed and tip-toed out of the room.

So that's it? I wasn't at all impressed. Needless to say, I was more curious than I was before; I just knew I couldn't do it. My brother would kill any guy that came near me, let alone popped my cherry.

Growing up with two men in the house, I knew a lot about how men thought, how their egos worked, and how to weaken their manhood, as well as how to strengthen it. They taught me to think like a man, get money like a man, and beware of all men. As sheltered and spoiled as I may have been, I was a beast when it came to my family. They were all I had. There was nothing I wouldn't do to keep them around.

***

It was Izzy's 16th birthday and we planned a party at Harlem's. The party was slammin', as all of our parties were. Manny held back no expenses. Izzy's money tree was 16ft tall and full of hundred-dollar bills. Preem, Daddy, and Manny were the biggest drug dealers in NYC. We'd eventually come to realize it, we dealt with it, and moved right along with it.

After the party, Reese, Izzy, Torey, and I hopped on the d-train and headed for C.I.; Coney Island that is. Reese was the only male friend that stuck around long enough for me to see what it was like to tongue kiss. I'd let him feel up on me from time-to-time. I was careful with that, though. Preem always told me to never start something you couldn't finish, never lead a man on, it could be dangerous, and all men weren't nearly as respectful as he was.

Reese was different. He liked me. He liked being around me. I could tell by his smile and the way he looked at me. He avoided Preem, but he was never really afraid of him. He figured, if he could keep the peace, he could stay around, and he was right. Preem tolerated him because he stood up to him. I think that told Preem he was really interested in keeping me as a friend.

"Is it just me or does anybody else want Nathan's"? I asked.

WET

"I could eat some cheese fries." Izzy replied. Torey and Izzy had been dating a while, since 4th grade actually. Izzy was a bit faster than me. She had two older sisters who damn near screwed the whole Fordham Rd. So, she knew all about sex, she just hadn't done it yet.

"I want a swinging car," Reese suggested.

"Me too." I replied.

Upon entering our car, a red swinging one like I always picked, I whispered in the attendant's ear to keep mine and Izzy's car at the top as long as he could, and Reese handed him a twenty dollar bill.

The attendant grinned. "Okay, go 'head up!"

On our way up, I noticed Torey handed Reese something and they both smiled and crossed their fingers. I disregarded the notion as I admired the background. I could see the whole city. It always made me feel larger than life when I rode the Wonder Wheel and literally sat on top of the world; even if it was for just a few moments.

Reese was looking good as hell. I wondered what was on his mind. He was quiet and seemed preoccupied.

"You good, Reese?" I asked

"Yes, Heiress," that was another nickname I had adopted. I nodded and replied, "I'm good."

He stood up and moved toward me, placing one hand on each of my cheeks. "You are my best friend and I think I love you." He confessed.

I was speechless. A few seconds went by and there it was... that kiss I'd been waiting for, those butterflies I longed to feel, they fluttered inside me. My eyes seemed to shut automatically, and his touch got even more graceful.

Our car began to sway in the sky. So, he held on tighter, still kissing me so sincerely. He stood me up and pinned me between himself and the doors of the car and

WET

began to dance with me. There was no music, but the sounds from the sky, the sounds from below, and the melodies coming from us both forced our bodies to move together.

I started to get that same feeling I got when Preem got with Kia. It was more intense though. I felt one hand slide up the slit in my mini dress and Reese began to softly explore the breeze between my knees. He watched my reactions. He knew when I was scared and would back off. He knew when I was curious and would engage. He understood that my flower hadn't bloomed yet and remained patient. *That* was turning me on.

Reese looked at me and asked if he could kiss me... on my other lips. I giggled like a virgin and nodded my head, yes. He sat me on the bench in our car, he spread and propped both legs up, one on each of his shoulders. He blew on my clit softly. I began to shiver.

"You aight?" he asked.

"I think so," I replied.

He took his thumbs and carefully opened each side of me, exposing my clit to the cool night's air, then he covered it with his warm wet lips.

Dear God, I thought. I couldn't close my mouth; trying to be sexy like on the soap operas, but I was feeling anxious and freaky as hell. I went with the ladder. I began to feed him, holding his head in both hands so I controlled his mouth's movements.

He ate all he could until I decided I wanted it all. *'Fuck it do you shorty'*, that's what Preem would say. I wasn't being a hoe because Reese loved him some me, and besides, I wanted to fuck him.

WET

Reese reached into his pocket and pulled out a condom. I bet that's what Torey handed him. I didn't trip, in fact, I asked if I could put it on.

He snickered "Hell yeah. It's your world Heiress."
That turned me on even more. I slid the condom on his dick slowly. It was kind of funny looking to me, because it was curved at the tip. I didn't have much to compare it to; however, I had seen some penises in pictures and on TV. His was fat and about as long as my foot without toes and bent at the tip.

After spitting all over my panties and me sliding the condom on, he flipped me around so I could enjoy the view of the city and he could enjoy me from behind. He moved slow and carefully, knowing it was my first time.

I was a little scared. All kinds of thoughts began to run through my mind. Would it hurt? Would I like it? Would he still like me after?

I gripped the gate of the Ferris Wheel car and let out a scandalous cry. He slowed up. "Are you ok, Harley? Your body is perfect, just like I'd always dreamed." He whispered into my sweetness as he continued to stroke inside me.

I noticed the hooked, curved, slight abnormality was hitting a spot I had no idea existed. I wanted to scream, and he knew it, so he gently covered my mouth with one hand and wrapped his free arm around my waist and thrusted in and out, breathing hard on the back of my neck. Sweet soft periodic kisses landed on my ear lobes.

159

I felt him thrust one… no, two more times. "Ahhhh mannn," he cried out.

Three. Four. Five more strokes. My whole body began to shake. He was literally holding me up. I was weak. I couldn't feel my legs. However, I could feel his sweat sticking to my neck, back, and ass cheeks. He seemed to have visited heaven.

As I turned to look at him, his eyes were gleaming, almost teary or glassy like he just put one in the air. He kissed me on the lips, the forehead, then he intertwined both his hands with mine. "No matter what happens from here, you will always be my first love and my best friend." He told me.

"Ditto," I replied in the midst of a pinky swear and a sweet simple kiss.

I loved Reese but something was missing. I felt like I was almost obligated to give him some. He had been around begging since forever and had always been an amazing friend. Besides, I was tired of being Harlem's only virgin. I was curious and horny too, I suppose. However, I was a bit sad I'd given myself to someone I knew I wouldn't spend the rest of my life with. I was sure of that.

***

It was junior year of high school. Izzy and I were so excited. We had major plans already mapped out for the year and after graduation. It was the time to begin placing our pieces on the board.

WET

Daddy finally let me get my driver's license and the keys to my Mustang I'd gotten a few years back. The **Heiress** plate went perfect with it. My 16th birthday wasn't for a few weeks, but Daddy and Preem knew I'd just die if I had to wait another day. So, they handed me the keys.

They both had this look. They looked like they were about to lose the most precious thing they'd ever known. Me! I could see it in Preem's eyes and Daddy just spit out rules of the road and how to maneuver through rush hour.
   "I'm gonna be fine boys." I assured them. "I'm not a baby anymore."

   Daddy looked at me. "You'll always be my baby," He sounded so sincere as he turned and walked away.
   Preem turned to me after we were alone. "Do you lil one and never forget who you are, Harlem's Heiress. Don't ever forget that! Do you, Shorty." He yelled in his Tupac *Thug Life* voice. I was sad that they were sad, but glad I was all grown up now. I had big plans for my future.

   The next day, Preem started asking how I wanted to celebrate my 16th birthday. I wanted to do something different this year. In my mind, this was the big one.

   I remembered Mommy used to always take us to Prospect Park. We would have picnics, go hiking on the trails, and ride the merry-go-round. I told Preem to take over Prospect Park, not thinking that he really would. However, he did just that.

   I woke up Friday morning. It was my birthday. I was so excited that I screamed, "It's my birthday! Capricorns

161

Starzpen

rule!" I ran through the house, thinking for sure they'd have breakfast or something going on. There wasn't nobody home, though. *Really?* Daddy was never gone this early and Preem usually woke me when he left for *"work."*

Oh well, damn. I figured I'd head to school, not thinking much of it. It was a good day. I got lots of cards and gifts from friends and some teachers who kissed Preem's ass on the regular. Izzy got us tickets to go see Mary J. Blige at The Garden. My girl always came through with the best gifts and I was grateful.

Maino pulled up and told Izzy and I that Daddy and Preem would meet us at the park. We hurried home to shower, change, and get fly before we headed to the celebration. Upon arriving at the park, I noticed a line of cars parked on the street. It seemed to be a parade or pep rally.

"Izzy, what's all that?" I asked.

"I don't know. Let's hop out here and see." She suggested.

"Maino, we're gonna get out here." I told our driver and he pulled over to let us out.

As we approached the park's entrance, I spotted Daddy on a huge stage talking on the microphone. Izzy and I looked at each other, both wondering what the heck was going on out there.

Suddenly, the beat dropped and someone started playing my song, *Real Love* by Mary J. Blige. She and Preem were acquaintances, so I'd met her a few times before. Izzy and I started dancing and singing along.

WET

"I'm searching for a real love, someone to set my heart free... real love." We swayed from side-to-side.

Preem ran over and led me to the stage. As I climbed up, Mary came out singing, *Missing You.*

Oh my God. I almost fainted. She even shouted me out as Harlem's Heiress in between song lyrics. It was amazing. This was the best party ever, Daddy and Preem literally shut down Prospect Park. They really came through. They even let me take a shot of gin while Izzy and I sang to Snoop Dog's *Gin and Juice.*

We were all having a great time dancing, laughing, hugging, and just loving up on each other, all for me. When the night began to die down, and people began to clear out, the terrifying sound of gunshots rang out.

Pop. Pop. Pop. Pop.

They were deafening. It was utter chaos. Screams filled the air from the street. Omg. Somebody got shot. I ran over and saw Izzy lying on the ground, bleeding. A man was laid out on the side of her, he appeared dead. Then, I saw Daddy sprawled out in the street with bullet holes in his chest.

Before my body could collapse, Maino swooped me up and I heard Preem yelling.

"Get her the fuck out of here, now!" He demanded with his pistol in hand, frantically standing over Daddy, crying.

Somehow, I broke away from Maino and ran back to where Daddy and Izzy laid, dead. I screamed both their names, wishing they'd just get up.

"Daddy, noooooo! Wake up, Daddy. Get up." I cried. Preem and Maino pulled me away again.

"Izzzy. Izzyyyy." I fought against them. She wasn't moving and Daddy was bleeding from the mouth. I knew that meant internal bleeding.

As sirens approached, Preem became angry and told Maino he'd shoot him if he didn't get me to car now. I wanted to stay to be with my family.

***

Once Maino got me home, he carried me in the house. Reese was there with a few other friends and some of Preem's posse. They were strapped up in my living room, guarding windows and doors. I was in shock. I couldn't believe what was happening.

My brother came running in the back door. He told Maino to get the truck out the garage so they could go to the hospital. I looked at him, as if to say, *'take me with you, please'*.

Preemo read my mind. "Come on, lil one. Let's go," he said.

On the ride over, everyone was silent. All of our beepers were going off and none of us cared enough to acknowledge the constant beeping. Approaching the emergency room's entrance at Kings County, I ran in to find Daddy and Izzy. Preem was moving in slow motion. He was scared to death at what we'd find.

WET

The doctor came out with an empathetic look. I broke when he told us Daddy died on the way to the hospital and Izzy… she was still alive, but in critical condition. In that exact moment, Manny came storming down the long hallway leading to Izzy's room. He looked at us and fell to his knees. I almost fell with him.

The doctor let us go in to see Izzy. She was in a coma. Her mom was dead, similar to mine, but she would never ever see her mom again. In my heart, I somehow always believed I would see Mommy alive and well, someday.

While Preem handled Daddy's arrangements, I never left Izzy's side. She died two day later, though. The day before I buried my father and my best friend, my sister dead… on my birthday.

I knew every birthday from then on would be a mixture of my life and their deaths. I would never celebrate another birthday the same. I'd shed tears June 6th of every year to come.
I spoke at Daddy and Izzy's funerals, wanting to pass out each time. As they lowered their bodies into the ground, pieces of me were buried too. I felt empty and numb; angry and hurt; sad and lonely.

I was alive. So, why did I feel so awful? Did I feel guilt somehow? They were all there because of me. Knowing that was far from the truth was one thing; however, convincing myself was another.

Preem was broken, but he was always good at being a pillar for everyone else's hurt. He was emotionless at times but I could see him die inside every time he walked past Daddy's room, his car, and every time we saw Manny, another piece of Preem would break off.

Manny was never the same after Izzy died. He stopped running the store and barely washed anymore. Everything changed. Things became dark.

Our dollhouses sat side by side in the basement of Manny's club. We'd go there and have our own party off the music above while Preem worked the club. I missed those days. I missed her. In a way, I expected Daddy would die soon, but not in a wishful type of way. He lived his life, for the most part. But Izzy had so much more to give.

Daddy's death ached and made me sad. I couldn't have him anymore. Izzy's death hardened my heart, yet somehow, it humbled my soul. They never found out who was responsible for the shootout. It may have been random. No one seemed to know anything. All we knew was that Harlem would never be the same.

After the shootings, Preem moved Maino in with us. I think Preem wanted some extra hands around. Maino was my driver, but Preem had taken him under his wing before I was even born. So, he was my friend too.

Jermaine, who we called Maino for short, was a silly dude that could fix anything. His real passion was cooking. Preem talked about sending him to culinary school. Maino was autistic. You couldn't tell at first glance, but he didn't try and hide it either. Sometimes, he even used it to his advantage. He would always say, '*people treat you like you dumb let them keep thinking you dumb.*' I ain't stupid," he'd say. "I just look like dis."

He loved Preem like he was his daddy and me... well, let's just say, if Maino had a little sister, it'd probably be me. Harley Pooh, that's what he called me. When Maino's parents died in a car crash, Daddy and Preem looked out for him and never stopped.

Oftentimes, when a parent passed on, the children usually worried about money and how they would survive. Not me though, Preem had vowed after Mommy left that we would never struggle, never be hungry, homeless, or poor! Little did I know; Daddy felt the same way.

Maino brought the mail in and I saw an envelope from Sam Starks. He was Daddy's lawyer. It was addressed to Preem and I. Opening the envelope I clearly saw a check with a note from Sam. It read:

I have already withdrew my fees from this settlement. As instructed by your father, the rest is to be split down the middle between you and your sister, Harlem. I'm sorry for your recent losses and will be here if you need anything.

I glanced down at the check amount and did a double take. *Huh? whaaat? 3.2 million dollars.*
"Preeeeeeeeem," I screamed. "Where did Daddy get this kind of money from?"
"Oh, that's the insurance policy he took out when mom died. We added you when you were born." Preem shrugged.

WET

Seriously, although the money seemed bittersweet, I couldn't help but feel like someone had to die for me to live lavish. I thought of all the things Izzy and I dreamed of doing after graduation. I made up in my mind I would do them all. In her name!

***

Graduation was near and I dreaded walking across the stage without my sister and my daddy with me. I felt like I was betraying Izzy somehow. I requested the school honor her by putting her cap and gown in an empty seat with her picture attached. They were happy to be a part of that tribute and decided to sit her right next to Daddy and Preem. They were a faithful funding source for my school. He donated big bucks. They kissed his ass also.

I couldn't crack one smile during the ceremony. I was holding back tears the entire time. All I could think of was these empty seats next to me and that damn college foundation commercial playing in my ear.

"Save a place for meeeeee!" It echoed on repeat.

The tears began to fall. Maino and Preem noticed and both placed their arms around me, in an attempt to block the pain. Sweet and all, but it didn't work. I was crushed. Deep down, I knew I had to keep pushing. I could already feel the gleam beaming off the pot of gold at the end of the rainbow.

WET

After graduation, Preem handed me the papers to my car. "Congrats, Lil One. You are now literally Harlem's Heiress. Wear your crown well and make us all proud." He smiled.

Maino jumped up and down like a little kid. "Salute, Queen. Salute!" He shouted while sucking on a blow pop.

I kissed him on the cheek and told him I would see him later. They stood there, watching me drive off like it was the last time they'd see me. I knew another piece of them was dying. Change was inevitable. How you embraced the change determined who you really were… as Preem would say. He was smart and thugged out to his heart, but he wasn't a dummy. He lived the life that was handed to him and wanted nothing but the best for the ones he loved.

I had my life all planned out in regard to my future. Isabella was a huge part of that. I called her that when she cursed me in Spanish, and she hated it.

We had plans to go to medical school and start a free clinic for women and children. Yeah, I could still do it, but I no longer had the desire to do so without her. I hadn't touched Daddy's insurance money yet. I really hadn't needed it. Preem had crazy loot and since Izzy's doll house days, I've never wanted for anything. My brother made sure of that.

The insurance money just sat in an account for the next four years. I had decided to go back to school, but for fashion design. I wanted to style runway models as well as create my own line.

Preem was still messing around with Kia, surprisingly. They decided to marry. She was all happy like she had won the lottery. Well, in a way, she did hit the jackpot. Kia had been around a long time. So, I knew Preem loved her.

She wanted me in the wedding, so we were out dress shopping and cake tasting one day. Kia got a call and stared at me the whole time she was on the phone.

"Harley!! Harley!! Call Maino. We gotta get to the hospital, now!"

"Why, Kia. What's wrong?"

"It's Preem." She screamed.

My heart sank I began to have flash backs of Daddy's and Izzy's bodies lying in pools of blood on the cold concrete. I started to feel my knees weaken.

"What? What, Kia? What happened?" I stuttered.

"Preem was in a car accident. He's in intensive care." That was all she offered as Maino pulled up, tires screeching. He hopped out to open the doors. Again, the ride was silent. No one said a word.

Reaching the hospital, Kia sprinted into the lobby where she ran right into Preem's ex. Automatically, they began throwing blows. Security was running up on them. I gestured for that scallywag to get the hell out of there

"They're getting married, bitch. Go home" I hollered.

Preem's ex looked down at Kia's hand and said, "Oh this motherfucker," and stormed out.

Kia didn't seem too fixated on the drama that transpired seconds prior. She knew she was number one and had been for a while now. So, she let her leave. However, I was heated. Man! I was so down to assist in having Preem's ex admitted to the emergency room after we beat her ass in there. I needed to hit something. I needed to release some pressure.

Racing up to Preem's room, it seemed like it took forever as we sped up the long lonely hallways. I could hear Daddy's voice, He was saying, "Preemo, what the hell have you done now, son?"

Somehow, I could feel Mommy too. It filled me up but terrified me at the same time. Kia was beside herself, cursing out nurses for moving too slow, crying and screaming because they wouldn't let us in yet.

Finally, after an hour or so, the doctors told us that we could visit, but only for a few moments. Kia grabbed my hand and we walked in together. I was so scared for us all. Preemo was all I had left. I begged God to make him get up. I pleaded with every angel for grace and mercy on his soul.

Preem was conscious and I was grateful. He looked at me and said "There go shorty. You really gotta woman up now, lil one. I think this may be my last stand," he let out a strained laugh, gasping painfully.

I began to tell my brother how much I loved him and needed him. I pleaded with him to find the strength to make everything go away. He grabbed my arm and pulled me closer, whispering in my ear.

"Always keep Maino near," His voice was so weak as he squeezed my hand with what seemed like all his might. "I told you I'd see Daddy before you, Lil One." He added.

"Maino, maaan!" Preem pushed out extending his fist toward him. Maino grabbed his heart with one hand and buried his face in the other.

"Ki Ki! Stay sweet, baby, you always been number one. Stay close." Preem was spitting blood from his mouth trying to squeeze out his last words.

"I love you too, baby." Kia replied, crying hysterically.

"Not yet, Preem." I cried. "I love you. What am I gonna do without you?"

"You gon' live, Shorty. You gon' be exactly who we taught you to be. You don't need me.

"But I'll miss you. I do need you!" I screeched.

"Harley, go get yours... you and mmm... mmm... Mommy." Preem's hold on my hand loosened as his head dropped back. I literally saw my brother float away. 93 million miles away, we'd say.

Suddenly, his equipment started beeping and lights began to flash. Nurses and doctors ran in, pushing us all out the door. I watched through the crack in the curtain as they tried to save him. His body was jerking with every hit from the paddles. No matter how hard they tried and how loud I screamed his name, he wouldn't wake up.

I was devastated, alone, and terrified to be in this world without them. I was now mourning not only my whole family, but my life as I'd known it. Any and all familiarity disappeared in that instant. Kia rested her head in Maino's arms, just to realize she would have to hold him up instead.

WET

Maino began to hit the walls, smack himself on the head, and bang his head on the walls, causing the doctors to place their attention on him. They ended up having to sedate him.

My brother took care of everyone he loved, including Jermaine. I knew I had to take over. Surprisingly, I buried my devastation quicker than I thought possible. I was sure it would resurface someday, but I couldn't wallow in self-pity. So, I did the opposite and decided to woman *up*.

Daddy, Izzy, and now Preem were gone. I was all alone; except for Maino. I was angry and almost bitter. I was sure after some time went by, Kia would fade away also. She never did though. Surprising to me, she stayed in my life and took on the role of Big Sis. I loved her for that; especially since I knew Preem really loved her.

I hadn't touched Daddy's or Preem's things ever since they passed. Their rooms and belongings were exactly as they'd left them.

***

I was about to graduate from NYU with a degree in fashion. *I made it,* I thought. I had to admit, Maino and Kia pushed me to my limits. I doubt I could have done it without them. We were supposed to be here together.

I was so scared I would fail; certain I couldn't do it without Izzy, my daddy, and I definitely didn't think I'd make it without Supreme.

WET

After serious debate, I made the decision to leave Harlem. There were too many memories. I needed to make new memories to share the old ones with. Harlem was the home of all the heartache and loss all I'd ever known. My root, my protector, my whole being was gone. Harlem was my everything.

While cleaning out all the items, I donated them to Goodwill and some of Preem's neighborhood homeboys. Of course, Maino grabbed what he wanted first. In the midst of cleaning, I stumped my toe on a floor tile that seemed loose. I pulled the panel back and there was a huge metal box down there. It was too heavy for me to pick up, so I hollered for Maino.

"Yes, Lil' One." He replied, making his way into the room with me.

"Come help me see what this is."

Maino pulled the box out and snapped the top back. I was in awe. We both gasped.

Maino started clapping and hitting himself in the head in excitement. Cash money! All hundred-dollar bills were in the metal box from what we could see. I wasn't impressed, I was more so surprised, wondering where all the money had come from.

Inside the container, there was a postcard from an unfamiliar place. I looked at the date and it was postmark stamped for twenty years ago, from Cairo. There was a key and a letter addressed to Preem. I opened it and immediately felt a heartbeat. It was Mommy. Twenty years ago!

WET

I was seven back then. That confirmed she was alive and well; at least when I was seven. The letter read as:

Supreme,

I couldn't handle the drugs alone. I couldn't handle the city's rage and Harlem's heartbreak anymore. I need help. I'm leaving the country and don't know when and if I will ever come back. So, I beg you, please look after Harley. She needs you. Joseph will wither and fade now that I'm gone. I always knew that. As selfish as it may seem, I'd rather see you happy than sad, watching me destroy myself along with everything I loved. I know you will be her rock. Please give her my contact when you think she's ready. I know she hates me for sure, but I can only do what I think is best.

Always,

Mommy

I began having vivid flashes of Preem right before he took his last breath. I could hear him as he pushed out his last words.

"You and mommy," That's what he said. My heart was pounding. I could feel it in my head like a migraine. Boom. Boom. Boom.

The envelope still faintly smelled like her, the whole box did. I didn't hate her, and I wasn't angry with her. Actually, I understood, accepted, and still loved her.

"This was twenty years ago." Maino said. "Long time ago, Harley. Long time." He said, snapping his fingers and making a song out of it. "Long time," Snap. Snap. "Long time, Harley." Snap. Snap.

I couldn't help but laugh and join in. She was in Cairo, Egypt twenty years ago. The wheels in my head started turning. Was she still alive? Was she healthy? Would she want to see me?

"Maino, you wanna go to Egypt?" I asked.

His face lit up. "To see Moses, Lil One?

"See Moses?" I asked.

Maino nodded. He loved the story of Moses and Pharaoh and the "water breaking apart" as he called it.

"Yes, Pharaoh's Village." I confirmed. "I'm gonna get somebody to finish this and go home to get some travel plans together."

I had it in my head I was moving to Egypt. My first thought was, *huh? Why?* But I figured why the hell not?

I got Sam on making travel plans immediately. He would know how to handle things over there after he tried for at least an hour to change my mind. Preem had no children. My best friend and father were dead. Maino was coming with me and Reese, well, Reese would be fine. I'd miss my friend though.

He could come too. I thought humorously, but quite seriously. Preem always told me to keep the loyal ones near and we went back to the playground days. I had to at least extend the offer.

My lawyer, Sam, took care of the condo and Reese declined the move, but promised he would come visit a few weeks after I settled. He promised to call and stay close, as if he were a cab ride away. He promised he'd hop a flight at the drop of a dime, if need be. I knew he would.

As much as I wanted Reese to join me, I knew things were how they were supposed to be. Deep down, I wanted him to find him someone. What we had as teenagers was a genuine love. He said he was and always would be my best friend and I would always be his first love. I teared up as we said goodbye, as did Maino.

Reese began to fade away as we moved toward the boarding gate. Suddenly, I saw Daddy, Preem, Izzy, and in the distance, I could see Mommy too. She wasn't with them, though.

They were all in white and Mommy was all glammed out. She had on a long black silk dress with red heels. She looked beautiful. I had never seen her dressed up. My hopes to find her in Cairo strengthened in that moment. She was the only blood I had left, the only automatic beat to my heart that still had a heartbeat. Mommy! I've learned that no matter how hard we try to convince our hearts that we are okay without family… friends… connections, everyone needed someone.

As I walked to my seat, I felt like someone was pulling life from me, draining me of my strength. I felt a wave of sadness. It was drowning me. I saw flashes of everyone, gone. The reality of change terrified me.

My root was completely exposed now, naked and vulnerable as fuck. I felt completely lost, but confident I was bred from beauty, brains, and boldness. I was built to withstand. Me, Maino, and my bags full of fear stepped out on faith and went for it.

WET

Harlem Meets Cairo

WET

I'd been here for a few years now and still no mommy. I purposely got my house directly across from the address the letter and postcard were sent from. Turned out, it was a local Internet café type spot. The owner said customers used their mailbox because it was a military drop box and the mail traveled safer and faster. I still had crazy hope, almost a certainty regarding my search. I knew if my mother was here, I'd find her. There was no way I could live in a city with my blood and not feel it. I could feel her. I knew it was just a matter of time.

After a while, I knew I wanted to leave Egypt soon. I wanted to find mommy and leave. Maino loved it here. Honestly, he would love it anywhere. I loved him and promised my brother I would keep him under my wing until I took my last breath, or he took his.

Cairo was a beautiful city. Its population reached 19.5 million. I couldn't get used to this third-world atmosphere. Poverty in the States was crucial, but here is it was unbearable to see. That is, if you had a heart anyway. Some communities had no running water, the children created toys from rocks and bones of dead animals, and sometimes the bones of dead soldiers. I would take Maino twice a month and drop off toys, food, clothing, baby items —whatever I saw a need for. Maino had the best time passing out the toys and they loved him too. As we pulled up in the trucks, the children would run past the truck with all the toys and run straight for Maino and I. They genuinely lit up when they saw us coming. The feeling was priceless. I couldn't live good if I sat by and watched them suffer while I could do something to ease their pain. My pockets were padded nicely; my family made sure of that. I often wondered what if they hadn't though. What if I was one of these people? What if I had to fend and defend for my livelihood?

Amina was my contact in the poverty-stricken communities. We met shortly after Maino and I arrived. She was an advocate for women, which was a mission in the danger zone here. She rescued women from abuse, prostitution, and any injustice served by the hands of a man. Amina had been a nurse in the U.S. Air Force for 20 years when she watched an attack on an orphanage that devastated her. After witnessing that horror, she never left. She made it her personal mission to make amends the best way she could for all the lives lost at the hands of the very country she was sworn to honor. When we spoke, and Amina bared her truths, she described watching heads blow off the bodies of infants. She wept over them, watching in shock as other nurses removed body parts that had piled up on top of other children. Bones of children whose bodies actually saved other children from the initial blast were common. Amina lamented the injustice and hypocrisy from the United States. She ran an underground assistance unit for the women wanting to escape violence and poverty, some even migrating to the U.S. in search of peace. She knew a lot of military officials and Embassy people that would help her with anything. She was well connected, and I always felt she would play some part in finding mommy for me.

After a few months of dropping off supplies and assisting Amina where I could, I decided to become more involved in the mission. We began making late night runs to Germany to transport women and children. Maino always accompanied us; he was still my bodyguard and would fight for and with me at all costs. I would do the same for him. His overprotective spirit increased tremendously when Preem died. I knew that feeling all too well. We were literally all we had and Maino was special with his autism. I was all he had. Truthfully, we were all *we* had, and that was alright with us.

The transport truck pulled up one night with a driver Mina and I didn't recognize. Maino saw the confusion on our faces and pulled out immediately.

"Who dat Harley?" Maino asked, gritting hard on the driver.

"Calm down and let's ask him, okay?" I replied in my therapeutic voice.

I walked over to the vehicle and saw a man that appeared to be frightened to death. I was at the window and his eyes were fixated on Maino posted up with the AK-47 looking menacing. He wanted to squeeze his fingers so bad.

Maino moved closer as I approached the window. I gestured for the man to roll down the window. He hesitated for a second then he complied.

"Hi, I'm Harley and you are?" I asked, as I scanned inside the vehicle for anything suspicious.

"I'm Von," he said. "Short for Javon."

Upon hearing the name, Amina quickly rushed to the window and asked for someone named Ishmael. "Ishmael is my half-brother; we share the same father," Von explained.

Von broke the news that Ishmael had been killed last night in an attack on Bahrain. He was going to pick up a mother and her four sons and help them get to safety. They were killed too. "Oh no!!!" Amina cried.

WET

Seeing her grief, my head fell into my hands in despair. Maino lowered his weapon and began to hum the theme song from the sitcom, *The Golden Girls*. As he hummed the melody, I heard the words in my head. *Thank you for being a friend.*

Maino sang it funny as hell but no one could muster up any humor out of the situation. Though I lived a rough life and had seen death firsthand too many times to count, this was heartbreaking and quite unbearable. Death was death no matter how it came or who it came for but, somehow this was different.

"I'm so sorry to hear about your brother, Von. We cared for Ishmael very much. He was dedicated to making a difference and he did."

"Yeah Ishmael, homeboy Maino gon' miss him like Preem! Say... say... say what up to Preem," he belted out looking toward the sky. Amina was silent, she looked as if the bomb hit her directly.

After we all took a few moments of silence Amina snapped out of it like she was a different person. "Let's go! Now! We are already late!" Amina yelled.

We all hopped in the vehicle and rode in complete silence with such a morbid atmosphere amongst us. It was a two-day trip to Iraq from Cairo. Halfway though we would always stop at this amazing bed and breakfast. It was Ishmael's favorite spot. We decided we would continue that tradition now to honor him.

WET

Aida was our contact. At the halfway mark she would meet us at the back entrance and have a full-course meal waiting. Now realizing we had to tell Aida about Ishmael, Amina and I decided we'd make something up and tell her in the morning.

We had our meals brought to our cabin so she wouldn't ask questions. Amina and Maino ate and went to bed. I couldn't sleep, of course, so I got a bottle of red wine from the cellar and sat on top of the mountain watching the night air whisk across the earth. From behind, I heard footsteps and a voice singing Joe's song, *Don't Wanna Be A Playa* in the most soothing voice. As I turned to see where this sweet sound was coming from, all I saw was teeth. It was Von and he was wearing the most amazing smile. Under the circumstances, I didn't expect that. It was beautiful though and he had an amazing voice. I hadn't necessarily noticed Von before, but I saw something a little different in this moment. Maybe I was just horny as hell. I hadn't had a good love making session since I'd left Harlem.

Von had the prettiest brown eyes that glistened as the light changed. His skin was evenly coated in a beautiful brown. Brown like... mmmmm... the caramel drizzle on top of an ice cream sundae. Smooth, sweet, and sticky as hell sounded like the ingredients to a nut recipe to me... I'm just saying.

"You have a beautiful voice, Von. Do you sing often?" I asked.
"Thanks Miss, and no, just in the shower. Do you want some company?" Von asked.

"Sure, have a seat. It's beautiful up here this time of night."

"Yes, the view is breathtaking," he said, looking at me like he wanted to eat me out right here, right now on top of this mountain. I blushed and started to speak but he cut me off and said, "You look just like...ahh well, never mind."

"Just like who? Like what?" I asked.

"Oh nothing," he replied. "Just favor someone I knew."

I brushed it off and asked what brought him to Cairo since he clearly was American. He explained how his mother was killed and he came for the funeral. Von said Ishmael begged him to stay and help with the mission, which was against all the rules. Ishmael and Von's father was an American soldier. Both of their mothers were killed because they were born. Ishmael didn't have much convincing to do. Von was all in.

Von told me about a woman his father sexed from time to time and how he and his dad really grew to love her. Von said she looked Israeli and passed for one in the community. Somehow, she even learned to sound like them, but she wasn't one of them; she just blended in well, at least until she spoke. Von said Taliban officials raided the compound and killed mostly everyone except for this one woman and about ten small children. He said he and his dad hid in a bunker while they watched the Jihadi soldiers take her and the children. Von said they would probably traffic them, enslave them, and then kill them. Maybe they would do all of that if the captives didn't kill themselves first.

"She took good care of me and my dad," Von recalled. "We miss her and I promised I would continue my father's search for her."

"What was her name?" I asked.

"Her name was Halo, and actually, you look a lot like her. You too could pass for an Israeli native. If I didn't know better, I'd think you were family," Von joked.

"Do you have a picture?" I asked.

"No, not with me anyway."

I just left it at that, but I wanted to know who this woman was. Was it mommy after all this time? Was it really? No, it couldn't be. I convinced myself this was me thinking with my heart and let it go. Could my one wish be this easy?

As the night went in, we rested on the rocks. I couldn't sleep at all. I kept replaying all these signs. Preem's last words, the letter Maino and I found, and now this. This was too coincidental. I had to dig deeper.

The warmth from the sun's rays woke me. Mina and the others were already packing up. Maino was cooking breakfast. He had grits, bacon, and fried eggs ready to serve us. We had a grill we took with us and other supplies to ease the third-world vibe for when we took these trips. The truck was all ready to go and we gathered to eat.

Suddenly, we heard shots fired. *Clack! Clack! Clack! Clack! clack.! Booom!!!*

"Grenade!!" I yelled.

Mina looked at me and we ran for the truck. Maino met us there, pulling the floor from the truck revealing an arsenal fit for soldiers. Von grabbed the rocket launcher and posted up on a high rocky area above us. We secured the perimeter and Maino covered us. The firepower was getting closer. We were uncertain of the target, so it was still too soon to bust back. One thing about living here the last few years, was it felt just like home, a fucking war zone. I wish I knew guns then like I knew guns now.

As soon as the thought occurred, I felt a sweet, soft wind sweep across my face and I swear I heard Preem say, *'Everything is just as it should be, shorty. Run it!!!'* I smiled to myself because the thought was so vivid it was like I could smell his scent.

But we were in action, so I used the thought to soothe me then I gripped the Mini 14 tighter, ready to unload it at the first thing moving.

Von whistled to get our attention, and we quickly realized we were the targets. He held up three fingers, which indicated three vehicles. He then held up one finger and pointed toward the threat. That was to indicate he was about to take out the first vehicle. As soon as he let off, Mina and I sprayed the second vehicle until the clips were empty. Maino tossed grenades back to back while we reloaded and resumed fire. Von took out the last vehicle and we didn't wait around to see anything else. We all headed for the truck, galloping like a stampede. We hopped in the truck and proceeded on our journey.

As we rode in silence, I thought to myself this had to all be for something. The end game had to be a win. I couldn't afford another loss. My heart couldn't take another break. We had a long drive ahead of us, 10 hours to be exact before we reached the Villa. I planned to take a long hot bath and hop in a real bed for a few hours. Our mission wasn't until 6 a.m. the next morning.

We drove a few more hours then stopped for lunch at a little family owned diner. I could smell the curry from a mile away. Maino and Mina headed straight for the restroom while I retrieved my bag out of the back of the truck. As I turned to close the door Von was practically standing on my heels.

"Did you need to get something too?" I asked pointing to the truck, somewhat surprised that he was all up in my personal box. He smelled good though. He smelled manly. No cologne, no after shave shit, just plain ole' clean man.

"No, I just wanted to see if you needed help getting something out," he replied.

"Oh no. I got it. Thanks, though."

Von hesitated for a second, as if he was uncomfortable. He stared at me in silence then said, "If I may be honest, Harley, it's your energy, I'm drawn to it."

In that moment, I was trying to use my discernment skills and narrow down the true meaning of that bullshit line he just ran. As I was pondering my response, Von had the nerve to reach out and raise my chin with his finger.

"Why Israel?" Von asked. "Why are you here? I know I'm here for some odd reason and I believe it was to meet you."

Me??? I was flattered speechless. His words sent a chill down my spine and my nipples did a slight tingle. The way he looked me dead in my eyes and spit that shit was so sexy.

"Is that so?" I replied.

"Yes. I do believe that is so," he insisted.

His topic of conversation was unexpected, to say the least. It frightened me a bit. I wasn't afraid of one specific thing; I was more afraid that I had no idea what I was afraid of. I hadn't felt a tingle in my nipples since I left Harlem but damn that felt nice.

Von proceeded to take my bag and close the truck doors. We walked into the diner where Amina and Maino were having no conversation. All we heard was smacking, forks hitting plates, and ice tapping against tall glasses of water.

"Girl, you better come eat. This is amazing!" Amina said between bites of food. "Mmm hmm, dis good, Harley!" Maino cosigned. After the waitress took our orders, Von and I headed to the restroom to freshen up a bit. I could feel him watching me from behind. He was so close I could feel the wind from his walk and the breeze from his admiration of his current view. I grabbed the door handle to enter the ladies' room and Von touched my shoulder. He stared at me silently, gazing into my eyes.

"You have a familiar sweetness about your soul," Von whispered. "I don't know why, but I feel a need to be near you."

He moved closer to me and backed me against the wall. I was stuck with my eyes locked in on his. We seemed to be speaking with our souls. This telepathy of the bodies was intense. Von slowly pressed his lips against my forehead and inhaled and exhaled deeply. My palms begin to sweat and I could damn near see the veins popping out of Von's pants. Huge veins too.

A woman came around the corner to use the restroom, and we both flinched. The woman saw us and stopped abruptly. She looked from me to Von and smiled.

"Ohhh, how I remember when me and my Johnny used to love like that," she said beaming. "He passed away a few years ago. You two make a beautiful couple. Hold on to him, little miss. I see forever in his eyes. You two kids stay sweet now." She disappeared into the bathroom and Von looked at me.

"Did you feel that?" Von asked.
"Feel what?" I replied.

He smiled and walked into the restroom. I stood there for a few seconds. Long enough to realize that I did feel that. We had an undeniable connection. He was gorgeous and all that, but it was more than that. He got inside me mentally, almost as if he saw right though me.

We finally joined Amina and Maino at the table. I ordered Darwood Basha, an Egyptian-style meatball made from beef and a special blend of herbs and spices. Von ordered the Gyro. *So traditional*, I thought. His choice of meal also told me he was not the average Egyptian. Gyro here was equivalent to canned meat in the U.S. They ate entire lambs here. Their meals consisted of many parts and was always full of flavor.

Amina and Maino both stuck their forks in my plate, and I gave them a look.

"Do we have a definite route cleared for this family, Von?" I asked.

"Yes we do," he answered confidently. "I will brief you all on your specific assignments when we resume riding."

"Ok cool," Mina said.

I dug a little more, asking Von some questions about the operation. It was basic prostitution, human trafficking, abuse by default. Maino and I had just recently joined the cause, but Mina had been at it for many, many years.

"How long have you been riding for the mission?" I asked Von. "Do you have any idea who's in charge? Cut the head off the snake and all that!"

"No, we don't, but we are getting closer," he replied.

We loaded up after an awesome meal and drove for several more hours. As we rode, Von explained all of our positions.

Maino would take the wheel and leave it running as we exited the vehicle. Von would clear a path for Mina and me to go in and get the children. The mother was downstairs waiting tables at the restaurant below her apartment. Her husband was at work, which was why we picked this moment to begin with. Easy retrieve, we thought.

Upon entering the apartment, we noticed the children were not there. As we moved back further into another room there was the mom lying in the bed with her throat cut. Her eyes were wide open with tear streaks as if she died pleading for her life. Her hands were both shut tight in fists as if she braced herself for the slice to her throat. Mina and I were in a trance for a few seconds then we finally made eye contact and reached for our weapons. Before we could turn the corner to exit the apartment, I saw Maino with his hands up and a man walking behind him with a pistol pointed at the back his head.

"Drop the fucking guns now or I empty his skull," the man promised.

We hesitated, hoping this wasn't real or that Von was about to come through like Zoe Saldana in *Colombiana* or some shit. Boy was I wrong! As we were led to a van parked in the back of the building, I could see Von on his knees with two rifles pointed at him. I tried to maintain eye contact with Maino. He was an 808 when it came to guns and a threat to his Harley. I had to let him know I was okay before he died making sure I was.

Mina had that look on her face. That look that said, *Not again, not more bodies. I can't be helpless.*

I was thinking the same thing. We may not have set shit off right away, but we were definitely not going out without a fight. We all knew that.

As we approached the vehicle and were forced inside, we saw the children inside. They were tied up and had scratches all over. The smallest one was hysterically gasping for air. I moved quickly to sit by her and immediately began to comfort her.

Von made eye contact and put one finger to his lips and used the other to gesture for me to stay calm. We passed that message on through us all.

WET

We drove for about thirty minutes and when the van stopped, I could hear a conversation between the driver and someone on a cell phone...

"Yes ma'am, we got more than we bargained for. Three girls... pretty too!" The man paused for a second and I assumed he was listening to whomever was on the other end of the phone. Then, he continued, "Well, maybe the two guys. Let's see if we can convince them to work. If not, we shed dead weight... Yes ma'am, we'll be here when you arrive."

The van doors opened, and the men snatched us out. They escorted us at gunpoint the entire time. They took us to a huge underground home made from the mountain's wall and its jewels. The jewels were made from an amazing rock formation dressed in marble stone and earth's gritty tone. It was so sexy that even in our despair, I still thought of fucking as I entered. Almost like sexuality was pouring from the seams between each rock. My hot box actually started to moisten. I was a bit deprived at the moment. I could use some dick, but it was the wrong time and wrong place. My mind was telling me nooooo but my body... my body was telling me yessssss!!! (Ooooh damn, that was the greatest album ever. Too bad mental and sexual health got in the way of good talent. I still liked the damn song though).
Well, whatever!! Don't charge it to my head or my heart, charge it to my ass since she was the one feeling all sticky right now. Walking down the long hall of rocks lit by candles and lanterns all I could think was what would Preem do? What would daddy do? What gutter shit would Izzy and I come up with?

Starzpen

They pushed us all into one room and locked the door. "Von, what the hell is going on? Who the hell are they? When they came for you, I fell behind them," I heard them say. "We ran up on good money this time. Yes, two girls and the little one will go quick."

Hearing the words, Mina trembled. "They are the traffickers, aren't they?" Mina asked softly.

"Yes," Von said.

"Why did they kill the mother?" I asked. "She probably tried to keep them from her children. It's a woman!" I belted out of nowhere.

"What's a woman?" Harley asked Maino?

"It's a woman in charge. I overheard them talking before they took us out the van. The guys kept saying, 'Yes ma'am,'" I explained. "This is crazy! Are they going to kill us Von?"

Von looked at me and I felt the air from a slight wind of fear. "No, my Queen. We are going to be fine."

Suddenly, the door opened and three men with guns rushed in and took stance around the room. They looked like they were looking at ghost.

Mina looked at me and shrugged her shoulders. "Why are they staring at me?" she asked, puzzled by their astonishment.

The children jumped into my arms while Maino looked like King Kong all bloated and posted up, ready to die if need be. The men remained silent when another man walked in dressed in a very expensive suit smoking a cigar.

The man chomped on his cigar and looked at each of us briefly. Satisfied, he bellowed, "Yes! Yes, good job boys." He did a double-take in my direction and his mouth hung open as he examined my face. "Hmm..." he said, while walking over to me. He grabbed my hand and held it in his. Slowly, he flipped my hands on each side and examined them closely.

What was he looking for? I wanted to slap him, but I didn't want to rock the boat just yet. Suddenly he dropped my hands and continued on his mission. "Rhonna will be here for the two women and the children shortly," he announced.

"And the men?" One of the guards asked.

"Leave them till she arrives. Get them some food and bathroom privileges," he decided. Then he looked directly at me curiously. He seemed puzzled since he first arrived. "You are beautiful," he said, barely above a whisper. "You look like... mmm... you look just like..."

All the men began speaking Arabic as they exited the room walking backwards, guns still aimed at us, but all eyes were on me. The door slams shut, and I could feel the children exhale. I could feel Maino let down his guard too and I felt Mina hurting as she remembered all we fought for and wondering would we be in the same dead place as that of those we dedicated our lives to saving. I couldn't think help but think that I just came here to find mommy. I came here running from heartache hoping to run up on the mend. *What the hell was I doing in the middle if this shit?*

"What are we going to do?" Mina asked.

'We are going to be fine, Mina,' I assured her. "We are going to get through this."

I knew Mina was tough, but this appeared to be too much for her, so she just began to sob. I'd never seen Mina

195

cry before. She was such a hard rock. She would die before she exhibited an ounce of weakness. But here she was crying. For some odd reason I was the calm one in the room. My optimism was on a thousand when I should have been afraid. These were jihadi soldiers derived from a militia group designed to traffic women and children across the globe as a sport. Not to mention the enormous going rate for this little girl would be an easy achievement for some pedophile. They brought us pizza which the kids and Maino, of course, enjoyed even under these circumstances. As hard as it was everyone except Von and I fell asleep.

There was a small whole at the top of the cave we were in that allowed night air to seep in and permitted us enough of a view to the stars to remember there was a God. It was refreshing. I found a few seconds of peace there.

Von startled me as he crept up quietly behind me, curious as to what had my attention. It was as if the few seconds of peace he craved for himself peeked out from my soul. I laid my head on the rock as a gesture of fatigue. A mentally, emotionally, spiritually draining fatigue. Von laid his hands on my shoulders and began to firmly press his fingers down like he was stroking piano keys. A sweet melody, soft but firm. Rough but lyrical, it felt nice. The air from the cracks in the cave's wall was beckoning cooler, more direct air, and what a beautiful breeze it was.

Suddenly I felt moist air grace the back of my neck. Mmm…good God! My body melted in my mind. I didn't know whether to be offended that he even tried me like that or let him slide up inside me and relieve some built up tension. I turned to look at him for clarity I supposed, as if I didn't know he would make love to me on Mars with no air if I was wit' it. We stared at each other, both searching for the green light. So, I flipped the switch on and clutched the back of his neck to bring him in closer. I was about to kiss him, but I was slightly hesitant. I gave one last look securing the green light when Von smashes his body against mine. He lifted my chin with his finger and wrapped his lips around mine. It felt so sweet! I exhaled as he touched me, then our tongues met as they began to dance to this oh so euphoric tune.

Von massaged my breasts with both hands. I couldn't stop if I wanted to. It didn't matter because I didn't want to anyway. He eased his way down the road until he was on his knees. Undressing me, he swiftly snatched my shorts down to my ankles and I stepped out. He gripped one side of my panties and with one yank, tore them off. He dove straight in with no mercy on his automatic rhythm. I was trying my best to stay quiet. Lord knows I wanted to fucking scream! Von saw my dilemma and sweetly wrapped his hand around my mouth. That shit really turned me on. He was eating my pussy with the sole intent of making me cum. He was concentrating on me and what my body reacted to.

He watched for when my clit hardened so he could put extra pressure on it. He watched how I moved my hips when he sucked on it like the sauce off sweet, slow baked barbeque ribs. He paid attention to the manner in which my breathing increased when he massaged the tip of my asshole with his forefinger while penetrating my pussy with his thumb. Ohhhh yesssss, daddy! That drove me bananas.

WET

My back pressed up against the cool rocks while his face pressed between my legs. It was about to rain. I could smell it in the atmosphere. Sure enough, the drizzle began to run down my face and I didn't try to move or hide from the rain. I welcomed it; it felt nice. The rain began to fall harder and Von came up for air.

"You alright, beautiful?" Von whispered.

"I'm great," I replied.

"That you are," he teased, right before lifting me up onto his waist.

I wrapped my arms around his shoulders and dropped my head backward. Von licked my neck just like I wanted him to while wiggling his waist, so his dick slid inside me on its own. The feeling was similar to a snake slithering up a thigh, no guidance needed, it just ended up where it fit. His dick fit perfectly inside me. We didn't move for about five amazing seconds. It was like the second my body touched the water in a hot tub taking in all the hot, steamy, moist goodness the moment had to offer. Then, he gracefully bounced me up and down until only he and the wall behind me were my anchor. I braced myself on the wall and gripped his neck while I rode the wave until I drowned him. He was a sweet lover, not rough at all, but the precise amount of force in the right places. The perfect amount of pressure at the perfect time. It was nice.

Von enjoyed my "bouncery" until he couldn't take it anymore. He placed one hand on the wall while he still held me up with the other and began pounding inside me. He moved like he was dancing to a reggae song. Really fast and hard, then he'd slow up with amazing timing and just grind his body into mine. The pressure in my clit and the beating of my cervix was about to make me lose control.

I gripped his neck harder, sucking and almost biting his neck, ears, and shoulders. He grabbed the back of my hair and looked me in my eyes.

"Can I cum?" Von hissed, panting and nearly breathless. I thought that was the sweetest thing ever. Like really, what man asked? Usually, they just nut and die! I was speechless until he asked again while slowing his grind a bit.

"Harley? Can I come?" Von repeated.

"Yes sir, please do. I wanna cum too," I whispered in his ear as he pressed his body harder on my hot spot like he knew exactly what would make be spit uncontrollably. And it did!

"Ohhhh shhhhhhhhh…" Von grunted into my face and I felt his knees buckle. My pelvis relaxed and his dick became soaked with juices. He was calm though. No ugly lovemaking faces, odd grunting noises, or hard old man breathing in my face. I can't believe I'm about to say this but... Von was perfect. This couldn't be real. I felt a near supernatural connection to him. I felt like he was made for me.

Suddenly, the door opened, and we scrambled to compose ourselves. I heard the children begin to cry. As I ran out to see what was happening, I saw three men and a lady standing in the doorway. Her face was covered but she had to be the boss.

Fed up, Mina yelled, "What are you going to do to us? These children need to be cared for!"

WET

The woman moved into the light and removed her head covering as she looked up. She locked eyes with me and I returned her stare. Von gasped in amazement. The woman moved toward me and touched my face with the back of her hand in shock.

The man in the doorway said, "I told you she mirrored you exactly."

"Mommy!!!" I screamed, right before I hit the floor and fainted.

***

I woke up in a beautiful garden home in the mountains if Iran. It was surrounded by forest and winding rivers. I woke in a beautiful bed covered with Arabic writing. I felt pretty out of it, so I stood and went to the bathroom to wash my face.

As I washed my face, flashes of the dream I had captured me. I dreamt I saw mommy. I dreamt I shared an amazing moment with an awesome, sexy man. I splashed some water on my face as if to wake me from this nightmare, but that didn't work. I ran to the door to see where I was and where was Maino, Von, and Mina?

I walked down a long flight of stairs to where I heard music and laughter. I began to move faster, not understanding how we went from being kidnapped and held hostage to waking in this huge house. I entered the room the noise was coming from and saw Maino eating. Of course, Mina was having a glass of wine. She raised her glass to me as I moved closer to everyone. Von sat staring at me with the strangest look on his face.

Starzpen

Confused as hell I asked, "What is this? Where are the children? The guards?"

Maino belted out, "Big surprise, Harley. Big, big, big surprise." Maino clapped his hands hysterically.

"What is going on?" I asked, really confused now.

"Do you remember anything from last night?" Mina asked.

"Not really, just the weirdest dream and a lovely encounter with...the rain," I caught myself before the words tumbled from my mouth and embarrassed me. Von and I avoided contact when I slide in that little private joke. I continued, "For some reason, I remember dreaming about Mommy."

A voice from behind me spoke up. "It wasn't a dream, Harley."

That voice! I turned my head so fast I felt my neck pop. It was her. It was my mother.

I looked to Von and I saw a tear stream down his cheek. Maino was pacing hysterically, clapping and screaming at the sky, "We did it, Preem!! We found her!! We found her, Preem!!!"

"The universe has a way of making sense out of what was meant to be. We have a lot to talk about, but if it's alright, can I just hug you?" Mommy said.

I was speechless, and I couldn't move. I still wasn't sure if this was reality or was I in another dream state.

"You look exactly like you did in my dreams," I told her.

"You look exactly like me. When my men told me they captured my twin, everything in me told me it was you. I left clues and always kept an eye on you. You've had a rough time. I thought at the time I'd just make it worse," Mommy explained. "I understand if you hate me."

I didn't hate her; I loved her and longed for a piece of me somewhere in this world.

I ran to her and said nothing. I just melted in her arms. I could hear Maino behind me, "Look Preemo, look at Harley and her Mommy." Maino clapped slowly, then broke out in a full applause.

Mina broke up this Kumbaya moment by reminding me this was the lady who has been the head of this trafficking organization.

"Where are the children?" Mina asked, angrily.

"They are fine. We found a family to care for them; they will be safe. Their mother should have never been killed. My men assured me it was purely accidental. The children will be safe and very well taken care of," Mommy promised. Von finally stood and spoke his peace. "Why did you leave us?"

I now realized my mother was the same woman he spoke of, the woman who cared for him and his dad. In a sense, she was his mother too. In all reality, he probably knew her better than I did. I remembered her voice, her scent, and her touch by the memories I fought hard to hold on to.

"I will explain to you all everything at dinner," Mommy suggested. "Please make yourselves at home and get some rest. Please, please try to understand that everything is not what it seems," she whispered as she readjusted her head covering before darting from the room.

We all took a moment to process what the hell just happened. After a few moments of us in complete dismay, Mommy returned. This time she was with only one guard. He stood guard at the door while she sat at the table gesturing us all to join her. What seemed strange to me was that he didn't appear to be guarding her from us. He appeared to be watching the door instead.

"Mommy..."

"Harley, please let me go first," Mommy insisted. I relax in my chair as much as possible, still in disbelief that I was sitting here with her after all these years in this horrific capacity. What could possibly be her reasoning?

"I know you have millions of questions but let me start by explaining my reason for leaving to begin with." She sobbed and wiped tears as she tried to tell me her side of the story.

"Let me stop you," I said. I am so sorry you went through whatever it is you went through, that it cost you us. Preem's daddy and me. I'm not angry, oddly enough. I never have been. I missed you and wondered if you were doing okay, but not once did I ever hate you. So, let's start there." I paused and took a big sigh.

"I read the letter you wrote Preem. I wish I had found it much sooner. But I was taught that all things happen in its own time. To rush, manipulate, or fake that would result in the "L" every time. I'm here; you're here. It's a beautiful thing. What I don't understand is what this is!! A woman was killed. Hundreds of women and children have been killed or forced into prostitution in exchange for their own lives. Is this who you are? Can you imagine what they would have done to those children?"

WET

"Yes, Harlem! I understand completely. I *was* them! I left Harlem and went to North Carolina. I only had a few dollars, so I got a hotel and a job at a diner nearby. I tried to save money to keep going and get my head right. I hadn't hit the pipe for almost five months. I was clean and doing great. One night I was closing up late one night and a van with two women inside pulled up and asked if they could use the restroom before I locked up. Me being nice, I said sure. I opened the door and pointed to the restrooms. The women walked in and the van doors flew open. I felt a stick in my neck like a needle and the next thing I remember I was in a cargo unit on a boat in the middle of the ocean. I wasn't chained or tied up. I was free to walk around. After a few minutes, I realized they didn't need restraints though. We were in the middle of nowhere. There was nowhere to go. A man approached me in the hall as I was still trying to grasp what was happening." She took a deep breath.

"He said come with me! I hesitated, too scared to ask questions but I followed him to a state room below. There was a man with a long fluffy beard. He wore a head dress like Osama or somebody. He stood and flung my hair, turned me around to see my entire body. He even sniffed me. I asked him who he was. He told me that the only important thing is who I was now. He said I belonged to him and I would either do what he said or be killed. He informed me clients would be boarding in one hour and I was to take them to Eva and wash her ass because she looked like she stank of trouble.

By this point, I realized what was happening. As they took me to this Eva, I saw young girls on the deck half-naked. Young girls, like eight, nine, and ten-year old. Men groped them and kissed them and were having oral sex right out in the open. I thought to myself, Dear God, I'd rather die. So, I jumped." Mommy shrugged.

"The water was freezing, and we were up so high I'm was sure the fall alone would kill me. As I reached the surface and realized I wasn't dead, I panicked. Where was I gonna go now? The sharks would've eaten me. I'm gonna freeze to death. I laid on my back and floated for a few seconds before a speed boat pulled up and pulled me aboard. I was taken to an empty room where they left me for four days, no food, no water, no bathroom. Just the four walls and the hard cement floor."

As Mommy recounted her story, Maino sat in the corner slapping himself in the head. He did that whenever he was angry. Mina tried to comfort him by sitting down near him and holding his hand. She laid her head on his shoulder and appeared to be sad herself.

Maino immediately reacted, rubbing her head, "It's okay, Mina. It's okay." Maino's level of compassion was off the charts. He couldn't bear to see anyone in pain. Mina was good like that; she would pick up on your strength and use it as a weapon against any weakness.

Mommy went on to tell how the men beat her for days as punishment for trying to run. They left her in that room until all the bruises healed. She was used as a sex slave for the dirty old men who couldn't afford what they considered to be a best seller. She told us how she was raped repeatedly by men, women, and sometimes both. She said she threw up constantly and often prayed they would just kill her.

Mommy then went on to tell us how she escaped to Cairo with a girl she became friends with on the ship. That woman turned out to be Von's aunt. His father's baby sister. Mommy told us they were taken to a party full of military officers. While there, a female captain left her car keys in the bathroom. Mommy said she grabbed the keys, snatched up Aisha and got away. They knew the mountains like they knew the lines in their hands. The ditched the vehicle and hopped on a refugee convoy vehicle.

"That's when you met daddy," Von said softly.

"Yes, that's where I fell in love with you and your father."

"But you ended up here. Back here. Was that by choice?" Mina asked.

"No, they took you again when they raided the camp, didn't they?" Von answered for her. Mommy began to sob and nodded her head. "Did they know you were there? Was it just another slave round up, or were you sought after?"

Mina asked. "It was both, Amina. When I returned here, Hafeek told me he never stopped looking for me. He was in love with me and often used me as his own personal bed buddy. He had become quite particular about the men he sold me to and usually only allowed the ones who let him watch purchase time with me."

Mommy shuddered at the thought. "So I've become sort of what your father would call a house nigger. I wanted to live so I figured, why not live good. At least until I found another way to get out of here and completely away from this end of the earth."

"Sounds like you've been through hell. So you want to leave??" Mina asked suspiciously.

"I've always wanted to leave, my dear. Believe me. Until your breathing becomes contingent upon what becomes a small price to pay after all the beatings, rapes, horrible acts of sexual violence toward children at the hands of grown men and women.

"The more comfortable Hafeek became with me, the more children I was able to keep under my thumb. I would find jobs around the estate for them. Keep them out of sight and out of harm's way as much as possible. Some, I was even able to convince had diseases and we should just let go."

My body had become a slab of concrete. Stiff and worn, yet still served its purpose. I've become numb but never hopeless.

"I could feel you on this earth somewhere, Mommy. I never thought I'd find you here like this," I said.

"I could feel you too baby, believe it or not. I dreamed of the day I could tell you I've always loved you and thought of you daily. I wondered what and who you looked like. How you talked, how you walked. You looked a lot like your father and a little of Preem as a little one. I must say you have grown to be the spitting image of me and my mother."

I turned to Von and asked, "Von, is this what you meant when you said I had a familiar spirit?"

"I wasn't certain then, but yes, I knew it was Deja vu and I had seen you before."

We all chuckled. All except Mina.

"You okay, Mina?" Von asks.

"I've been here a long time as well, and I've seen these people go to major lengths to protect their organization. I don't know if I trust her. She's *your* mother, not mine!!!" Mina pointed out.

I was a bit annoyed, but I did understand. I looked at mommy and asked, "What are they going to do with us?"

Mommy sighed, "They are going to offer your friends a job. If they refuse, they will be shot on sight. Amina is going to be killed. They know who you are and are celebrating your capture. They even joked about placing her head on the bones of her dead husband. Hafeek doesn't know who you are yet Harley. He hasn't seen you all yet. However, his right hand keeps saying how you look like someone. He claims he can't put his finger on it yet. His plan for you is to… well, he wants you to be his wife. He won't kill you until he's sure that you won't cooperate.

"They trust me because I have become one of them in a sense. Literally trying to save the lives of some of the young children I see come through here every day. I'm allowed to go out alone now. No guards! I take children to doctors' appointments and shopping. They only allow the older more seasoned ones to go and they will put a bullet in the heart of anyone who tried to run," she informed us.

"Has anyone ever made it out?" Von asked.

"Yes a few, but not many. More than 90% are hunted and killed."

"So wha…whaaa...what's the plan?" Maino stuttered.

"Yeah, what is the plan?" Mina mimicked with major attitude.

"Well, I have a few loyal soldiers who care for me and will help us. We have to make it to the Embassy in Bahrain. I have friends there."

"Wait a minute, I have a question," said Mina. "If you have all these friends, why haven't you tried to leave before now."

Mommy stood and pulled her shirt up to her breastbone. We all gasped at what we saw. A stitched line extended from one end of her waist to the other. Dear God, I whispered.

"Von, you remember when they raided the camp?" Mommy asked. "Well, no one but your dad and I knew it, but I was pregnant with your father's child. When the doctors came to examine, they found I was carrying a child. Hafeek ordered them to "cut it out.""

Looking down at her belly, she sobbed. I ran to her and just hugged her so tight. She sat back down in the chair and lifted up her skirt about mid-thigh.

Mommy said, "This is the first time I actually tried to run. I stole a horse and about two hours into my ride a sniper hit him directly in his head. Without the horse I would never make it to Bahrain. I found a cave and I had a few supplies as I prayed someone would pass through and help me. Hafeek left me in the desert for a week before they came and recaptured me.

"When I returned, they hung me upside down from a tree and beat me with the soaking wet tail of a camel they killed just for that purpose. They beat me for hours. Then tied the camel's still bloody tail around my thigh and left me tied to the tree while night fell. I grew more and more terrified as the sun sank, knowing wildlife would pick off the scent of the camel's blood. Buzzards began to eat the tail from my leg. Pecking and chewing on my flesh also.

209

Starzpen

"Suddenly, I heard a truck and shots were being fired. It was Hafeek. He untied me and gently laid me in the back of the truck. Hafeek was a middle man then; his father was in charge. He was killed by a man whose daughter was raped and murdered by his men. Hafeek was proud to take his father's place. He was ten times as ruthless and a hundred times more evil.

"When we returned to the house, he had the other girls take care of me. I was in so much pain and I couldn't fathom there was much worse than a Brooklyn corner. I thought this was my punishment for leaving you all behind. Now it seemed it was all worth it. The countless children able to live normal lives with normal families. The lives we've saved secretly for years, and now you. Harley, all this was for this moment right here, right now. Amina, you've been with the mission for quite some time now," Mommy stated matter-of-factly.

"How would you know?" Mina answered sarcastically.

"Have you ever met your handler? Have you ever met the person in charge of the underground mission? You were in Fallujah a few years ago moving a young mother and her two sons to Cairo. You were all nearly killed trying to get out of there. With one of the boys on your back and the other hand in hand with his mother, you ran for your lives. The fire in your eyes, the determination on your face. The love for others manifesting in the form of tears flowing from your eyes as you begged God for mercy was inspiring."

"Whaaaa…What are you talking about, mommy?" I asked. "Mina? What the hell???"

Mommy continued, "I asked God to send me an angel to help me get these people out. Out of nowhere, a stampede of horses came storming through blocking us from the bullets. There seemed to be hundreds of horses. They served as a wall between us and the enemy. The stampede pushed them back and us closer to safety. Then there she was! It was YOU. You sat atop a white horse. You were armed wearing a head dress. You pointed to the west and there we saw a helo. You ordered the men behind you to launch rockets once the horses moved out. That gave us time to board the helo and make it back to Cairo. We would have died had it not been for you. I did what I had to do to stay alive. I conformed to my circumstance to allow others to live as well."

"Mommy, let's go home!" I cried. "Let's just GO!"

"In order for me to be free I must shut this whole organization down."

"But why? Why is it your problem? You've done more than your part!" Von yelled. "No matter what we do today there will be others ready to take their place tomorrow. But what does matter is what we don't do today."

Maino sat in the corner as if someone were telling him a story. Mina looked like she was in another place completely. Trying to take all this in and still figure out what we were going to do. I could suddenly hear Preem say, *dying is not an option lil one!! Let's get it!*

I saw flashes of Izzy wearing the boxing gloves we got for her tenth birthday. She was in fight stance as if to say, *bitch suit up and let's go!* Like we did before we handled some hood biz. I smiled and Maino hopped out of the corner.

"Shout out to Preemoooooo and Blu Izzy. We love you," Maino shouted. Tears just fell from my eyes uncontrollably. Maino felt what I felt. He sensed them as I did. That was confirmation we fought, or we died fighting. We had three advantages.

One, failure was not an option. Two, we had Mommy, our secret weapon and our one element of surprise. The third and most powerful, we had heart. We were all built with it. Now it was time to truly do what we always knew we could do. Survive!

Von walked over and laid his hand on my back and rubbed it as if he were comforting a dying puppy. I just looked at him and smiled.

I fell into the arms of the love seat near the window and tried to make sense of all this. Nothing made sense. I couldn't even hear Preem, Daddy, Izzy... nobody was here with me on this one.

Mina walked over to me and held my hand. Von didn't know what to do or say at this point. One thing I was certain of, all of this had to be the divine purpose from day one. I looked at Von now as the love of my life, as if we were destined to be in love. I was sure he mirrored my feelings. I could feel it. He filled a spot in my spirit that he fit into perfectly, like dropping pudding into a glass bowl it sets in and conforms. Clearly, he was made for that spot. The reality was that Cairo was my destiny all along. Harlem was my teacher. Brooklyn was my punisher. New York City was my root. Egypt would be my saving grace. Egypt would be the gateway to the beginning. Egypt would truly earn me the right to my name. I was Brooklyn's best student. I am Harlem's Heiress. I was one of New York's finest.

Starzpen

After gathering our thoughts and composing a plan to make it to the Embassy in Bahrain, we decided to get some rest. We were all quite fearful but ready for what tomorrow would bring.

"Harley, I have to go," Mommy said. "I will make sure the children are ok tonight. At the start of sunrise, be ready to move. Samuel will drop off instructions in the night. Hafeek will be here by ten a.m. We must be long gone by then."

"Ok, I understand."

Mommy wrapped her arms around my whole body and squeezed me so tight. Before letting go, she whispered in my ear,

"I'll die before I separate from you again."

I whispered back, "As will I Mommy."

She turned to Amina before leaving and thanked her for all that she did.

Amina grabbed her heart with both hands and while holding back tears, she replied, "No, thank YOU. For just being you. Thank you for being for all these people what clearly no one had ever been for you."

Mommy left and Mina rushed to me and laid her head on my shoulder. We embraced, both feeling like we'd been thrown out of a 747 in mid-flight. Maino slept on the sofa and Von stared out the window in utter shock himself.

Von looked to us and said, "Ok ladies, enough with the tears. Let's get packed and get some sleep. We have a long road to Bahrain, and something tells me it won't be a walk in the park."

Though no one could sleep like Maine, agreed. Amina snuggled up under Maino on the sofa while Von and I pulled two love seats together, pushed them up against the sofa like the forts me and Izzy used to make and climbed inside. Von wrapped his arm around me and I fit perfectly in the nook between his armpit and his body.

He took one hand and laid my head on his chest and said, "Sleep, Beautiful. Tomorrow we fight for one more tomorrow."

"Mmmmm...one more day," I mumbled.
The next morning, Amina was up first. She woke me up too.
"Harley, look." She passed me an envelope with a letter inside. They were instructions from mommy:

Harlem,

Samuel will be there to take Maino and von to the meet spot. You all leaving together will look odd. Samuel was to take them to a briefing aka beating to get them ready for work or burial. He will bring them to me. Exactly twenty-three minutes after the men leave Sharifa will pick you and Amina up the children are with me now. There are weapons and everything you'll need to make the trip to Bahrain in your vehicle. I see a smooth run due to Hafeek not arriving until late morning.
Be safe and I'll see you in a few hours.

Before I could put the paper down the door opened. It was a woman in a nurse's uniform.

WET

"I'm Sharifa," she said forcefully. "We must go now! I just overheard the men say Hafeek will be here earlier than he is supposed to." Sharifa turned to me. "Halo, your mother and the children are already gone. They will await our arrival at the Embassy gates."

Von was up now gathering Maino. Amina was in full solider mode, throwing Teflon protective vests, goggles, ammo, and all kinds of shit now. Full beast mode. I loved her this way. I was so wit' it. Preem and the guys always handled the gutter shit. Now it was my turn to show the world what little girls were really made of.

While we prepared, I had a moment of silence with Izzy. That bitch would cut off her right arm if I needed one and I would do the same for her. I felt a moment of sorrow for myself because I wished she was here. Then I heard her voice. *"Get up sis! Do you!!! Live bitch!!!"* I could see her as if she was here, smiling and blowing kisses, throwing up fake gang signs and shit. Oh, how I was sinking into this whole life loss in my heart. I had to turn this into my motivational fuel to fire up this ride we were about to take.

We all scurried up our things while I convinced Maino to go with Von. He wasn't happy about separating from me, but after major convincing he finally went and got in the truck with Samuel and Von.

Sharifa took me and Mina out the back door into a tunnel under the mountain. When we reached the inside of the mountain, we came to a cave with a small cargo railroad. We hopped in while Sharifa hit a button and the cargo train took off. We rode in silence watching our backs, ready to light this tunnel up if need be.

We were riding for over an hour when the railroad suddenly jerked so hard I nearly fell out of it.

"Everybody ok?" Mina asked, looking around.

"Yeah, I'm good," I answered.

"I'm ok too," said Sharifa.

"Let's go! The bus will be here in five minutes."

As we exited the tunnel the sunlight burned my eyes but in the shadows, I saw Von and Maino waiting.

"Harleeeeey!!!" Maino screamed, running toward us with his arms wide open. *He's such a big baby,* I thought. Then, out of nowhere bullets started flying.

Clack! Clack! Clack!

I hit the ground swiftly, crawling toward Maino. Pain ripped through my gut as I realized he wasn't moving.

Dear God, not again!

"Mainoooooo!!!" I screamed.

I finally reached him and flipped him over to see where he was hit. A smile tugged at my mouth when I realized he was vested. I quickly patted him down to confirm he wasn't hit. There was no blood, so I sighed in relief and tried to wake him up. I shook him hard enough to rattle his brain and smacked his face harder than a scorned lover.

"Maino! Maino! Maino!" I cried. "Wake up baby!!" I continued to smack his face, but he just would not wake up.

I heard more shots and looked up to see Mina unloading into the vehicle that was taking shots at us.

Von yelled, "RPG!!!"

We all braced for the boom, praying Von hit his target. Amina and Sharifa emptied their weapons in an attempt to keep cover on me and Maino. The RPG hit the mark and the blast woke Maino.

"I'm ok, Harley," Maino assured me, struggling to grab his pistol from his waist.

"Relax baby! Can you walk?"

"Yeah, Harley. Yeah, I'm good, I'm good. Get in front of me. On three, we run," he instructed. "One... two... three... Run Harley, run!"

We made it to the bus without incident. Looking out the rear window I saw Mina and Sharifa with this huge blast shadowing them. The look on Mina's face was priceless. She reminded me of Angela Bassett burning the Bimmer in *Waiting to Exhale*.

Von jumped down off the top of the bus and started the engine. We all boarded the bus and took seats screaming at Von to move! Now!

As Von rocketed the bus forward, Sharifa informed us that the attack was an amateur attack. "They work for the jihadi soldiers," she explained. "They recruit them as scouters for food and a little clout. The ones who get the best products get the paying jobs," she explained.

"So that wasn't Hafeek? How can you be sure?" I asked.

"If it was, we'd be dead," Sharifa assured us.

We had a few more hours before we reached the American Embassy in Bahrain. We weren't safe until we got there. We all dozed off a bit but Maino stayed up front armed and on guard for Von the entire time. Mina and I peeked in and out of sleep while Sharifa sat in one spot praying and chanting for most of the ride. We zoned out until we heard Von announce our arrival.

"Rise and shine, beauties; we have arrived!"

We pulled up to the Embassy gates when suddenly there was a loud noise coming from behind us. The guard began to close the gate, running and speaking Arabic in their radios.

Von looked at me and yelled over the commotion, "Run!"

Me, Maino, and Mina hopped out the side window of the bus. We tried to run behind the Embassy when I saw Mommy.

"Harley Harleyyyyyyyy! It's Hafeek!"

We had nowhere to go. We were trapped.

"Drop your weapons," the guards ordered.

"Fuck you!" Maino yelled. "You drop yours first."

A motorcade pulled right up on us and a well-dressed handsome man stepped out. He walked toward me and wrapped his hand gently around my throat.

"You... you are her daughter. So I will kill you first, the man said.

We all knew we had to make a move. I could hear Izzy in my ear saying, *Do or die bestie, what you gon do?* I made eye contact with Mina and Maino and sent them a message with my eyes. *I'm going for mines.* I knew once I made a move my peeps would follow suit.

I reached in my pocket and pulled out a grenade, pulling the pin simultaneously. I had stashed a few before we left Iran. I figured they'd come in handy. By now U.S. forces had their weapons on the gate so no one crossed without permission, not even us. They would shoot us too. I moved as close as possible to Hafeek, almost hugging him. He actually looked terrified and unsure if I was bold enough to let go.

I heard one of the Embassy guards yell, "Hold fire!"

As I looked I saw mommy pointing and explaining. This was my chance. I stuffed the grenade in Hafeek's coat pocket and pushed him backward as hard as I could in an attempt to protect myself from the blast. I was thrown across the street anyway.

Maino pulled out and it began to rain bullets from all corners. Von swooped me up off the ground and threw me across the gate where mommy and the children were. Von tried to run back to get Mina and Sharifa when one of the men from Hafeek's camp opened fire. Sharifa went down. Then Mina tumbled down too.

"Noooooooo!!!" I screamed, trying to get up but still shook from the blast. "Minaaaaa! Mainoooooo!"

Maino dove over to where Mina laid while Von took out the last few of Hafeek's men.

Suddenly it became quiet enough to hear a baby breathe. Sharifa was hit in the throat. She was dead. Maino was hit in the arm, but he was okay. He was still on top of Mina. I couldn't see if she was moving.

"Minaaaaa!!!" I yelled.

Maino picked her up and took her to the gate. The Embassy guards and medical staff tended to her for a minute or two when one looked up at me putting two thumbs in the air. Hafeek's men dropped their weapons once they saw the snakes head on in the tree. Mina was alive. She was hurt but she would be okay. My heart began to beat again in that instance, thanking God she was okay. Yet I still grieved for Sharifa. She risked her life to save us. She gave up everything to help us. She was mommy's friend, that made her mine too.

The Embassy guards began rounding up Hafeek's men. Mommy rushed over to me and said, "You are exactly who I dreamed you'd be. Your brother and father would be proud. Where did you learn to fight like this?"

"Harlem, Mommy! Iron sharpens iron, right?" I replied, still out of breath and in major pain.

A helicopter picked us up to take us to Germany where we could receive medical attention. We stayed there a few days. Before being released, we were visited by the Department of Homeland Security and a few FBI agents. They came with the local news station to honor us for dismantling a huge jihadi sex trafficking operation. As the cameras and microphones were pushed into our faces, we were all thinking the same thing. In unison we shouted out our thoughts all the way to the tarmac.

"Sharifa! Sharifa! Sharifa!" We wanted to honor her.

Arriving in Germany, I realized this was my passion. I wanted to help others fight for the divine right to fight for themselves. I was born to be wild straight out the womb. Figure I'd put it to good use. Besides, I got a huge rush when I saw Hafeek's whole head land in that tree.

WET

On this journey through life, the starting line always seemed 93 million miles away from the finish line. Suddenly, a shooting star appeared dead center in the universe and the sun seemed like a small thing in comparison to the possibilities.

WET

Three Wishes

WET

I don't know about you, but I wasn't afraid to say I loved sex; good sex, though. Not the waste my time with ya' dysfunctional bullshit type. I didn't care for the *let-me-get-it-up* bullshit, acting like it was the first time your dick ever acted a fool... little dick slumped over like a slab of Italian sausage. What I needed was some good, back loosening, uterus massaging, clit-still-thumping-tomorrow type of fucking. Listen, I needed a man to snatch me by the back of my head, slam me up against a wall, and slide himself inside me. That was the kind of love making I craved.

I was single. I answered to no one and paid my own fucking bills. Having a man around was for pure pleasure. I called them when I needed them, sent them home when I was done with them, and ignored them as I indulged in a couple of other hobbies. For instance, his brother... maybe.

Yes, yes, and yes. Shut the hell up. I practiced very safe sex and I did my best to ensure my partners did as well. I had the perfect man all rolled up in three. Why should I deprive myself of good dick? Hell, this pussy was pretty juicy, so it kept them coming' back multiple times for a reason.

Seriously. For example, my baby, Tank. He was a beautiful cherrywood shade of chocolate goodness. He was buff as hell nice and rugged with a beautiful face. Sadly, Tank couldn't eat pussy worth a damn. He was forever fuckin' up my nut, moving his mouth at all the wrong moments, wanting eye contact and shit. I wanted to shout, "Boy, eyes on the prize. Look down there. It might help you navigate through this maze."

WET

I always had to tell him shit, instructions and what not. *No, nigga. Get it right or get the fuck up. I'm not in the business of teaching yo' ass shit. So, go practice on a mango and call me when you can make me come.* Those thoughts never left my head, but they should have. However, Tank, now this brother was thugged out to the bone. His dreads hung shoulder length and were about an inch thick. They smelled like pineapples and coconut oil. He stood about 6'4 and rocked a scruffy but sexy goatee.

Tank had a dick the size of my arm, literally. Make no mistake, he knew how to work that shit like a magic wand dipped in diamonds. He knew just how to make it worth my while. Royalty! Good God!

It never failed, I'd nut uncontrollably every time I fucked him. I was a hard nut to crack, so kudos to him. That was a great accomplishment. His dick game spoke volumes and that made him worth keeping around. On another more subtle but sweet note, I played Bruce. This babe was an older guy. He was a nice-looking chocolate, clean-cut dude. He wore suits and expensive snakeskin shoes and shit. That prettier than me crap was somewhat of a turn off, sometimes.

Needless to say, he came with wonderful perks. Bruce had major paper and didn't mind giving it to me. He would stroke and suck on my clit perfectly. He kept his face planted in my pussy for hours, coming up for air from time to time. Then, going straight back in, licking, sucking, and talking to my pearl. One time, I thought his ass was down there snoring.

Bruce was a slow gentle lover. His dick was small, though. It reminded me of squash... cookies! What the fuck? I had to chuckle at the thought. He was good for about eight minutes, including foreplay and clean up.

Bruce was good for a quickie when I felt like one. That amazing fucking mouth he had, though... His tongue felt like it was perfectly designed just for my pussy. He served his purpose well.

Bruce was slightly cocky. He knew I loved it when he had a late dessert inside my Candyland, and he didn't mind letting me know I'd miss that tongue if it ever went away.

I let the dummy think that shit. It costed him hundreds of dollars plus tax every week for an ego boost from the queen. He was in love with this pussy and would bow down to my every command. So, I let him talk shit. I let him think he was in control and decided in my head that if he ever pissed me off, I would play with my own pussy in his bed, just to show him that he wasn't a necessity and was so very easily disposable. I could do what he did and better.

In a perfect world, good sex, good food, and good living was fabulous. However, when your heart beat, you couldn't control its tempo. Even me, there wasn't much I gave a shit about these days. I was literally just doing me and having a ball doing it.

I guess we all had somewhat of a weak spot when it came to our hearts. We couldn't control who it beat the hardest for; that skipping of melodies when you were in their presence, the knot in your stomach seemingly attached to your soul… that beating that forces you to crave them, even in your sleep.

Antonio was that for me. He was my heart string. He was my husband on the low. I'd marry his ass if I ever decided to stop being selfish. If I ever decided to knock down this wall life had me build, he would be my rider on the other side. However, that would mean settling for one wish, giving up my "eat it too", cutting one cake for the rest of my life. Antonio. Mmm… yesss. Lawwwd, have mercy! This motherfucker was Heaven sent.

Tonio was from the Dominican Republic. Butterscotch coated his skin, he stood at 6'2 height, and his eyes were like the sunset, breathtakingly gorgeous. He had curly jet-black hair that looked, felt, and smelled of well-groomed fresh flowers... fluffy carnations. He had the cutest ears. I liked to grab them while his face was nestled between my legs. Mmmm, I thought about him doing just that. I'd grab them tighter, pulling his mouth closer up my thighs. Then, I'd stop, take a break, and clench his ears as he passed my pussy with a light wind from his breath.

He'd tease me, heading straight up to my belly button with the very tip of his tongue. Oh my God! Damn, my pussy was wetting up just thinking about his loving.'

Antonio was a semi-professional baseball player, soon to go pro. His body was cut the fuck up. It was graced with beautiful curvy biceps from shoulder to shoulder, rock solid lusciousness from his edible abs to that huge bulge in his pants. He was just fucking dope all around.

WET

Tonio was a fucking beast in the bedroom. He didn't fall short in any area. I figured out off the rip that nights with him would always end in the morning or the morning after that... or the morning after that. We usually dipped off for a weekend or more. Tonio was dope like that, fun, fine, and fuck worthy!

He too was worth a fortune that definitely added extra drip to his saucy sexy ass. Antonio wasn't like Bruce or Tank. He wasn't having no quick hit and go home action. He wanted to cuddle, hold hands, and go for walks in the beach. He had made it clear on more than one occasion that he wanted to marry me. He was in love with me and he knew I knew it. Truth be told, I was crazy about him too. I think we were in a relationship as much as I was willing to "*relate*" right now.

I just wasn't ready to be somebody's wife again. Cooking, cleaning, having to tell somebody when, where, and why the fuck I was leaving. Hmmph, he'd turn around and be fucking the next bitch the whole time. Fuck that. I was no longer putting anyone in the position to fuck my life up. I wasn't going to lie to myself. I wouldn't disappoint me. So, why the hell would I ever give anyone else a chance to? I preferred to have the freedom to fuck who I wanted. Bottom damn line, you can listen to the rest of this shit and still abide by your own choices. But I hope you keep reading, my love. It gets juicy.

Anyway, Antonio was my fuck me, *make-love-to-me*, and *hear-me-when-I'm-silent* lover. We were in a different place emotionally though. Neither Tank nor Bruce could come close. Tonio knew exactly when to hold me, and exactly when to spank my ass, making it jiggle. He could tell if my mood was screaming, "swing me by my ponytail and fuck me."

Antonio knew exactly when to just love me. Nevertheless, I was still single and did what I wanted, how I wanted, and when I wanted to do it. You're probably wondering, if he was so great, why not just be with him and just him?

I bet you think I'm a hoe too, huh? Greedy? Selfish? Nasty? Well, hell yes, I'm all of that. The last time I checked, I was signing these checks. So, I could really give no fucks about an opinion. Nevertheless, I guess I was hoeing a bit, because I was all about getting the coin. To be frank, the dudes I dabbled in… pffft, I didn't even have to ask them for anything. Hell, when Bruce's horny ass was around, I didn't even have to wipe my ass when I peed. Though, I've acquired many coins of my own, you couldn't put anything in my pussy if your coins didn't pierce my pockets.

Money really wasn't a deal breaker for me, because I wasn't looking to ever be tied down or taken care of. I took care of my damn self, so I didn't need a man. I was my own boss, in every sense of the word. Fuck you and what you convinced yourself you had to offer. I already had my own shit, that was my swag.

Asking me what I brought to the table? Really? First off, I didn't want you at my table unless you were fucking me on it. Second, I wasn't bringing nothing to your raggedy ass Rent-A-Center table because I had my own table and all the shit I needed to go on it. I wasn't in the habit of feeding niggas unless it was edibles coming from my pussy. Third, were you paying for this fucking table you were asking me about?

Tonio knew where I stood with the label thing. That girlfriend/boyfriend title shit. Nope, I wasn't with it. He dealt with it in hopes that he would eventually win me over. He absolutely didn't know I was still taste testing, condom-safe and all.

I was sure he would be angry. Oh well, I didn't really give a fuck. I did, but I didn't, if that made any sense. I was on another page when it came to living my life the way I wanted to.

I've had some awful relationships and some terrible experiences in the past. Now, I just wanted to LIVE! I vowed to let every decision I made from now on be solely based on the rhythm it put in my heart. Completely driven by what I wanted, I vowed to be still until something or someone moved me. Besides, Antonio wasn't going anywhere. He was whipped, fucked up. Tonio was crazy in love with me and this juicy, juicy!

He especially liked when I twirled my tongue around his dick, as if I were cleaning the drip from my ice cream cone… all the way around. That drove him bananas. He slapped me once, lightly, yet aggressively. It startled me, until I looked up at him. It was so cute. His eyes were closed, one hand gripping my head, the other resting on his hip. His head was tilted toward the ceiling. He wasn't himself in that moment. Yeah, I knew how to take you there. He was in another space, so I let him have that one. Besides, that shit was sexy as fuck, watching him enter wonderland and me helping him get there.

Yessss, that was the sexiest shit ever. I had it my way, like Burger King and I liked it that way. There would have to be some sort of cosmic intervention in order for me to change my orbit. Some things never happen, I always thought that. Have you ever noticed we only feel that way about the things we believe can NEVER happen? I learned to thank God for all the things that NEVER happened, though. That was my true saving grace.

It was Friday, Bruce was flying back in town tonight. He was already texting me about some fur coat he saw online, wondering if I was free tonight. Antonio was on tour in Italy. They had about four more games left in the season. I figured I could get my pussy done up and some change inside a new purse, why not?
I texted Bruce back.
Yes daddy. I missed you. I want to go to the Poconos for a few days. I could really use a break.
I added a tired worn out emoji. He quickly replied to my text.
Easy. I'll have a car bring you to the condo at nine. You can tell me what else you want then.
Yes sir. Can't wait. I replied.

Little did he know, he was about to send me on a trip to see Antonio in Spain, some spending money, and a shopping spree. I knew he was with it, though. He liked throwing money around. I believe it was a defense mechanism for coping with his male inadequacies. I felt sorry for him, sorry that he didn't realize we were all inadequate and ignoring the fact that perfection didn't exist. You wasted less energy being who you are than that of who you thought *WE* thought you should have been. But, whatever.

I was here for it, all day long baby! Listen, when God got ready to sit me down, he would. Right now, I was going to enjoy sharing the juicy fruits of my pussy with select sticks. Stella got her fucking groove back, so why couldn't I?

In the shower, getting ready for my evening with Bruce, I started craving Antonio. It was unusual and completely subconscious. Vivid images of he and I flashed repeatedly across my visual

I stuck my face in the water to wash away this semi-haunting feeling that had come over me. I ignored the flashes and continued washing. The trickling water from the shower was now giving off flashes of Bruce sucking on my clit. I was horny as hell.

My car was here, and I was feeling sexy as ever. Draped in my pearl white one-piece off the shoulder jumpsuit. My neck-angled hair was cut into a shoulder length bone straight bob and my lips were poppin' with my nude Fenty matte lipstick.

I decided to do something different tonight. I was feeling adventurous and wanted to have some fun. I told the driver to call Bruce and tell him we were picking him up instead. The driver chuckled. He thought it was cute. I asked him to close the partition and call Bruce to come down when we pulled up.

"Yes ma'am," he replied, smiling from ear to ear. I began to remove my clothes. Underneath, I was wearing this little red laced one-piece under garment. It had spaghetti straps and snaps at the crotch. I kept my shoes on. Bruce loved to watch my heels on his shoulders while he was tasting me, looking in awe from his peripheral.

Arriving at the condo, I heard Bruce questioning the driver. It was funny. I could tell the driver thought so too. Bruce finally calmed down and suddenly snatched the car door open.

"Man, come up. It's c-c-c-cool." He stammered, staring at my half naked body in amazement.

I literally watched his dick spread; like the popcorn bag rose as the heat built it up. He had to realize God's grace on his sexual spirit. He began smiling sinisterly and stuttering. Finally, abruptly hopping inside, he realized I was wide open, nipples like raisins, clit pulsating. I opened wide and he went right in.

"Oh, damn." I moaned as the driver asked where we were going on the intercom.

"DC to get some crabs." I replied.

"DC it is" Bruce yelled back.

"Yes, sir. Let's ride. Hit the button if you guys need anything."

We ignored him as Bruce continued to pleasure me. My feet were planted on the roof of the limo, my ass cheeks rested in Bruce's hands. He was holding on tightly, bouncing my ass back and forth, sucking on my clit.

WET

"Ohhhh, maaaan. Mhmmm. My god. You do that shit wonderfully every time." I moaned.

"I love this pussy, Cyn. Marry me," he whispered.
He didn't mean it. It was just the *fuck me* talk for him. He slid me on top of the seat so my ass cheeks were on the headrest and his knees were on the seat. He peeled my legs apart and dove in like he was in the ocean about to do the breaststroke.

So softly, Bruce licked around my thighs. First, my right thigh. Then, my left, kissing my knees while tickling my nipples with the tip of his fingers.

"This shit feels amazing." I squealed.
The car was moving smoothly with just enough rock to aid in my arrival. Bruce would nut just eating my pussy. He would eat it again so he could regroup and fuck me for about four minutes. So, really, if you thought about it, it was a win-win for me.

If I wanted some dick, I had to get my pussy ate first. You're a damn liar if you said you weren't down for that. I let him eat that shit, nap in it, and wet on it all the way to D.C. That equaled mortgage, a couple of trips, some pocket change, and his Amex for my shopping spree. Besides, me and Bruce were good friends. Who better to fuck than a friend, right? No strings. No obligations. No explanations Just good, wet, adventurous sex for me. It was quite pleasurable for him too; expensive, but out of this world and so much fucking fun.

WET

We were riding through Delaware, both resting, still naked, sipping champagne and nibbling off the snacks at the bar. The driver asked if we needed a rest stop. Quickly, we both replied, "NO!"

I was hungry as hell and I knew Bruce was also. Still, my taste buds were fixated on those D.C. crabs and what I wanted, I got. I laid down flat on my back, figuring I'd sleep for the next two hours of riding.

Wishful thinking. Here comes Bruce. I wanted to tell his lil' dick ass to go up front with the driver so I could get some sleep. Instead, I went with it. "Oooh, mmhmm baby." I faked a moan. "Take a load off daddy. You wore me out."

Just like I thought, he agreed. "Ah, yeah baby. Daddy fixed mama's pussy up, huh?"

"Yeah, daddy. Come here. Lay ya' face in my lap. I just want to feel you breathe on my pussy." I said. That shit was sexy as shit too. You would have thought I worked for a damn sex talk line or some shit. Yes, bitch, you did that. I had to pat myself on the back.

"Yes ma'am." He replied, planting his nose and mouth comfortably on my well-groomed garden.

Needless to say, Bruce accosted my whole pussy area the entire ride back. I just laid back and played pillow princess, hopping on his face, bouncing and grinding my ass on it. I wasn't wasting one drip. I wanted it all… I meant that literally and wholeheartedly.

Bruce would irritate me sometimes, tickling and slow stroking my pussy. *Boyyy, eat that shit up like its shrimp and grits. Spank my clit with the back of your hand. You gotta be aggressively gentle, though. You gon' fuck it up without the right balance. I need just the right amount of pressure when ringing the devil's doorbell.*

I was coaching him into making me orgasm in my head. I knew he would be straight for about a month after all that. He usually was out of the country on business and would hit me up when he was in town. I could care less what went on beyond me. It wasn't my problem.

Sometimes, Bruce took me with him. We'd been to Tokyo, St Thomas, India, and the Philippines; extravagant trips with the best excursions ever. Bruce liked the best of everything. He liked me. So, he liked me to enjoy the best of his everything. It was a dope arrangement and I liked him, so that helped. See, I'm wasn't just out here fucking people for money. I was living! Try it instead of sitting there reading about my chronicles. I was enjoying this shit. My pussy stayed wet on the regular. Girl, you better go get you a Bruce!

Bruce booked my round-trip flight to Spain and a suite at the amazingly luxurious and historic Hotel Maria Christina. He also left an open-ended tab for spa and boutique visits. I was gonna surprise Antonio with a sexy distraction and it was just great that I could splurge a bit. I hopped on the first-class flight early the next afternoon after a quick bite to eat and a manicure. I had a long flight, so I made sure I packed my laptop so I could get some work done.

I had a few more classes before I was able to open my practice. Oh yeah. let me introduce myself. I'm Cynthia, you call me Cyn. My practice was all about releasing the alter ego, doing what they say we shouldn't, working your sexuality to the highest levels of orgasm possible.

Why the fuck not?? I found that many women complained about a man not being able to make them climax. They, ok we, often boasted about the ability to create our own explosions. So, think about it ladies. If you could achieve the most amazing nut by yourself, imagine if you could train your body to produce that same energy when enjoying someone else? Make him or her MAKE you come. When I say make, I mean that in the most literal sense; that *don't-stop-do-whatever-it-takes-until-you-bust* lovemaking. Use his or her body for whatever it took to get there. Like Usher said, that's what it's made for. Go on and hit it. That's what it's made for.

We gotta stop saying he fucked me, queens, and start saying I fucked him! He was gonna come, trust me... unless he had some dysfunctional shit going on. But, yeah, all a man needed was a place. We needed emotional companionship. Hell, I needed mortgage, flights, car notes, red bottoms, dinner, shopping, and cuddling. Shit, and that was just to name a few. He had to at least be able to do more for me than I could do for myself; otherwise, what was the point? I didn't like nobody like that. It was a fucking reason I allowed a man to enjoy my presence.

After some blog entries and answering a few emails, I fell asleep watching a movie. It was *Australia*, my absolute favorite of all times. The love story between the aboriginal boy, Hugh Jackman, and Nicole Kidman was phenomenal.

WET

I must have fallen asleep because I woke to the flight attendant telling me to buckle up for landing in ten minutes. I felt the wheels hit the pavement and a flood of excitement rushed me. I couldn't wait to see Antonio. I couldn't wait to fuck 'em on some Italian landmarks, in some dope ass Italian shoes. Yes, shoe shopping and great sex in one of the most romantic cities ever. I was with it.

I had a car pick me up so I could surprise Tonio. I decided to go to the stadium where practice was held and have lunch with him. As the car pulled up to the curb, I saw Tonio outside. He seemed to be walking a young lady to her car. I asked the driver to wait a second before I got out so I could observe this shit a bit more.

She kissed him on his cheek as he opened the door. Then, she got in and pulled off. That wasn't no fan kiss either. I decided, in that instant, I wouldn't mention what I saw to Antonio. Whoever she was, I was not about to make it easy for her legs to just fly open.

Besides, I wasn't tripping. I knew Antonio would fuck up and do exactly what men did. Sell out! They were disrespectful, greedy as fuck assholes and they always had an excuse or wanted to blame you, talking stupid shit like, *"you don't suck my dick enough or, you always got an attitude."*

Shut the fuck up and admit you had to use all these women to convince yourself that your raggedy, funky, lil' dick wasn't really as bad as it sometimes seemed. *Oh, let me go fuck Tasha and see if I can still last at least four minutes.*

237

Starzpen

WET

No, let me call Lisa, she nibbles on the tip. It'll stay hard longer for her.

Antonio was really getting a dose of protein from two other sources. I decided to make the rest of Antonio's time here surrounded by me. I planned to shut lil' mama down. This pussy, this dope ass mind, and this amazing love I had for myself. She won't stand a chance. I'll play nice for now.

I waited about five minutes before entering the stadium. Tonio spotted me at the gate. "Aye, let her in, Sam. He hollered, running towards me. The gate opened and he swooped me up, slamming me on top of the car.

Everyone was watching, smiling. Some were even recording and going live from their social media. I sometimes forgot how big of a star athlete he was, even in another country.

Antonio stuck his tongue completely down my throat, He did it so sweetly it screamed, "*I miss you, baby. Can we please fuck right here?*" My legs wrapped around his waist, arms around his neck, and we twirled and twirled, kissing, missing, and loving' up on each other.

I didn't want to argue and fuss about no bitch. She was no threat to me and if he wanted to go, trust ladies, he was going. So, just had to make him want to stay. I decided to give him every opportunity to fuck over me but every reason not to want to. With his dick consistently resting on the back of my throat and his balls hitting my cheeks on the regular, I do believe the bag was secured.

"Hey baby, I missed you." He said.

"I miss you too, baby." I replied. That was really code for, *yeah motherfucker I'm glad I pulled up when I did.*

"You can wait in here. Let me wrap up practice and we can go." He told me as we arrived at a room in the stadium. It was like a hotel room. It had a bed, television, bar, and an amazing bathroom. I assumed it was for out of town guests.

Antonio had a roommate, so the arrangements Bruce made for me were perfect. The Maria was so romantic and sexy. I had already made up my mind I was gonna get me some dick right here, though. I was jet-lagged, tired, and my body was aching for a fix and a quickie would be love right now.

Watch me goggle his dick and make him drop to his knees. Or, at least want to. He'd have no choice but to exit via my pussy before we headed out. Besides, I was already naked in the kitchen, eating the fruit left on the counter. It was in a gorgeously woven basket. Sweet too. I decided to place some pineapple wedges and grapes between my legs, made a lil' pussy platter for him.

Tonio walked in and dropped the clipboard and towel that was in his hand. He headed straight for me. With one leg propped up on the faucet, he planted his foot on the counter.

The fruit looked amazing against my skin. Vivid colors graced my thighs, awaiting his nibble.

"Yessssss gawwwwd!! You got time for a little snack, Toni?" I asked.

WET

He grabbed an apple from the counter and turned on the faucet to rinse it. Oh, you forgot my legs were open. He was rinsing all the fruit with cool water, just a trickle though. I noticed how careful he was with the water pressure. It was a gentle stream running down my legs.

He bit the apple and kissed me sweetly, still chewing, putting the apple near my lips to share. I took a slight nibble and rubbed my fingertips across both his nipples. He mirrored my actions, gracing my nipples, slowly looking at them like they were diamonds. I held my head back to expose my neck. He knew what to do next. I had a pressure spot there. He would suck on it perfectly. It would ignite every part of me. Only, he could do that; which I found dope and somewhat annoying... annoyed that he makes me wonder.

He placed both hands gently around my neck using his elbow against my calf to turn off the water. Twirling his tongue around that spot on both sides, he caressed me with the tip of his finger. My God I was weak. I gripped both his shoulders and arched my back.

"Let me look at you, Cyn." Tonio whispered, backing up as he helped me off the sink.

I stood ass naked, one finger in my mouth, the other rubbing on my clit. He grabbed a bottle of apple Crown Royal from the bar and poured a shot. He poured that shit all over me.

"Don't fucking move," he commanded. I stood at attention and dared not move and fuck up this nut.

"Yessss." I began to reply.

WET

"Shut the fuck up, Cyn. Right now. I'll tell you when and what to speak. Got it?" He growled, slapping me on my ass. It stung, but I knew that was my pain before pleasure. So, I shut the fuck up like he asked.

With Crown apple now running down my torso and landing in my belly, trickling down my thighs, Tonio caught every drip. On his knees, he weaved himself between my legs as I stood in a perfect "A", legs spread precisely the way he wanted them, licking and slurping sweet apple flavor off my hot, wet, butterscotch color-coated body.

"Grab my head, mami." Tonio commanded.
I grabbed it, moving my hips to the tune of his tongue. "Ooh baby." I whispered, grabbing my ass cheeks tightly. I felt the tip of his fingernails. I liked it.

"Did I tell you to talk?" He asked, smashing his whole face into my pussy. Oh my God! He was not playing. He missed this juicy booty. I wanted to come so bad!

Suddenly, Tonio jumped up from his knees and lifted one leg up, resting it in his arm crease, he rammed inside me so hard. It almost hurt, but I liked that shit too. So, it was cool. Sliding in and out, slamming me between his dick and the wall, he looked at me. "Say my name, Cyn."

"Toniooo!" I whispered, moving his ear so it touched my lips.
"Say it again. What's my name baby?"
"Antonio, my love!" I replied, weakening by the second. Still fucking me, he snatched my ponytail, swinging me around and slung me onto the bed, face down. My knees

241

were at the foot as he thrust my stomach upward, forcing me on my knees, hands planted in front of me one on top of the other. He wrapped one arm around my neck, almost in a headlock and crept up inside me, slowly enjoying the moment.

I could tell he was all in, watching his dick go in and out. I squirmed and pleaded for him not to stop. Slapping and punching my nipples, Tonio was in absolute beast mode. Hell, he had me growling and purring and shit.

"Umm umm umm umm, ooooh. Baby," I squealed, trying to get out the words between our fuck me vocals.

"What, Cyn?"

Harder. Bang. Bang. Bang. The headboard was hitting the wall. He was doing this amazing long, slow, deep stroke. It didn't take long for him to nut.

I could feel his dick hit every wall, every nook and damn cranny I had. He dropped his head in my shoulder and caught his breath a minute.

"Let's go babe." I whispered.

"Hell naw, that was just a warm up. I gotta get you right." He countered. We both laughed.

"It's all good. This one was for you." I assured him as I kissed his forehead and gestured toward the door.

"Will some housekeeping come in here, bae?" I asked.

"Don't worry about all that, Cyn. You good." He responded amused.

"Well, I just don't want my DNA floating around in here."

We both laughed as we assembled ourselves for the exit. Paparazzi was everywhere. We both knew they'd be

WET

waiting outside. All smiles, of course. Hand in hand, we walked out of the stadium. People were screaming his name, asking for photos and trying to get him to sign balls. Little did they know, I had already signed, sealed, and suck them.

Security was making a path as the driver opened the door. Antonio gave one more wave and posed for a few pictures before we left. The whole ride over, my phone was blowing the fuck up.

Did I give a fuck? Nah. Antonio knew where we stood. He never cared about my phone's activity before. But, somehow, I still cared about what he thought. Antonio was growing on me a little too much for my comfort. I was beginning to feel like I was somebody's girlfriend?

I decided to smoke a joint and loosen up for this trip. I was still dreamin', livin', and lovin' life.
"Give me some weed, Tonio." I asked
"You wanna smoke, bae?"
"Yeah, I'm going to smoke in Italy." We both laughed.
He reached for my hand like married couples did, hold hands as they rode and shit. Don't get all mushy and emotional with me, man.

Nevertheless, with a subtle hesitancy, I clamped my fingers between his. It felt nice. I felt safe... taken care of. Was I feeling love?

I knew we said it to one another, but I was 39 years old and I've never felt for anyone what I felt for Antonio. I had never shared a friendship with anyone like I shared with

243

Starzpen

him. My body didn't quiver for anyone, not even me like it quivered for Tonio. I never knew love, so I had no example to piggyback off of. All I had was my heartbeat, my pussy moisture levels, and the ability to make me laugh.

Tonio topped the charts in all those. However, I didn't want to be in no damn love, shoot. I just wanted to do what I wanted to do, damn. Why shit had to get so tongue twisted and difficult. I didn't go through this shit with Bruce and Tank; probably because I didn't want their asses like that anyway.

I could have another Bruce in the morning, one with a big dick too. Hell, Tank's ass was definitely a dime a dozen as well. He was cool, but totally disposable.

Ultimately, I decided I was going to enjoy this trip to the fullest and just rock with my boo. It wasn't all bad. Or, was I opening Pandora's box? For some reason, I had this flash of pain, an internal pain; a slight visual of red flags, but nothing specific. I had reservations about everything and just about everyone, so I ignored it. They said you should never ignore your gut, but I did.

The Wish That Mattered

My practice had grown beyond belief. I had no less than seven clients a day. Everyday. I had to hire an assistant and expand my office space. Not to mention, expanding myself.

I had no time for anything. I cut back tremendously on the time I spent with Tank. He had a big dick and all, but when I saw one in Priscilla's sex store just like it, I thought, *damn what a waste of time.*

Sex was really all he was good for. I still dabbled in Bruce's bank account from time to time: not that I needed to, though. The business was soaring, but Bruce was into buying property, taking huge life changing trips around the world, and expanding the dollar on purpose. Those were the types of people I decided to surround myself with, ambitious people, those that motivated me to move mountains.

Bruce was the kind of person that desired to believe in me, so he showed me how to believe in myself. He invested in me and taught me how to invest in myself. He wanted to build with me on a business level and we had pretty good sex. Nevertheless, neither of us wanted anything permanent. It was perfect just the way it was.

He was about to purchase the property in my name for my new office space. We decided on seven percent lifetime take for him. I did that so even if the sex stopped, we would still build in other ways. He was and always would be my friend. Now, circumstances did vary upon situation, but overall this was fact. See, ladies, when women expressed love, we generally expressed it through loyalty, nurturing, and affection.

WET

Ok, simpler language, we cooked, cleaned, and sucked his dick, regularly. Most men were quite the opposite. A man would take you to dinner; however, if it was McDonald's or Tavern on the Green, it would tell you where his mind was.

For example, a big mac would satisfy your hunger. However, Tavern on the Green would stimulate your mind. You weren't getting that without some thought, a bit of care, and a sprinkle of interest beyond the booty... my three wishes all rolled up in one. They each served a purpose. I had convinced myself I deserved them.

I had made a believer out of the liar in me that kept saying, "keep ya' pussy wet at all times, you deserve it. Maintain a mountain in your pocket, adding to it consistently. You're worth it. Enjoy life, no matter the fucking cost. You only live once. Enjoy it while you can."

I wasn't afraid of committing. I just didn't want to. I didn't feel like being lied to, disappointed, and fucked over. So I avoided giving a fuck at all costs until I couldn't anymore.

***

Tonio and I decided to go zip lining across the ocean. We were having an amazing time. The weather was perfect a slight ray of sun was shining with just the right amount of breeze. The water sprinkling as we glided from one end of the pier to the other was refreshing. Dolphins jumped in and out of the waves, just breathtaking.

Starzpen

Suddenly, I heard something snap and the line jerked. I heard Tonio say, "Oh shit. Noooooo!" He said it right before his body hit the water like a two-ton rock.

"Oh my God," I screamed. Jet skis and speed boats scrambled to his location. They loaded Toni up and headed full throttle to shore. I hopped on a nearby jet ski and followed.

Once we arrived at the hospital, the doctors worked on him for hours before giving us an update. Finally, he came out and told us Tonio was paralyzed from the waist down. I couldn't move. I couldn't react. I was speechless, on top of crushed, with a whole lot of what the fuck running through my mind.

"Is he awake?" I asked.

"No, not yet. He is still sedated quite heavily. Let's let him rest through the night and you can see him in the morning," the doctor advised.

I wasn't having that shit though. "Umm, well, I'll sit with him until he wakes up," I told him.

"Well," he said hesitantly, not yet realizing I wasn't asking. "Ok, but you get some rest as well. I'll make sure the staff does all they can to make you comfortable."

"Thank you," I replied sitting there looking at Toni like this was extremely difficult.

Basketball was his first love. *This is going to break him*, I thought. Somewhere in my heart, I didn't believe Tonio would stay this way, no matter what the doctors said.

In my heart, in my gut, I saw him on his feet. I prayed all night that he would come through this like the champ he was.

I woke up to the nurses taking Toni's vitals. His eyes were open. Cleary, he had been crying. I jumped up and ran to his side, immediately.

"Hey babes." I cooed. He just looked at me with the most intense pain in his eyes. "How you feeling?" I asked.

"Like I fell out a plane," he answered humorously. "The doctors say I may not walk again. The nerve damage to my spine from the fall was so severe, it paralyzed me from the waist down." He explained softly, almost as if he was embarrassed.

"I know. That's what they said, but I know a man that can say different. I don't believe that for a second and neither should you."

He offered a half smile. "I guess marrying me anytime soon is really out of the question now, huh?"

I shrugged. "Let's not worry about stuff like that right now. I need you to put on your faith gear and let's get ready to make liars out of the doctors," I demanded. "I called your mom. She's flying in this evening. I have a car ready to pick her up."

The nurses came in to run some tests, so I stepped out. I headed down to the chapel and just sat there. My heart was heavier than normal. Something was missing. *Cynthia? Are you giving a fuck?* I asked myself.

I had compassion for Tonio's injuries and the long road to recovery he'd end up on. This was different. This felt like...L... Lo...Love. I was sick to my stomach at the thought of losing him. My heart dropped as he did when he fell. I felt helpless, lonely, and in love. The thought of Tonio not walking again devastated me.

WET

Bruce and Tank seemed like small things to this giant emotion. Could I live with him not walking again? That never once crossed my mind. I knew I'd never leave his side, even if he never walked again. His mouth was moving just fine, and I fed off the way he loved me. It was the sexiest thing in the world, and it made me love him even more.

***

After a few weeks we were able to fly Tonio back to the states. I moved in with him and his mother came too for a few months. He went through test after test, experiment after experiment, and got disappointment after disappointment. I was waiting for my mind to start telling me I needed more than a wheel chair and an awesome companion. It never did, though. My heart did a complete 180 and led me down a path of mind over matter. Quality over quantity. All that cake and eating it too was putting weight on me that I could no longer carry.

Tonio's love for me was refreshingly welcomed. Even though I'd convinced myself I didn't want forever, ever again, I came home from work to an amazing candlelight dinner. Tonio had waiting. He was all fly and smelling good. It was a welcomed surprise. We hadn't let our hair down since the accident.

Toni's mom left as I was coming in. She hugged me and said, "thank you for all you do for my baby. He loves you and so do I." She kissed my cheek and walked out, giving Tonio two thumbs up behind my back. I saw her reflection in the glass door as she opened it.

WET

Wondering what he needed luck with, I asked, "what's up, babes? What you and moms in hear doing?" He smiled and said, "sit babe."

I complied. He began to tell me how he knew all about my extracurricular activities with Bruce and Tank. He had known it all the time. He never said anything because he wanted me to choose him on my own without the angry ultimatum or the do the right thing pressure, because I felt like I had to. He went on to explain that he may never walk again, and he would totally understand if that was an issue for me.

Honestly, contrary to his well warranted insecurity on the matter, it wasn't an issue. It didn't bother me anymore than it bothered him. If he was sad, I was sad for him. If he hurt, I hurt with him. The way he looked at me even at my worst was confirmation enough for me to offer him my whole heart in return.

He pulled out this huge diamond ring from his shirt pocket and said, "I'm prepared for a no, but my faith is set for a yes on a thousand."

Without hesitation, I hopped in his lap and said, "I thought you'd never ask. Yes! Yes. Yes!"
"Yes?" He repeated skeptically. "You sure, Cyn? I won't hold it against you if you can't handle it.?

"Antonio, I've been scared to love you back this whole time, hence Tank and Bruce being my plan B and C. However, the instant I got a feel for what it would be like without you, I knew. So, yes, I love you and I will marry you, ride with you... Ride ya' face for as long as you'll have me," I added seductively.

Out of nowhere, I heard a sneeze. "What the hell was that?" I frowned. "Oh, you got a bitch in here, Toni?"

"It's me. It's me." Tonio's mom yelled. "I'm sorry y'all. I had to be here in case you hurt my baby, Cyn."

We all laughed and suddenly Tonio got up walked toward me. He got down on one knee and placed this humongous ring on my finger. I almost fainted. It was perfect. I couldn't have asked for a better proposal.

Tonio's mom was in tears and so was I. Hand in hand, heart to heart, we walked... together, straight to the bedroom. Me, Tonio, and my one wish. We'd live, love, and laugh for an eternity.

Sometimes, the most enticing three wishes would be drowned by an ounce of faith, a pop of love, and a whole lot of orgasms leading you to your one true wish.

WET

Toni's Reign

WET

I pulled up at the truck stop, unannounced, with good news to share with my husband, Rudy. I had just gotten the news of a major movie producer showing interest in my book. He wanted to put it on the big screen for the world to see. The truck stop was unusually empty with only about two trucks in the lot.

I thought it was strange that the truck and Rudy's car were both parked there. As I moved closer to the cab, I noticed the truck rocking. I stood still for about thirty seconds, observing the movement of the truck.

"This your pussy, daddy. Want me to bounce it on ya' face?" The strange woman's voice burned my ears. It was evidence of betrayal.

I abruptly climbed up onto the driver's side of the truck and looked through the window. I saw a nicely rounded, size ten, buttercream colored honey completely naked bouncing wildly on her husband's dick. Rudy laid on his back with his hands behind his head.

I frowned. "What the fuck? I bounce better than that," I said. The little slut bucket jumped off top of Rudy and grabbed some nearby clothing, trying to cover herself. Rudy gathered his items, trying to cover up as well. I never understood that. You were okay being naked a minute ago, but now you suddenly wanted to hide in shame?

"Really? Get yo ass up! No more fun for y'all TODAY!" I screamed. "My one and only question is, why this truck ain't moving? Well, it's moving alright, but where is today's pay?"
"Our bills paid, man! Baby, listen. Let me explain."

"Let you explain that you fucking this bitch in the truck you supposed to be making money with? You couldn't fuck her after? Stupid!" I yelled.

"Toni!! Baby," he started. "You don't be wanting to fuck me, though. You always working and don't pay me no attention. You know I love you," he lied.

I studied the jump-off. "Don't you work at Nieman's? I've seen you before?"

"Yes, I work there," she answered, scared and trembling.

"Please don't try to fight her I told her I was separated." Rudy said, looking all stupid in the face, probably praying to God I didn't blow up his truck. However, I was going to leave him with his truck and his nut. He was going to need em'.

My mood was different, much different than even I expected. I didn't feel the need to pull out my gun and exit pure iron into their brains. I oddly avoided the urge to throw a book of lit matches in the gas tank. I had honestly fallen out of love with Rudy the first time he cheated on me. It didn't affect my heart. He just played on my intelligence a bit and missed a day's worth of dough. This just confirmed for my head what my heart already knew. It was a wrap! Done. Rudy and I had been together since junior high school. I guess I've been trying to hold on to that piece of me, fearful of what and who I was without him.

Rudy and I had clearly out grown one another. I just never thought passing my pussy around would remedy that for me. Needless to say, men were different, and I knew that. The woman in me lost interest years ago. Sex with Rudy became dull and robot like. I had more fun with my fingers and my pillows. I would always know when he was cheating because I kept getting yeast infections, obviously from these slutbots he had been forcing me to share juices with.

I stopped sleeping with him all together after that. What I had in mind for the real ending was crazy as hell. I wanted a sense of fulfillment that differed from anything I'd ever done. Things I only thought about and saw in books and movies.

Today, I felt on top of the world, as if the universe just shifted in my favor. It was almost like cat woman when she hopped on her bike in all black leather for the first time with a new confidence. The rush was enormous, the sense of power was extraordinary, and the erotic juices flowed through my pussy when I thought about the magnitude of the sexual satisfaction I truly craved. It made me wet and horny. I also wanted to have a little fun with this idiot for a while for all the lies, disrespect, and bullshit I put up with. I was going to make him sorry he didn't put more effort into fucking me and loving me properly all these years. The way missy was looking on top of him in the truck. It was apparent I've been missing out.

I decided not to tell Rudy about the movie deal I'd landed. He paid no attention to me anyway, so he probably wouldn't even find out until it released.

I received a major advance check for royalties from the book, didn't tell Rudy that either. Before I divorced his ass and moved on with my life, I wanted to have some fun. I popped in to Neiman's to holla at Lil' Miss Truck Stop.

WET

When she saw me, she tried to run into the dressing area. I followed her and backed her into a corner. I was somewhat amused by how frightened she was. Yet, I reassured her I wasn't there for petty drama. "What is your name?" I asked.

"Sunni," she replied.

"Hi Sunni. I'm Toni," I told her. "I believe we have formally met already."

She frowned. "Ok, so why are you here Toni, at my job? That was a one-time thing with Rudy. I was just bored and felt like fucking. I wasn't tryna hurt or wreck anyone's home," she explained.

"No worries. It was already wrecked, boo boo. You get no credit. Anyway, enough about Rudy. I'm here for a different reason," I explained.

She looked suspicious, puzzled, and scared to death. "Okay," she mumbled.

"I just got a deal for my book and I want to execute some of the things on my bucket list."

"So, what does that have to do with me?" She asked.

"Well I was hoping you'd be able to help me."

"Help you how?" She asked.

"I wanna fuck repeatedly with different people, in my house. Hopefully Rudy walks right in." I told her.

She laughed and paused for a minute before saying, "wow, that's a bit scandalous don't you think?"

"Yes, but I've dealt with scandal, as you're well aware. Time to dish out some of my own."

Sunni hesitated for a few seconds and then said, "Ok, I'd love to help you. On some girl power shit. I guess I do owe you one."

"Yes bitch, you do," I answered sarcastically. We both laughed.

WET

"What exactly did you have in mind?" She asked excitedly.

I handed her my phone to view my bucket list. Her facial expressions while reading were telling a story of its own. She was so with it. Before I could say a word, she typed her number in my phone and called herself.

"I love this idea of being so carefree and doing what you feel. I think I know exactly how to execute this task. "

"So, you'll help? Point me in the right direction? Introduce me to some willing participants?"

"Absolutely, my love. This is right up my alley." Shockingly, she agreed and asked when I wanted to get started.

I'll text you later with details," I replied.

"Ok, and Toni, I'm sorry about Rudy and all."

"No, you're not! You were lovin' that shit. He do got a big dick, though." I called her out on her lie.

"Yes he does! But just in case, I am sorry."

"Don't be, love. It was over way before you. But word to the wise, be careful. You may not be so lucky next time. You'd both be dead if I gave a fuck."

As I turned to walk away, Sunni called out to me. "Here, take this discount card for the store. By the looks of that list, it'll come in handy."

I took the card and told her good looking out and I'd talk to her later. Number one on my list was a threesome. I wanted a threesome with two women and myself. Then, two men and I. Finally, a man, a woman, and myself. It was Sunni's job to make the connections. I knew she was single and freely mingling. So, I was sure she'd know just the right people.

WET

I never had a one-night stand or been real loose with my snacks. Being tied down in this loveless marriage had opened me up to exploring new things.

The next night, after Sunni and I plotted on this escapade, I went to Neiman's to pick up a few items. Those five-year-old moo-moos and pajamas weren't gonna work for what I had planned. I used the 50% off coupons to purchase a few sexy items for my future single life runs. After shopping, I headed over to the spa to get a mani/ pedi and the landing strip groomed. I felt like the million-dollar advance I'd received and was looking like I was coming down the spiral stairway at the Playboy mansion. I put the wine on chill, booted up my Pandora to the *Fuck Me Now* playlist and waited for my guests to arrive. I hoped Sunni did good and didn't ruin my night with mud ducks

I knew Rudy would be home around seven, so I timed my nut perfectly. No bedroom for me. I wanted to be fucked beyond imagination in the kitchen, the first room visible when entering the house.

The doorbell rang. I was sure it was my blind fuck dates. As I peered through the peephole, I saw this fine ass hunk of man with green eyes and his skin looked so smooth that you could drink it; a mocha latte with whip cream and a cherry on top for sure.

As I opened the door Sunni came from around the corner. Surprised to see her here, I still invited them both in anyway. "Toni, this is Snoop. Snoop, Toni." Sunni introduced us.
"Hello, Big Sexy. I said excitedly.

259

Starzpen

WET

"Hi, beautiful," he replied.

"Hey, Sunni. What are you doing here?" I asked.

"Well, I was thinking the best revenge on Rudy would be me here when Snoop puts this shit right here to bed," she answered, pointing and probing my pussy. "I can help."

I knew the threesome was on my bucket list, so I didn't trip and similar to myself, she was a baddy. Rudy did have good taste. I smiled devilishly. It would be great for Rudy to walk in and see his lil' honeypot with her face in my ass and me riding the shit out of this fine hunk of chocolate she brought with her.

I had never been into chicks, but I left no boundaries when creating my list. I had specific projects and characteristics I'd requested, and Sunni did a great job. His name was Ghost, no not like James St. Patrick from the show *Power*. He was Ghost way before that.

"Anywho", I walked over to the bar and poured everyone some wine. Half-naked in this hot little white nightie, my wand curls trickled down to my ass. Coconut oil shined my collar bone as well.

"Mmm hmm, sexy as hell, Sunni. I was expecting some old, dried up hag. You're gorgeous," Mr. Sexy smiled.

"I did good, huh?" Sunni perked.

"Yess! You did," He and I said at the same time.

Sunni took a sip of wine before taking off the double-breasted coat she was wearing. That's all she was wearing. She positioned herself behind me and wrapped her arms

260

Starzpen

underneath mine, massaging my titties subtly. I felt all tingly inside, not sure if I was diggin' this girl on girl action. Yet, I was still curious and quite turned on.

While Sunni caressed my body, she softly blended with each curve. Swaying my body with hers, I vibed to Tank singing his latest hit. That fucking hot mocha latte of a man walked over, he dropped straight to his knees, loosened the snaps on my teddy with his teeth, and put my whole pussy in his mouth. His bottom lip was slightly softer than the top one.

Toni was kissing my neck while Ghost sucked my mango dry. I heard smacking coming from my pussy. Grabbing both my thighs and peeling them apart wider, Sunni held one leg up for him, bumping and grinding her clit on my ass. Holding Ghost's head so my clit rested perfectly on his tongue, I found his rhythm, my pussy was slow dancing with Ghosts' face. Sunni began to tap on my asshole, making my knees weak.

"Ooh, damn. Yesss. Yesss. Yesss! Oh, my goodness! Right there. Put your tongue in my pussy." I wanted to scream. I had a husband; a live-in pussy licker and it never felt that good.

I'm so deprived. I thought.
Shit! I was about to come in his mouth, and he was down there looking like he was ready for the flood.
"How that pussy taste, baby? You like?" I purred.
"Hell yeah." ghosts said.

WET

Then Sunni asked, "and how about you, miss? How you feeling?" She still was firmly pressing her clit against my ass, subtly stimulating her own pussy.

"Ummm," Sunni moaned, moving her body up and down, grabbing and clutching my thighs.

Ghost rose up, wiping my juices with his hand and letting Sunni taste my juices running off his fingers. "Mmmm, sweet pussy. What was your husband thinking? All this good sweetness, he could have had us both." She shook her head and we both giggled. Ghost grabbed Sunni by the waist and laid her on the kitchen table. She opened her legs and began playing with her hotbox.

"Mmm, yes baby. I'll be right there," Ghost said. Before taking care of Sunni, he scooped me up and straddled me over her face.

"Yes, Toni. Bring that pussy here she demanded. Ghost pulled her body to the edge of the table with me on top, kissing me and rubbing each breast, while ramming his dick inside Sunni.

The harder he fucked her, the harder she went on my clit.

"Umm umm umm ummmmmm," I moaned.

Bam. Bam. Bam.

Finally, Rudy was home. He was standing in the doorway with his mouth open. Ghost's dick was still going in and out of Sunni while his hands and her tongue made amazing music with my body. Ghost looked up, as if to say *'should I stop.'*

For some reason, I didn't think Sunni passed on the memo about the "*get back at 'em*" shit. "Hell, no." I belted out, breathing hard as hell, working hard for the nut. "Don't stop, Sunni. You're tearing my pussy up."

I dropped down uncontrollably, face in her belly button, Ghost pounding harder and harder with his hands on his hips. I could tell she was about to come, so I arched my back and fed her my pussy while holding her legs up, making the "V".

Griping her ankles and bouncing my ass on her face, I held her legs apart, keeping her body in place so Ghost could beat the pussy up. Watching him pump weight in and out all thug-like and rugged was sexy as hell.

"Sunni, I knew you was a hoe and it's over, Toni. You're in our house? In our kitchen? And who the fuck is this swole ass, pretty boy looking nigga? Toni!" Rudy yelled. He was losing it.

Me in a sixty-nine position with my pussy getting major attention, I watched Ghost fuck the shit out of Sunni in full HD.

"Oooh, babyyy!" I screamed. Then, I focused on Rudy. "Come watch me come in ya' girlfriend's mouth. You wanna hold her face still for me? Aaahh, come on, baby. Come with me." I moaned.

"Rudy, ya' wife's pussy tastes great." Sunni taunted.

"Bitch, fuck you!" Rudy spat.

"Ooooh, yes. You hear that, Ghost? You can fuck me. I wanna come wit' Sunni."

He went harder and deeper. With each thrust, I got the aftershock as she bounced back. "Yes, sweet, soft exotic moans and groans came from all of us.

"I'm gonna come again." I screamed, looking straight into Rudy's eyes. I smiled while I worked my body... around and round, grinding and swaying on Sunni's face.

In the midst of my climax, Ghost grabbed my throat. With one hand still stroking my nipples and pumping his big wet mocha colored dick inside Sunni, He stuck his tongue gently in my mouth. Sunni's hands were smacking my ass cheeks. That intensified the nut.

"What the fuck?" I screeched.

Ghost tightened the grip on my neck as Sunni palmed my ass, keeping it still while she sucked me dry. "Shit. That was the best sex I've ever had," I said, still catching my breath and wiping the sweat from Ghost's forehead. It was dripping profusely on Sunni's stomach.

I turned to Rudy. "I see you enjoyed standing there watching that."

He snarled. "I done fucked both of y'all and don't want neither of y'all. So, please get the fuck out my house."

Still on top of Sunni, I sat up. "This is my house. You can take the truck I bought you to maintain a living and YOU can get the fuck out. Your lil' side lunch box over here eats pussy better than you ever did." I growled.

Looking embarrassed and pitiful, he turned and walked out. "Fuck y'all," Rudy called over his shoulder, telling me he'd be back for his things tomorrow.

As he slammed the door, we all burst out laughing. "Yo', that man is fucked up right now. You savage, ma. Sexy as fuck too. I hope you beautiful ladies feeling as good as I am." Ghost said. "You two make a good team."

We both giggled and sipped from the wine glasses we'd left on the counter.

***

Starzpen

WET

Rudy waited a week before contacting me. He finally texted saying he would be by this evening for the remainder of his belongings. I could see he'd come by and picked up a few of his things while I was out, no doubt. I dreaded this conversation with him. It would be the final tie between he and I. I wanted to wish him well and part on a cordial note.

I heard a car pull up, so I went to the window and peeked out. *Sunni? And who is that?* I snatched the door open, looking somewhat annoyed and confused that this motherfucker just decided to pop up at my crib with company no less. She was smiling with a bottle of apple Crown in one hand and a Sprite in the other. Walking toward the door, she looked at me and said, "Ready for round two, gorgeous?"

I was shocked and speechless, so I stayed silent. Sunni continued inside the house. "Come on you guys. Let's have some fun." Two guys hopped out the backseats and walked in also.

"Umm, Sunni? What the hell are you doing? And who the fuck are they?"
"Girl, I'm doing what you asked me to do." She simply replied. "Now, you wanna get ya' pipes readjusted or not? These motherfuckers fine and both got big dicks. And, they will eat ya' ass like sweet baby back ribs. Now, you down or nah?" She commanded.

I was hesitant but nasty as fuck anyway. It was a bonus that they were both fine as hell. "Sunni, you should have called first." I sighed, contemplating.

"Girl, stop tripping. Come on in here and get you a shot."

"Rudy will be here soon to pick up his stuff." I told her.

Grabbing my belt buckle, she ran her hand between my legs gently. "Good, now he can watch all three of us terrorize this pussy," she whispered. "Look at them," she added. "You need this and you know you want it."

I walked inside and over to the bar to fix a shot of Crown. Before I could touch the glass, Sunni grabbed it and said, "Let me. You go get acquainted with the twins."

Twins? I didn't even notice the twin thing. One had on a hat and sunglasses and the other had a hood on. I walked over and slowly began to undress one of them. Starting with his socks, I kneeled down slowly, asking his name.

"Dre,' he replied.

Mmmmm, Dre. You have some sexy ass lips."

He blushed slightly. "Now can you imagine what I planned to do with them?"

Sliding up into his lap, I unbuckled his belt, then pants. Taking a drink from his glass with one hand, he pulled my neck toward his dick. I rose up and removed his shirt. Unexpectedly, his brother scooted up behind me and began removing my shirt, one button at a time.

"I'm Tre, the brother said. I could tell he was the aggressive one."

Dre had a soft touch with a smidge of thug mixed in. Tre was rugged, his swag was demanding and forceful, yet sexy and a bit intimidating. Sunni was at the bar in her bra and panties, getting drunk as hell.

"Tre? Can Dre eat my pussy first?" I asked

WET

"Hell naw," he replied, flipping me on to the floor on my stomach. He smashed my head into the carpet and slid his dick inside me. That shit glided right in like a frank fits the bun.

Bam. Bam. Bam.

Sunni walked over and knelt down beside me. She began stroking my back, head, and neck like I was a fluffy cat, rubbing her body against mine, purring almost. Then, Dre joined us as he rose off the sofa, removing his clothing. His huge abs were rock hard. They both had brown sugar-coated skin with arms like two fully loaded AK 47s. Their dicks were identical. They were both long and smooth with pinkish tan tips.

Dre's dick had more veins bulging out than Tre's. That meant he was ready to bust one juicy move and it was over for him. Tre flipped me over onto my back while Sunni laid my head in her lap, giving Dre some major cheek action. Tre threw my legs in the air.

"Think you can take that heavy load coming at ya?" Sunni smirked, stroking my head.

Tre slapped my clit with the tip of his dick, running it across my pussy hole, then back to my clit. Dre's knees buckled while Tre was massaging my insides perfectly. Sunni was snacking on Dre's dick like it was a melting popsicle.

Tre slid his dick out, still stroking it with both hands. Dre walked over and backed us into the wall, ramming his whole dick inside me from behind. Arms around my waist,

WET

Tre slid down both my legs with his tongue. Then, he spread both moist lips apart, sticking the tip of his tongue directly on my hotspot. I couldn't feel my legs.

Damn, Dre was stroking slowly from behind, slightly nibbling on the back of my neck. I was feeling like I could walk on air. Sunni was on the sofa watching us and ramming her fingers inside her pussy.

"You gonna come for them, Toni?" She yelled from across the room. "Look at me," she demanded. "Come for me." She hopped up off the couch and started toward me. Stopping first to grab the belt from her dress pants, she swung it, hitting Tre on his back.

His head went all in, moving round and round up and down my pussy. It was dripping all in his mouth. Dre's dick was soaking up all the rest.

Sunni kissed me and fondled my titties, putting each nipple in her mouth and sucking on them. "Dear God, I can't breathe. You gonna come for me, Toni?" Sunni whispered.

Dre replied for me. "Yes, she's gonna rain down on Tre in a minute."

"Yesss, don't stop. Right there, baby. Make me come. I'm gonna come." I urged them to keep pleasuring me.

"Come on, Toni. Let it go." Sunni said while Tre was holding my pussy lips open for better access to that spot.

"She's coming boys. Bring it in." Sunni said laughing, knowing I was through. Dre still popped my pussy for leftover juices and Tre was still on his knees slopping up

268

Starzpen

WET

the drip. Dre knew my knees were weak, so he carried me to the sofa and laid me down, resting his head on my shoulder.

Out of nowhere, Tre slammed Sunni's head in the table and slid inside her. She was grinding and throwing it back on that horse sized dick like it was electrical. In. Out. Dre had her bouncing it back.

Tre and I watched like it was a flick on the screen. Yes, lord. I had to see what his fine ass looked like from all angles. His abs tightened with each thrust. Sweat dripped on Sunni's ass and Dre lightly smacked her on each cheek, repeatedly.

"Hell yeah, daddy. Fuck this pussy. Go fucking harder," Sunni purred. Sunni gripped the table and Dre gripped her waist. Her face was planted firmly into the marble tabletop, ass in the air, bouncing like Jell-O.

Dre's head fell unannounced on Sunni's back. He was jerking and moving his hips round and round while he was still inside. Sunni laughed, grabbing her titties, moaning and taking it all in. Tre rubbed my legs, enjoying the view. I was still semi trembling from the amazing nut I had worked up.

Sunni and Dre got dressed. Oddly, Tre and I fell asleep right where we were.

When I woke the next morning, I felt like a dude. My first thought was, *why is this clown still here?* My second thought was, *ummmm, do I smell feet up in here?* And lastly, I was wondering if I was dreaming or was my pussy literally

Starzpen

on swole. That shit was great last night. But I had to wake him up before he thought he supposed to be here.

"Tre! Tre? TRE!" I yelled, annoyed as hell.

He jumped up, looking around, trying to figure out where he was. When he seemed to remember, he calmly laid back down.

"Oh no. Tre, everybody is gone. This was fun and all, but you have to go."

"Oh, aight aight, Toni. No problem. Why you so upset this morning? You should be feeling great. I know I am." He tried telling me.

"Well, that's good, but it's also over." I replied with a slight attitude.

He looked at me while lacing up his shoestrings. "You think we could go out to eat or something?"

"Go out to eat? Ummm all this food I got in here, I don't need to be wasting money eating out." I frowned.

"Well, can I come over again? Maybe for desert?" He asked.

"Look, Sunni brought you here to fuck me. You did that and it was amazing. However, I'm not looking for any complications."

"Your pussy in my mouth repeatedly? That's a complication? I didn't ask you to marry me. I just asked if you would keep me company from time to time." He was persistent and he was nice looking, but what the hell did he really want? He had my attention though.

"Well, Tre, leave your number and I'll fuck you later." We both laughed as he exited. However, we both stopped dead in our tracks when we saw Rudy pull up in the driveway. To avoid any confrontation, Tre quickly got into his car and pulled off.

"So, this what you doing? You're a whore now? You got niggas coming in and out you now? Listen, Toni I know you're mad-"

Mad? I laughed in his face. "I'm not mad, Rudy. I'm numb. I'm tired. I'm over you. You are selfish, greedy, and you don't deserve me. Get yo' shit and get the fuck out. There is no more us. There will be no forgiveness. You lose, babes. And from now on, I can do whatever I please. Toni is about to reign down on life. And that no longer includes you."

"It's like that Toni? So we over? Just like that? Over a quickie?"

"Rudy, it's been over or the quickie wouldn't have happened. It's not about you fucking Sunni. I've come to realize there are millions of Sunni's. In my mind, there should have been only one Rudy and Toni. I wish you the best life ever and truly hope you find whatever it was I couldn't give you."

"Toni, don't do this. I'm sorry. I love you."

"I believe you. That's what's so funny, Rudy. Because I love me too. I love me sooooo much that I can't get comfortable with your kind of love. I can't accept the cold, hard truth that I wasn't enough. I can't live with knowing I settled for almost. So, I love you my friend, but this chapter of our lives is over. It's the inevitable turn. You just accelerated it." I kissed him on the lips like we used to one last time. I could feel time drain from my body like a soul from the dead. I felt the hurt somewhat from a lurking feeling of failure when it came to my marriage. Yet, my heart smiled as it was released into a world of possibility. I planned to embrace possibility and nurture my new beginning. I was going to live beyond belief.

Unable to accept my decision, Rudy turned and headed back to his vehicle, mumbling that he would be back to get his things when I was not around. "Goodbye Rudy, and please stay in touch and let me know how you're doing from time to time," I called after him.

Rudy suddenly stopped and turned to me. "You never truly know what you have until you no longer have it. That is so cliché, but so painfully true. I love you, Toni. I always will."

"I love you too, Rudy. Take care." He pulled out his phone and snapped a picture of me waving goodbye. I thought that was weird, but I guess he wanted to remember the day he lost the best thing in his life, all the while me feeling like I was just born... a lioness unleashed. Game over.